THE
EXECUTIVE
ORDER

TOM WINSTEAD

Library of Congress Identification #1-8993539281
Library of Congress Registration Number TXu2206781

Paperback ISBN: 978-1-09833-143-6

Question: "Who wins in a showdown between the Executive & Legislative branches of our government?"

Answer: "There can be no winners—only losers!"

We the people

*"The people are responsible for the character of their Congress.
If that body be ignorant, reckless, and corrupt, it is because
the people tolerate ignorance, recklessness, and corruption."*
President James A. Garfield, *(1831-1881),*
Reverend, Minister of the Gospel.

EXECUTIVE ORDER

Principal Characters

GOVERNMENT

JOE BRADLEY	VICE PRESIDENT OF US
NANCY PATRICK	SPEAKER, US HOUSE OF REP,
SENATOR LINDSEY SCOTT (R)	SENATE MAJORITY LEADER
HAROLD REED (D)	SENATOR, MINORITY LEADER
SUSAN BRICE	CHIEF OF STAFF FOR POTUS
JOHN BEAMAN	PRESIDENT'S INTEL CHIEF
BILL WINTERS (R)	REP., U.S. CONGRESS
DENNIS WILSON, (D)	REP., US CONGRESS
ROBERT WALTERS	DEPUTY SECRETARY OF DEFENSE

MILITARY

ADMIRAL VINCE DAWKINS, USN	CHIEF, NAVAL OPERATIONS
COLONEL JAMES "BULL" MILLER	GITMO COMMANDER
GENERAL DAVE MABRY, USMC	COMMANDANT, USMC
GENERAL GARY "DUTCH" HALL, USMC	SE COMMAND COMMANDER
GENERAL MICHAEL "MIKE" HOLDER,	CHIEF OF NATIONAL GUARD
GENERAL PAUL MOSELEY, USAF	VICE CHAIRMAN, JOINT CHIEFS
GENERAL SAM DRAKE-FORD, USMC	CHAIRMAN, JOINT CHIEFS (Residence: Anacosta-Bolling)
LT. COL. RON PHILLIPS	DEPUTY COMMANDER GITMO
SERGEANT PENNY FULBRIGHT	SECRETARY TO COLONEL MILLER

SPECIAL AGENTS

MEL PIERSON	FBI DIRECTOR
RICK WINSTEAD	SPECIAL OPS / COMMUNICATIONS
TOM BECKWITH	CIA DIR. RECRUITMENT & TRNG
CHIP REESE	ASST. DIR. SECRET SERVICE (WH)
DAN BLACK	DIRECTOR SECRET SERVICE (WH)

OTHER CHARACTERS

DAN JOHNSON	DRIVER OF DAVE MABRY'S CAR
GARY SPENCER	SECURITY GUARD
PETE & PAUL	COMMUNIATION WORKERS

PROLOGUE

The day-to-day fight and struggles to keep the gates of Guantanamo Prison (GITMO) closed, at all costs, and not releasing any of the dangerous, imprisoned, battlefield hardened, terrorists is the sworn goal of Colonel James A. "Bull" Miller, Commander of GITMO. He has vowed on the graves of hundreds of his fellow warriors, fallen on the field of battle, at the hands of these jihadist bastards, that he will take any and all steps necessary to keep from releasing them! Including refusing to obey a Presidential Executive Order! And if it becomes necessary to replace the President of the United States, by whatever means it takes! Little did he know the ultimate price—it takes more than a coup to stop a coup!

"_United States presidents_ issue **executive orders** _to help officers and agencies of the_ _executive branch_ _manage the operations within the federal government itself. Executive orders have the full force of law **when they take authority from a legislative power which grants its power directly to the Executive by the Constitution,** or are made pursuant to_ _Acts of Congress_ _that explicitly delegate to the President some degree of discretionary power (_delegated legislation_). Like both legislative statutes and regulations promulgated by government agencies, executive orders are subject to judicial review, and may be struck down if deemed by the courts to be unsupported by_ *statute or the Constitution.* **Major policy initiatives require approval by the legislative branch,** *but executive orders have significant influence over the internal affairs of government, deciding how and to what degree legislation will be enforced, dealing with emergencies, waging 72-hour length strikes on enemies, and in general fine-tuning policy choices in the implementation of broad statutes." (Wikipedia)*

"WE hold these Truths to be self-evident, that all men are created equal, that they are endowed by their Creator with certain unalienable rights that among these are life, liberty, and the pursuit of happiness. That to secure these rights, governments are instituted among men, deriving their just powers from the consent of the governed, that **<u>whenever any form of government becomes destructive of these ends, it is the right of the people to alter or to abolish it, and to institute new government,</u>** *laying its foundation on such principles, and organizing its powers in such form, as to them shall seem most likely to affect their Safety and Happiness. Prudence, indeed, will dictate that governments long established should not be changed for light and transient causes; and accordingly all experience has shown, that mankind are more disposed to suffer, while Evils are sufferable, than to right themselves by abolishing the forms to which they are accustomed.* **But when a long train of abuses and Usurpations, pursuing invariably the same object, evinces a design to reduce them under absolute despotism, it is their right, it is their Duty, to throw off such government, and to provide new guards for their future Security. . ."**

(The Declaration of Independence, July 4, 1776)

CHAPTER ONE

It was a horrible, unbelievable night with merciless screams of terror filling the hot, steamy, and stale night air. Terrifying squeals from the scores of desperate men wailing and begging for help. Cries of, "They are torturing me, someone please—I'm dying, they're killing me!" The pleas and screams of pain from the frantic souls only bounced off the thick, unhearing uncaring concrete walls of the prison cells. Clanging sounds of metal slamming against metal, more screams, more yelling and howling, "Get me out of here! I'm dying. Somebody please help me!" "You nasty, filthy American Infidel pigs are killing me; let me out, I'm going home soon! I will have your heads on the end of my sword. Allah be praised!"

Suddenly, a hand grabbed him by the collar of his prison uniform and lifted him completely off the ground leaving his feet dangling. The southern sounding voice of the big hand came out loud, clear and strong, "You ain't going nowhere but to hell, you 'sum-bitch!" The big hand threw the mouthy prisoner back across the wall of his cell. Scared and suddenly very quiet, the prisoner turned his head to see who had jerked him up and threw him; all he saw was one big, tall U.S. Marine Sergeant standing outside the cell door with a smile on his face.

The screaming and yelling and threatening stopped as quickly as it had begun; the cacophony of voices turned to loud fits of laughter, replacing the screeching and yelling. Suddenly, the air became filled with stinking, acrid smoke rising from inside the cell blocks. Mattresses burning! The slow burning material of the cotton-filled mattresses created foul clouds of smoke that drifted upward into the night wind, which carried it along for the ride. The night air quickly became filled with the sinister smell of urine and feces and no telling what else the prisoners had done on the bedding. The nasty, foul smell rose and drifted across miles of the Island of Cuba.

"We are going home soon and you filthy-ass American Infidel pigs will still be here!" More laughter, "You cannot do anything about it. Your President has said that we can go home and be free; he has signed the order already! Maybe we will see you another time on the battlefield where we first met. We will have your heads! The President is our friend and ally; you are helpless American pigs. We will be in heaven with our virgins and you all will be in hell! Allah Akbar!"

One hundred armed U.S. Marines had surrounded the prison fortress and established a perimeter; as one, they slowly began to move the line closer, tightening the perimeter around the compound. No one gets out and no one gets in, except whom they wanted. Another fifty U.S. Marines, half armed with automatic weapons, half with large fire hoses and clothed in firefighting equipment, entered the gates of the compound where the shrieking, laughing prisoners were gathered, screaming filthy comments at the firefighters and guards, "We are going home and you will stay in the prison; we will be free men." More laughter.

The lead firefighter, a senior, seasoned non-com, grinned and looked back over his shoulder and nodded. Suddenly the air, the cell blocks, the entire compound was filled with high pressure water from half a dozen large fire hoses! Prisoners were knocked over, end-over-end when the water hit them, slamming them against the walls of the cells lifting them completely off their feet, slamming them down against the concrete floor, upending the contents of the cells turning beds upside down, extinguishing the flaming, stinking, bedding.

The fire hoses would open and close intermittently; as soon as prisoners could get to their feet, another powerful stream of water would knock them down again.

There were screams of, "You cannot do this to us; we are American prisoners of war. You cannot treat us this way; please stop, stop! The Geneva Convention protects us!"

"Tell it to your friend, the one who is sending you back home, you assholes!" someone shouted.

—Lieutenant Colonel Ron Philips, Deputy Commander of this paradise in the South Atlantic, called Guantanamo Bay or GITMO for short, was back at his desk after the prisoner's passions had quieted. It was late, but before calling it a night, he completed his Report To The Commander: "Activities, Events, Disturbances" of the evening. Then, he went to bed.

As I walked through the door into my office, a hand with a cup of hot coffee reached out and said "Good morning, Colonel Miller, I saw you coming and already had the coffee made."

"Thanks, Penny; after the weekend events, this is a good beginning for a new week."

I sat down at my desk and picked up the reports from the various teams and their responsibilities. I shuffled through them one by one until Ron's report came up, it read: *All quiet and peaceful in the compound and cells. No unusual activity.* I smiled at Ron's report, and then picked up and opened the large envelope that had just arrived from the Department of Defense (DOD). It was marked "OFFICIAL" on both the front and back covers.

Inside was another large envelope, this one marked "TOP SECRET." I opened it and inside was a cover sheet that was also marked "TOP SECRET." I removed the cover page and began reading: "Executive Order 13492." It had come directly from the White House, through the "five-sided palace" known as the Department of Defense (DOD), and was signed by the President of the United States himself:

By the authority vested in me as President by the Constitution and the laws of the United States of America, in order to effect the appropriate disposition of individuals currently detained by the Department of Defense at the Guantánamo Bay Naval Base (Guantánamo) and promptly to close detention facilities at Guantánamo, consistent with the national security and foreign policy interests of the United States and the interests of justice, I hereby order as follows:

"Bullshit!" I said, talking to myself, or maybe just thinking out loud; I already knew what was coming next; "Transferred to another 'United States detention facility', my ass! We can't—I will not—send these Al-Qaeda assholes to the mainland where they can blow up something there. I'll shoot the bastards myself! They've already killed too many of our troops in Afghanistan and Iraq. I'm not about to sit by and watch them kill our families too."

I kept reading: *Sec.3 Closure of Detention Facilities at Guantánamo. The detention facilities at Guantánamo for individuals covered by this order shall be closed as soon as practicable, and no later than 1 year from the date of this order. If any individuals covered by this order remain in detention at Guantánamo at the time of closure of those detention facilities, they shall be returned to their home country, released, transferred to a third country, or transferred to United States detention facility in a manner consistent with law and the national security and foreign policy interests of the United States.*

I'm not transferring them anywhere, I thought. *I'm going to appeal this nonsense.* "Khalid Sheik Mohammed, one of the top Al-Qaeda leaders before he was captured; Ramzi Bin Al-Shibh, connected directly with the September 2001 hijackings; Abu Zubaydh, linked to Osama Bin Laden and several other Al-Qaeda cells. These are just a few of the more dangerous prisoners we keep here. One hundred eighty-two detainees considered too dangerous to send back to their own countries—plus, another six hundred we think are less dangerous.

"No way in hell! I will NOT release them or send them to some 'country club' prison in the U.S. I don't know what, but something has to be done and some-damn-body has to do it!"

I was so pissed, I guess I must have been talking pretty loud to myself; the door popped open and my secretary rushed in. "Are you alright, sir?" she asked, adding, "I wondered who you were yelling at; I thought maybe I had screwed something up!"

"No, no, Penny, everything's okay," I replied. "I'm just upset at all this crap about releasing these bastards and sending them to the mainland."

Sergeant Penny Fulbright was one tough soldier and a good secretary, always there and ready to help with whatever needed to be done. She usually anticipated my needs and was ready with an answer, or would just hand me a cup of coffee and smile. She was usually right too. Before being assigned to GITMO, she was a Psychological Operations (PSYOP) team member and had served a tour in Iraq and two in Afghanistan. As a PSYOP Specialist, she fit in well here with the different jihadist terrorist nationalities we "entertain." Her training and experience in psychological warfare came in handy when trying to deal with these butthole of society detainees.

Not to mention that Penny was a very attractive, blonde, mid-thirties, career-minded person with fifteen years in. Her husband had been killed by an IED in Afghanistan three years ago while on patrol. She had seen some combat and came under fire. She hated those sorry sons-of-bitches about as much as I did.

I took another look at the Presidential memorandum dated December 15, ordering Thomson Correctional Center in Thomson, Illinois, to be prepared to accept transferred Guantanamo prisoners. *No DAMN way!* I thought.

Colonel James A. "Jim" (aka "Bull" by close friends) Miller! I sat there thinking and reflecting on days gone by. I had received my commission the hard way—on the damn battlefield—not through some school, like most. And there had been many different battlefields. I was the senior non-commissioned officer with the U.S. Army's Rapid Deployment Force—made-up of the 1st and 2nd Ranger Battalions and the 82nd Airborne when we hit our first combat role.

"Operation Urgent Fury" it was called, and we hit the island of Grenada in 1983 in a low-altitude airborne assault. The mission: to save a group of U.S. medical students studying at the island medical university. Hopefully, the mission would also restore the former democratic government and get rid of the dictatorship that had taken over.

Immediately running into more opposition than we had counted on, we found ourselves fighting trying to save our own ass, trying to just survive until we could get established. Suddenly, a grenade exploded nearby. I turned just in time to see Captain Dan Smith, our platoon leader, blown apart.

I realized that now I was the ranking non-com and person in the field, so I quickly re-grouped the men and assumed command. We were taking fire at an alarming rate. We had to do something, and fast. We "hunkered" down and told the men to provide fire-cover for me. I made my way around and behind the machine-gun nest that had us pinned down. I lobbed a couple of grenades into the nest and opened fire with an old Thompson .45 caliber machine gun that I picked up from one of the dead commie soldiers.

After blowing the nest to hell and back, and running out of ammo on the Thompson, I grabbed up a thirty-caliber, M19 Browning machine gun, threw two bandoleers over my shoulder, and scared shit-less, ran screaming like a mad-man. I rushed the enemy at a full-run with the .30-caliber blasting in every direction as I ran.

It must have scared the crap out of those Communist-Grenadian Army bastards because they turned and started running in the opposite direction. I didn't stop until I ran out of ammo and they were out of sight. I went back to the command center and began helping load the wounded and dead on a helicopter that had been called in to pick them up.

Somebody told someone that I had done something special and should receive a medal for it. About all I remember is that those sons-of-bitches were shooting at me and I was going to shoot back.

Two months later, when all the fight was out of the pro-communist Grenadian Army, General Schwartzman personally pinned the Silver Star on my chest while I stood at attention. As he came close enough to pin the medal on, the General told me that I was now Captain James "Bull" Miller. He said I was getting a battlefield commission as a captain.

In reading the citation, General Schwartzman said, "In complete disregard for his own safety, Sergeant Miller rushed the enemy machine gun nest and destroyed it, killing a large number of the enemy. Again, in complete disregard for his own life and safety, Sergeant Miller, thinking of the safety of his men, and having run out of ammunition, picked up an enemy weapon and rushed the remaining enemy position until they dispersed and retreated."

Leaning back in my chair and putting my feet up on the desk, I thought, *That was a long time ago, I don't remember all of that. I just know; you shoot at me, I'm going to shoot back.*

Now, here I am, "Colonel Bull Miller," Commander of GITMO. It could be worse, I guess. Hell, I'm lucky to be alive. I have seen combat in the invasion of Panama; I was even with the troops in that damn politically made disaster and chaos in Mogadishu, in Somalia; and every war since, in one way or another. I've been in Kosovo, Afghanistan, Iraq, and the Gulf.

Hell, I thought to myself, *Those weren't wars; those were just political campaigns. We didn't go in to win or kick ass and get out. We were just trying to satisfy a bunch of politician's egos and help them win elections. They didn't give a shit about the troops!*

But what the hell can a "dime-a-dozen," bird-colonel do about any of it, I thought. *Well, somebody has to do something, even if it means getting shot by a firing squad, so it may as well be me.*

I had plenty of time in service to retire, and nothing much else to lose. I picked up the phone and called base operations at the GITMO air field. And set-up a 0600 flight for the next morning, Friday, to Eglin Air Force Base (AFB) in Florida—headquarters for the Southeast Military Command.

A long-time friend from Vietnam, Marine Major General Gary "Dutch" Hall, was commander of the Southeast Command. He had injuries and medals to show from Korea and Vietnam: a Silver Star and a Bronze Star from Korea; two Bronze Stars with a couple of oak leaf clusters for valor from Vietnam; holes in both shoulders; shrapnel in his back; one leg missing from the knee down; and wearing a prosthesis for a leg and foot. "Dutch" was one tough marine. He had refused to let the Corps discharge him for "medical" reasons. He put up a helluva fight until he convinced a couple of review boards that he still had a lot of fight left in him.

I grabbed my phone and dialed Dutch at Eglin AFB. After all the times Dutch and I had spent together, military protocol wasn't that important.

After the third ring, "General Hall's office," a sweet, lovely sounding voice answered.

"This is Colonel Miller at GITMO," I said, "Is General Hall in?"

I thought to myself, *Penny sounds prettier and sexier when she answers my phone.* Just then, Dutch picked up,

"Bull Miller, how the hell are you?" He began. "I thought we were going to get together a couple of months ago."

"I'm doing great, Dutch. Just wanted to let you know that I'm coming your way tomorrow morning and wanted to drop in on you if your schedule permits; I've got some things I'd like to discuss with you," I said.

"Come on up; we'll have a drink or two over dinner at my house, so we can have some privacy. You know, I've got some stuff running around in my head too. I look forward to seeing you," he replied.

CHAPTER TWO

As the military Lear jet aircraft touched down at Eglin AFB and rolled to a stop in front of the base operations building, I looked out of the window and saw a military staff car sitting there. It had a flag mounted on the front bumper; the flag had two stars and was flapping in the breeze. Well, I thought, *Old Dutch has come out to greet me.* But I wasn't too sure what he would think after I told him on the phone what I wanted to talk about. That was a plus! Maybe Dutch wouldn't offer me a court martial after all.

As I stepped off the bottom step, I saluted my 'two-star' friend, and he returned my salute. We shook hands, smiled at each other as we walked to the staff car. There was no rank involved—just two old-time, combat friends making up for lost time by bringing each other up to date on their activities since the "wars."

As we approached the car, the driver saluted and opened the door; we returned the salute and got into the back seat. Dutch told the driver to take us to the Officer's Club.

"Breakfast is on me," said Dutch, "We can catch up on what's been happening and tell some 'war stories.' Besides, I want to hear more about what you have in mind about this GITMO closing crap. This is not the time to be thinking or talking about closing GITMO and moving those jihadist bastards here to the mainland."

"My thoughts exactly," I said.

Mulling this over in my mind, I thought, *I believe I have found an ally in General 'Dutch' Hall.* I knew Dutch had really close contacts in the Pentagon, up to and including the Chairman of the Joint Chiefs. Sometimes, when Dutch was called to Washington, he had lunch with the Chief, the Secretary of Defense, and other VIPs from different departments and agencies.

We were seated at a corner table in the main dining room of the "O" club.

"It's nine-thirty. Let's have a late breakfast and see if we can solve the world's problems. It shouldn't take more than an hour," Dutch said and laughed.

I laughed too, saying, "You'll change your mind when you hear what I want to talk with you about."

"That sounds pretty serious," said Dutch.

"It is. This most likely will be the most serious conversation you've ever had," I told him, and then added jokingly, "In fact, you may even want to recommend me for a court-martial."

The waitress came, took our order, and then left us to our conversation.

"Dutch," I began, "you recall my telling you about the Presidential Executive order I received from the White House, and how upset I am about it?"

"Yeah," he replied. "I also remember how pissed you were when you called me." He hesitated and then continued, "I can't say I blame you for being upset; I don't like it either. How many lives have we lost trying to capture that bunch? And now they want us to send them to some 'country club' prison in our own country. Besides, we have spent millions on these Jihadist SOBs. They've lived better at GITMO than they, or their families, ever did or even knew existed. I'm sure as hell not going to be the one to transfer them to some stateside facility."

I reached in my briefcase and pulled out the Executive Order and handed it to him.

"Read that and tell me what you think," I said.

Dutch took the paper from me and started to read. After about a minute, he laid the paper on the table between us. He looked out of the window, deep in thought, saying nothing—just looking out and keeping silent. Several minutes passed before he looked back at me.

Just then, the waitress brought our breakfast of scrambled eggs, grits, bacon, toast, and more coffee. We ate in silence, both of us in deep thought. After eating, Dutch looked up.

"Bull," he began speaking, "We've got a problem in this country. I've been doing a lot of thinking lately. I don't know just how to fix that problem, at least before the next election cycle. I'm not even sure it will be fixed then; depends on who goes in. Bull, you and I . . . have always faced problems, and never considered that they might be too big for us to handle. We just got busy and took care of the situation. I'm not sure how we can handle this one, or if we even ought to get involved."

After a moment's pause, he continued talking. "I know what I'd like to do to some of those bastards. Come on. Let's head over to my office," he said as we got up and headed out to his staff car.

Dutch continued talking as we drove to his office, "I wonder just what is going on in the President's mind for him to consider moving some of the most dangerous individuals in the world to one of the states. It doesn't make much sense."

"According to the news, his 'advisors' are going along with him," I said. "They're not telling him all of the potential dangers involved in having them in a civilian prison. Besides, he doesn't have the constitutional authority or the 'balls' to order the transfer on his own. He has to go to Congress, and they have to authorize such actions. Just look at the background of his so-called advisors; several are Muslim, and his top advisor, his Chief of Staff, Susan Brice, swore allegiance to the Muslim faith, on the Koran I believe, when she was appointed and sworn in," I added.

"Depending upon his motives," Dutch sort of mumbled, like he was deep in thought, "I think it borders on treason. It's like 'aiding and abetting' the enemy."

Still thinking out loud, he continued in a very soft voice, "Seems to me that the constitution says something about getting their just powers from the consent of the people, and if they don't, the people have the right to change or get rid of that government and put a new government in place of the bad one."

"Dutch, do you know what you're saying?" I asked. "Man, if the wrong person was to overhear that remark, it would mean court martial for both of us! But, I will have to say, I have been taking a close look at the constitution myself, these past several days."

Arriving back at Dutch's office we went in; I sat in front of his desk in a large, dark brown leather chair. Dutch sat down behind his desk, checked his messages and told his secretary to hold his calls, unless someone "extremely" important called.

Dutch turned to the credenza behind his desk and pulled out a book. He opened it to a pre-marked page and started to read out loud, "WE hold these Truths to be self-evident, that all men are created equal, that they are endowed by their Creator with certain unalienable rights that among these are life, liberty, and the pursuit of happiness. That to secure these rights, governments are instituted among men, deriving their just powers from the consent of the governed, that whenever any form of government becomes destructive of these ends, it is the right of the people to alter or to abolish it, and to institute new government, laying its foundation on such principles, and organizing its powers in such form, as to them shall seem most likely to affect their Safety and Happiness. Prudence, indeed, will dictate that governments long established should not be changed for light and transient causes; and accordingly all experience has shown, that mankind are more disposed to suffer, while Evils are sufferable, than to right themselves by abolishing the forms to which they are accustomed. But when a long train of abuses and Usurpations, pursuing invariably the same object, evinces a design to reduce them under absolute despotism, it is their right, it is their Duty, to throw off such government, and to provide new guards for their future Security. . ."

Dutch stopped reading at this point. He looked up at me, "Bull, can you make a trip to D.C. next week?"

"You're the boss; I can do anything you tell me to do," I replied.

"Okay; I'll set-up a meeting with the right people, and depending on their schedule, we will tentatively plan on hitting the 'big city' next week, or whenever it's convenient for them," Dutch said and thoughtfully added, "We better keep this under our hats for now."

CHAPTER THREE

Dinner at Dutch's house was pleasant, and Susan, his beautiful, "trophy" wife, had prepared a dinner fit for a king, or maybe more like two aging old military guys who didn't know when to call it quits.

We went into the den; Susan left us and said she had given the maid the evening off, so she was going to do the dishes and clean the kitchen; then she was going upstairs to do some reading. Dutch and I could spend some time catching-up on the old days.

Dutch picked up where we left off in his office, "Bull, evidently, you and I have been on the same 'wavelength' for some time, without knowing what the other was thinking. And what we are thinking is extremely dangerous. Hell, it is down-right scary! But we are not the only ones thinking like this," he said. "There are several people, who are way 'above-our-pay-grades,' who don't like what's happening to our country. And they want to do something about it before this President takes the nation so far down, there will be no getting back up."

Dutch was beginning to get his "ire" up, and his face was starting to turn red.

Then he looked directly at me and said, "I've fought too long and hard, and lost too much, and so have you, to let some shit-head

President, who doesn't have any idea what's going on, tear the country down around us."

Then he declared, "I'm just not going to sit by with my thumb up my ass and let it happen!"

I let Dutch talk and didn't interrupt. He needed to get this off his chest, and this was the time to let him do it. Besides, I needed a strong ally.

"Bull, you and I have been in battles that we didn't think we would get out of alive. In fact, we're damn lucky is the only reason we're still here now. But we knew it. We chose to die for our country and fight the battles necessary to keep this country safe and secure.

"Somewhere in the past, someone said, I think it was one of the founding fathers of this nation, when they were trying to establish this country and keep it by the people and for the people, said something to the effect that: 'we mutually pledge to each other our lives, our fortunes, and our sacred honor. . . .'"

Then in probably the most serious voice I had ever heard from him, Dutch stated, "You know, Bull, that's exactly what you and I, and anybody else that thinks like we do—and who are willing to act on it—will be doing. We will be pledging, to each other, and to the people of this great nation, our lives, our fortunes, our futures, and our sacred honor. But then, we—you and I—have been doing that every time we went into a fire-fight or battle against an enemy. We pledged to each other our very lives and our future and whatever honor we still had!" Dutch finished his summation.

I looked at Dutch and said, "Dutch, every fight we ever got into, we didn't know if we would get out alive or not. This one is no different. If, or when, we get into it, there is no retreat. We can't call in air support like we did in Vietnam. There won't be any forward controllers on the ground to guide us.

"We are on our own. Just you, I, and anybody who decides to support us. Do we go, or do we abort?" I asked.

CHAPTER FOUR

As we got off the plane on Thursday afternoon at Andrews Air Force Base, just outside Washington, DC, for a long weekend in the nation's capital, a pre-arranged staff car was waiting to take us to base ops and drop us off so we could check-in. Then, we were on our own for the weekend. No VIP special arrangements. In Washington, colonels and major generals were dime-a-dozen and rated no special treatment or recognition. That's probably a good thing, under the circumstances of our being in the capital city.

While Dutch took care of signing us in on the base, I called Enterprise Rental and got us a vehicle with unlimited mileage for the weekend. I had no idea where we would be heading and who we would be seeing. Dutch had set-up all of the meetings.

The Enterprise car arrived and Dutch got in on the driver's side, I on the passenger side, and we left Andrews AFB heading for the city.

Dutch said, "I've booked us into the J W Marriott, just across from the White House; it's convenient, quiet, secure, and probably the best place for meeting."

I wasn't sure what he meant by "secure." Quiet and convenient, I understood.

"We're having a little get-together tonight at the home of General Dave Mabry," he said. "Dave is an old friend; we go way back, before Grenada. In fact, he was involved in something called the 'Tanker War' in the mid-eighties, between Iran and Iraq. He earned his stars the hard way; he has the scars and holes in his body to show for it too. He is Old Corps all the way. He says he is Marine born and bred. He usually ends his conversations with 'Semper Fi'."

I knew that by "Old Corps," he was talking about the Marine Corps. I had never met General Dave, but I knew he was Commandant of the Marine Corps, with offices in the Pentagon. He was the Number One man in the entire corps. Even though Dutch and I had been in Iraq, Afghanistan, and several other scrapes together, I had never had the opportunity to meet General Dave.

We pulled up to the entrance of the J W Marriott Hotel and were met by a valet and bell captain who opened our doors, greeted us, and got our luggage.

We got checked-in and went up to our rooms. I looked out of the window and could see the White House and just beyond it the Washington monument. As I looked at this part of America, the United States of America, and thought about what it stood for, chills ran up my spine. I mumbled out loud, "The **UNITED** States; not the DIVIDED states! No way would I let one person, no matter who or what he is, destroy more than two-hundred years of fighting for freedom, for liberty, for the rights of every American. I could never stand idly by and watch someone destroy the dreams of all who had been born or had earned their right to the American dream. What is it the old lady standing in the harbor of New York has on her pedestal, 'Give me your tired, your hungry, your weary. . . .'"

The knock on the door brought me back to the present. I opened the door and Dutch came in. He walked over to the window. "Have you looked out?" he asked.

"Yeah," I replied.

"This is why we are here, Bull!"

"Dutch, I cannot just sit by and watch our country go down the drain and not do something about it. I just can't do it. I can't sit by and not do something about it, even if I'm not sure about what I'm doing; whether it's the right way or the wrong way," I replied.

"That's why we're here, Bull," he repeated. "You and I are not the only ones who feel that way. That's why we're here. We will have dinner at Dave's house. He lives a little ways out of town, near some little town west of here, out in the country; I don't know who else may be there, but Dave knows what we are thinking. He feels the same way and knows others who have been talking about doing something. We will let Dave start the conversation and see which way he leads it, and what he, and the others say and think. Dave and I have discussed this Executive Order crap before; most military leaders feel the way we do about releasing the detainees to some country club prison here in the states."

Dutch was going on, "Dave gets pretty fired up just discussing the prisoners. He says they all should be hung; they helped plan the World Trade Center mission, plus they're responsible for the beheading of dozens of other Americans. Some we don't even know about yet."

I went over to the beverage cabinet, opened it, and told Dutch, "You've got a choice of Pepsi, Ginger Ale, or a shot of Jack Daniels; take your pick."

"Let's just grab a quick drink in the lounge before we leave," he said as he walked toward the door. "I've got time for about 'forty-winks'," he said. "I need it too."

"Suits me," I replied.

CHAPTER FIVE

I met Dutch again in the lounge just off the lobby at seven o'clock, and we both had a gin and tonic to settled our nerves a bit, but mostly to let the "going home" traffic get out of the way. Walking to the parking garage to get our Enterprise car, we talked about what to expect from the evening.

"I think we may be in for a little surprise tonight," said Dutch.

"What do you expect?" I asked.

"I don't know for sure," Dutch replied, "I just have a feeling deep in my gut about this. I can't quite put my finger on it, but it's been there since we got to DC."

"Is that a good feeling or bad?" I asked.

"Don't know," he said, "just a feeling."

We got into the car and headed west, with Dutch driving, taking Constitution Avenue past the White House to the 16th Street bridge over the Potomac River where we hit Highway 50 West. General Dave lived several miles outside the small town of Paris, Virginia. It was about a forty-five minute drive from the Pentagon, longer if traffic was heavy.

As we got out of town and out of traffic, I asked Dutch, "Do you know who will be at this little 'get-together' tonight?"

"Not for sure," he said, "but I talked with one of Dave and my mutual friends this afternoon, and he mentioned that he was meeting with Dave this evening at Dave's place, and was looking forward to seeing me again. So I gather he knows what we will be discussing. He carries a lot of weight, and I don't mean pounds. His name is Paul Moseley; he's the Vice Chairman of the Joint Chiefs. He is four-star Air Force. I don't know who else will be there."

After about forty minutes, we came to a white, parallel fence that ran along the side of the road. A good quarter of a mile later, we turned onto a hard, clay road, between more white, parallel fence that ran a good two-hundred yards up to a beautiful, old, southern style, home. The house looked like something out of *Gone with the Wind*.

General Dave and his wife Anna planned to retire soon. It would just be the two of them since their three children were married, scattered to different places around the world, and raising families of their own. Dave and Anna had bought a small, twenty-acre ranch where they kept a couple of horses and a cow or two along with some ducks and chickens that roamed freely. The acreage was planted in hay for feeding the horses and cattle. But more likely it was just to give the general something to keep him busy during his retirement years, and, probably, to keep him out of Anna's hair.

We pulled into the circular drive in front of the house and parked off to the side of the driveway. There were two other non-military style cars there. We knew they didn't belong to Dave, but we didn't know who they belonged to either.

When he saw us, Dave stepped out of the house, followed by someone I already knew—Admiral Vince Dawkins, Chief of Naval Operations. Vince and I were from the same small town of Sumter, South

Carolina. In fact, we were from the same neighborhood, our houses just a couple of blocks apart.

"Bull Miller," he exclaimed when he saw me. "I haven't seen you in a 'coon's' age. The last time I saw you, you were climbing aboard a chopper heading for Grenada. I was a 'shave-tail' ensign on the Saratoga, at the time."

The USS Saratoga was one of the navy's finest battle-hardened carriers that set the standard for other naval vessels.

"Hey Vince! It has been a few years since our paths have crossed. I never made it back home very often after I enlisted. I lost track of most of our old friends and team-mates. You were so far ahead of me, when you graduated and left for the navy, things were not the same any longer," I said. "Hell, you kept everything stirred-up around the neighborhood, and school. Life around Sumter got boring after you left. But I finally finished school, worked a few months, and then joined the army. I was happy to read about you getting your fourth star and moving up to the chief's slot. It couldn't happen to a nicer guy!"

The navy could never have picked a better guy to head up naval operations. Vince was always very dedicated to whatever he was doing; and he was a detail man. He wanted to know all the facts before he acted or made a decision; then, just get out of his way and leave him alone to do the job.

"Dave and I have been through a lot together through the years," Vince said; "He and I were lowly 'shave-tails' on the same ship one time. He was Marine and I was Navy. We didn't go through the usual rivalry that most put up with, even if it's good-natured, in fun, and full of crap," he laughed.

"We became fast friends and have been for almost thirty years; I guess one, or both of us, will be retiring pretty soon," he added. Then, thoughtfully, he said, "We think alike on a lot of things, and talk frequently; especially about the way things have changed and keep changing in the military, and, in the country," he exclaimed!

"I don't like it either," I told him, "Dutch and I have talked about all the stuff that's going on, and it's getting the best of me. I've got to do something about it or I'm getting the hell out!"

"Sounds like we're on the same page, Bull. Dave and I have had some conversations along those lines also. Neither of us are quite ready to pack-it in and retire; not just yet anyway. Besides, we don't like the idea of turning tail, retiring, and letting the country go to hell in a hand-basket," he said! "We've fought too long and too many wars to let that happen!"

Just then, another car turned in off the highway and headed up the driveway toward the house. As the car got closer we could see that it was General Moseley. General Paul Moseley from the Air Force; he is the Vice Chairman of the Joint Chiefs of Staff. There was going to be a lot of "stars" at this meeting tonight.

I mentioned this to Dutch and he gave me a look that told me I shouldn't have said that! He quickly told me that there were no "stars" or "VIPs" at this **get together!**

He also let me know very quickly, that this was not a meeting! Just a group of old-time, military "buddies", getting together for dinner, a few drinks, and telling "war" stories. I got the message, loud and clear! There would be no "rank" here tonight.

Just then, Paul Moseley walked up and slapped Dutch on the back; then they shook hands and exchanged greetings. Dutch said, "Paul, I'd like you to meet another old-time friend and a "helluva" good officer. He is even greater when you're in a tight situation and he shows up. Paul, this is Jim 'Bull' Miller; he heads up our 'club' at Gitmo."

Paul smiled and said, "Nice meeting you, Bull. I don't envy your job right now. I've heard of all the pressure you guys are under down there, trying to run a country club for a bunch of terrorist assholes instead of running a prison for a lot of crazed maniacs that ought to be put away permanently."

Paul then hesitated for a moment and then smiled and said, "Sorry about that; I kind of get carried away when I think about what's going on in our country these days."

"We feel the same way, Paul," I responded; "I lie to my staff, and remind them almost daily, by telling them that it isn't necessarily a bad thing. That according to our intelligence, and the President, it's necessary in order to illustrate that we serve justice. They don't believe it for a minute! They know I'm just spouting a bunch of crap."

"Maybe that's because you're still full of crap, Bull," said a voice behind me.

I turned and knuckled bumped General Michael "Mike" Holder.

"Mike, where the hell you been keeping yourself?" I asked. "I haven't seen you in a month of Sundays."

Mike was the chief "honcho" of the National Guard Bureau. Guard units across the country were under his command. He was a good man to have on board, in case of problems in his area.

Mike replied, "They keep me hidden away in that five-sided 'prison' they call the Pentagon. I think someone is afraid I'll get into trouble if they let me out."

Just then, Dave came out and announced that dinner was ready. Anna was out of town for the weekend and had gone to spend the time with their daughter Lucy, husband Sam, and six-year old twin grandsons in Miami.

Dave called out, "Hey, everybody, I want you to meet 'Bubba,' a good friend and the best bar-b-que 'chef' outside of North Carolina. I'm not much of a cook, so I got 'Bubba' and his catering friends to do the job for me. It's guaranteed good!"

Then he added, "It's good, old-time, southern barbeque, with rice, hash, baked beans, slaw, and deep fried corn-dodgers. Just doesn't get any better than this! So come and get it and serve yourself, there's plenty."

We lined up on the long sun-porch that stretched from one side of the house to the other, where the caterers had set the tables and the food line. And that's when the chatter began, about the "old days." At some point in all of our careers, we had stood in the "chow" line out in the field, somewhere in the world. Probably more "war stories" would be told at this gathering than at any other in a hundred years. And a lot of them just may be true!

When we had eaten our fill, and pretty well "stuffed" ourselves, Dave said, "Let's go to the den where we can visit and have a drink while these folks can get this cleaned up. I know they are anxious to move on."

We gathered in the den and Dave went to one wall that was lined with books on shelves. He reached on the inside of the center where two shelves came together, pushed a button, and the shelves opened, revealing a small bar. The inside of the bar was made from Mahogany and featured a mirror on the back wall. It was well stocked with some of the finest also.

Dave said, "Help yourselves, gentlemen; there's plenty and there are several different mixers too. But you have to mix your own; I'm no bartender."

As we stood around the bar talking, Dave said, "You guys know what kind of crap we have been putting up with these past few years; well, Bull Miller is getting the brunt of it now. Bull was telling me the other day about the pressure that's building up for the closing of 'GITMO.' In fact, I think he has already received the executive order from the White House and the Pentagon."

That was my cue, so I spoke up, "Yeah, I've got to 'transfer' twelve of those bastards next week; back to some neutral 'allied country'. Neutral, my ass! Every one of those supposedly 'neutral allies' want to stick it to us. We release these twelve and they will be back on the line within days."

I was obviously pissed, and it showed. I added, "We'll be shipping a few of our guys back in flag draped coffins in a matter of days."

Paul Moseley spoke up and said, "Yeah, my boss and I were talking about it just yesterday. He's pretty pissed about it, too. He said he was tempted to throw it in the trash can. But figured he would have to go back and dig it out again, anyway."

Vince spoke up and added, "Sam said he was going to fight it all the way to the top." Sam Drakeford was the Chairman of the Joint Chiefs and had direct access to the secretary of defense, and practically to the Oval Office itself, pretty much anytime he wanted it.

After sitting around and talking about the situation at GITMO, and the overall situation within the military complex, the budget cuts, the force reductions, cut-backs in training, etc., for over an hour, Dave cleared his throat and said, "Gentlemen, what are we going to do about this whole mess?"

He let that sink in for a moment. "We know that if we speak up and vent our thoughts, we might as well kiss our careers goodbye! Nevertheless, we all seem to agree that it is up to us to take some kind of action . . . in order to . . . in order to save our country!"

Paul chimed in, "I think we agree that we have to do something, but whatever action we take, we must plan it extremely carefully and not talk about it openly with anyone but this group, until we decide on a plan of action. Let me speak with Sam next week and get his thoughts.

I'll get word back to each of you with what he says. I know how he feels and we have talked about it on several occasions."

Dave spoke up, "Whatever we say, or do, this must never look, or be construed to be, a military coup! The people would never understand or go for that."

Everyone nodded their heads in agreement; many muttering, "It can never look like a coup by the military, not in this country."

With that, Dutch said, "Gentlemen, I don't know about you, but I'm not getting any younger, and the nights seem to get shorter. I think Bull and I are going to head back in and call it a day. We have to get an early start back South in the morning. Dave, thanks for the great bar-b-que and hospitality; tell 'Bubba' that it's some of the best I've ever eaten. Guys, let's stay in close contact and see just where we go from here."

The others echoed the feelings and prepared to leave. Dave saw everyone to the door and bid them goodnight and Godspeed, and said, "We will be in touch soon and continue where we left off tonight."

On the way back into D.C. to the hotel, Dutch and I discussed the whole idea of—what was probably the most improbable—and likely, the impossible-mission we had ever encountered. How in "God's green acres" could we take control of the United States Government, at the highest level, or, put someone else, who had not been elected, in that position?

The more I thought about it, the more concerned, and scared, I became.

Suddenly, Dutch spoke up, breaking the silence, "We will have to get some others involved; some folks who outrank us by a long shot. We must get some congressional leaders in on this if it stands any chance to succeed!"

"Dutch, this isn't something we can handle by phone or email, or some standard communication. We are going to have to handle any discussions with a great deal of caution."

Dutch responded, "We'll have to move quickly on this, Bull. I think we better plan on getting back up here toward the end of next week. In the meantime, I'll talk with some of the others, and see if we can get together with some of the congressional committee members who we know, and who feel the same as we do. I've heard a number of them mention that it was time to get that asshole out of the oval office before he completely destroys the country."

After a rather harried and sleepless night, Dutch and I boarded his plane early Monday morning and headed back to Eglin Air Base, Florida. Then, it was back to GITMO for me.

CHAPTER SIX

Back at my desk at mid-day on Monday, I started going through the accumulation of papers that piled up since I left on Thursday. As I picked up one marked "TOP SECRET" from the Secretary of Defense, I knew it wouldn't be good news.

"BULLSHIT!" I yelled, loud enough that Penny came bursting through the door.

Penny Fulbright, with her long, blonde hair, tucked up on top of her head so that it would fit under her hat, came charging in. She was still relatively new to Gitmo and not used to my yelling out every now and then. She had made an initial impression of being intelligent and efficient; not to mention, beautiful. I made her my secretary.

"Everything is fine, Penny," I told her. "Just some more bullshit from the Pentagon. It looks like we're going to have to release twelve of our 'guests' and send them to Qatar. Hell, we'll probably pay for another vacation for them before they start shooting at our troops again."

Penny said, "Colonel Bull, you scared the 'willies' out of me when you yelled like that," as she headed back to her desk.

I was fortunate to have her working for me. She kept my schedule, and me, straight.

After a few minutes of thought, I pressed the intercom.

"Yes, sir?" came the sweet voice of Sergeant Fulbright.

"Penny, see if you can get General Dutch Hall at Eglin on the phone for me," I told her.

"Yes, sir," she replied.

About two minutes later, Penny buzzed me, saying, "General Hall is on line one, sir."

"Thanks, Penny," I told her and got on the line with Dutch. "Dutch, you won't believe what I found when I got to my desk this morning."

"Calm down, Bull, I just got off the phone with Dave; he found the same thing when he got to his office. I thought he was going to have a coronary. In fact, he told me to call you so you wouldn't have a stroke when you got the message. He has already spoken with Sam, head of the Joint Chiefs, and he said that his hands were tied. In fact, he had talked with Bob Walters, the deputy chief honcho at DOD (Department of Defense). And, according to Bob, this came straight from the White House itself. I quote, 'The assholes are to be released forthwith, and transferred to the government of Yemen!'"

"That's a real quote?" I asked, laughing.

"Well, almost, but not exactly. I added my own thoughts to it," Dutch added. "We've got two weeks to work out the details and ship them out. I'd like to ship them out in body bags."

"My thoughts exactly! I would gladly escort them back personally," I returned.

"Bull, are you free on Thursday, and can you get back up for another run to D.C.?" Dutch asked.

"Hell, boss, I can go anytime and anywhere you say," I laughed.

"Hear me out on this, Bull. *There ain't no bosses* on this mission. We're all in this little venture together. Who was it that said something to the effect, *We mutually pledge to each other our lives, our fortunes, and our sacred honor?* Well you and I have talked about that before; that's what all of us are doing now," Dutch said. "If we carry this through, and screw it up, we will all probably be shot, won't have any fortune or future, and our 'sacred honor' will suddenly be dishonorable! This is really serious stuff, Bull."

Dutch sounded very serious, concerned, and in deep concentration.

"I'll see you on Thursday, Dutch," I told him.

After we were disconnected, I sat back and thought, *Dutch really needs some time to clear his head. He's gotten really deeply involved in this. I hope he doesn't have a stroke over all this crap. He's too close to retirement.*

Early Tuesday morning, I was sitting at my desk mulling over a bunch of papers when Penny stuck her pretty head in the door, looking kind of puzzled and said, "Colonel Miller, there's a Senator Scott on the phone for you."

"Thanks, Penny. I wonder what he wants. I hope he's not planning to come down to visit. We've got enough 'official bullshit' on our hands now without adding more. Put him through, Penny," I told her. "Let's see what he is after."

Penny went back to her desk, still perplexed at talking with a senator.

Senator Lindsey Scott, **the** "big dog" in the senate—Senate Majority Leader. I wondered if he's coming down here to the "boonies?" I know he's been raising hell about the release of detainees.

My phone buzzed and I picked it up. "Colonel Miller here, Senator Scott. How are you?"

"Just fine, Colonel," came his reply. "I wanted to give you a call and see if it would be convenient for me to drop in on you one day next week."

"Of course, Senator; any particular day you and your party will be here?" I asked.

"There won't be a party, Colonel Miller, unless you and I have a drink or two and call it a party," he laughed and added, "I will be coming alone. I want to talk over some things I have going on in my head and I think you're probably the right person to discuss it with. How would a week from Thursday be? Will that work in your schedule? Since it's heading into the weekend, I hope neither of us will have to rush."

"A week from this Thursday will work just fine with me, Senator. I'll look forward to your visit," I lied. No military post ever looks forward to a congressional visit. *I wonder who has complained now*, I thought.

"By the way, Colonel, don't go getting yourself and the staff in a 'dither' about some 'big-shot' senator coming to look everything over. As I said, I will be travelling alone and this isn't an official visit, and I sure as hell don't feel like any 'big-shot' anything. I'm just as confused about what's going on as you and the rest of the country are," he added with emphasis.

"Yes, sir Senator, I understand and I will look forward to seeing you next week," I repeated.

We both hung up and I sat back in my chair and put my feet on the desk, deep in thought about what in hell would the Senate Majority Leader, of the U.S. Senate, want to talk with me about!

"Penny," I yelled out, without bothering to hit the intercom.

"Yes, sir," she said as she came rushing into my office.

"Penny, next week Senator Scott, the Senate Majority Leader, will be paying us a visit. He's coming by himself, so I have no idea what it's concerning. So, if you could just double-check on everything that he might be interested in and be sure we're okay; and maybe we should keep this quiet. Especially since we have no idea why he's coming," I told her.

"Yes, sir; I'll take care of checking things out," she said as she left.

"Oh, Penny, one other thing," I added.

"Yes, sir?"

"See if you can get General Hall on the line for me."

"Will do sir," she said, and left my office.

About five minutes later, she buzzed and said, "I have General Hall on line one, Colonel Miller."

"Hello Dutch, how are you? What's happening in the 'real' world of the good ole' U.S of.A.?" I asked him.

"Nothing new here, Bull. How about you, anything special happening at the country club in Cuba?" he asked.

"Well, I'm not sure, Dutch. The damnest thing; I just got off the phone with the Senate Majority Leader, Senator Lindsey Scott."

"What?" Dutch said with surprise in his voice. "What does he want?"

"He didn't say, Dutch. He just asked if it would be convenient and fit my schedule, if he came down here to GITMO a week from this Thursday."

"What did you tell him?" Dutch asked.

"Hell, Dutch. He's the senate majority leader. What could I tell him but 'of course, senator; come on down,'" I answered. And then I asked Dutch, "Have you heard anything, Dutch? The senator said he was coming alone and not to make a big deal out of it; he just wants to talk with me."

"Hmmm," Dutch mused. "I haven't heard any talk or rumblings about anything. I will kind of put some 'feelers' out to see if anyone else has any idea what the senator is up to. You're still coming up on Thursday this week, aren't you? Dutch asked.

"I'll see you Thursday about mid-morning," I replied.

CHAPTER SEVEN

My plane touched down at Eglin AFB a little after eight on Thursday morning. Dutch was there to pick me up and we headed to the Officer's Club for our usual breakfast when I was at his headquarters.

Sitting there, eating pancakes with crisp bacon and good, black coffee, I began telling Dutch about my phone call with Senator Scott. "Dutch, I don't know what to think. He's coming alone, not bringing any staff or entourage with him, like the usual official congressional visit; especially since he's the senate majority leader. Hell, he's the head honcho up there! What's your opinion? What do you think he wants, Dutch?"

"Damned if I know, Bull. We know he and the President are on opposite sides of practically any issue that comes up, and I do know that he has raised hell about releasing any detainees, and he really gets his hair up when the President mentions closing GITMO," Dutch said. "He must want to talk with you about that, and get your opinion."

"Well, he told me not to make any special arrangements and not to worry about preparing any reports. He said he just wants to talk to me. Hell, I don't have anything to prepare for, or about," I said.

"Well, Bull, I would do just that. I wouldn't worry about preparing anything and just wait to see what's on his mind. I sure would like to sit in on that with you. Normally, a congressional visit would go through regular channels, down the chain of command. If this was normal, I would have received notification through my command," Dutch said thoughtfully.

"Maybe we'll find out something about it this weekend in D.C.," Dutch added. "It's going to be a pretty interesting weekend, I believe."

"Where are we staying this time, Dutch?" I asked him.

"Same place, the Marriott across from the White House; I've already made reservations and have a car lined up, as before."

We finished up breakfast, went to Dutch's office to pick up some items he wanted to carry with him, got his luggage, and headed back to the flight line and base ops to file a flight plan to DC.

We arrived at the Andrews Air Force Base just outside D.C. at about two-thirty in the afternoon, picked-up the rental car and went straight to the hotel, checked-in, put our luggage in the rooms and went down to the lounge for a quick sandwich.

While we were eating, I asked Dutch what the plans were.

"All I know is we're supposed to meet with Dave, and maybe a couple of others, around eight-thirty this evening for a late dinner at a restaurant over in Georgetown," Dutch replied.

"Great, Georgetown will be a good, non-descript place to meet. I don't know what Dave has in mind, but a few old friends getting together over dinner shouldn't draw too much attention," I said, maybe a little nervously.

There's a lot of history in Georgetown. It's rich in culture and is the kind of "in" place to be now days, especially with the younger, business-elite crowd, and politicians who are trying to become known and make an impression in the Nation's Capital.

It has its "dark-side" too. Many deals, both business and political, and, I'm sure, criminal, have been made here. There have been a couple of famous—or maybe I should say—"infamous" killings and suicides here, some, with rather vague White House connections too.

All of this—history, culture, the finest of dining, deal making, killings, suicides, spying—a little bit of everything in the small area of about one square mile.

Only in America! I thought.

CHAPTER EIGHT

Dutch and I arrived at our designated "non-meeting" place, the "Filomena Ristorante," one of President Clinton's favorite restaurants in Georgetown while he was in office. Located near the end of Wisconsin Avenue, the Filomena provided a beautiful view of the C&O Canal, and a lot of the Washington Harbour area, including the "famous" Foggy Bottom, as the area is known, and which has its own reputation.

We were met by the maitre'd who lead us to a small, reserved, private room near the back of the main dining room—a "room with a view," from both sides. Although it was a private room, the wall separating us from the main dining area was glass. The glass wall was framed eloquently by beautiful, but heavy draperies that hung from ceiling to floor, providing some hint of privacy to those in the room. The room, and our table, overlooked the canal and the Potomac River and much of the Harbour area. As we sat down our waiter, dressed formally in black waist-coat and pants with white shirt and black tie, appeared ready for our drink order. Dutch and I both ordered a scotch and soda to sip on while we waited for the others.

Looking through the "glass wall" into the main dining room, we spotted several familiar faces from the House of Representatives, and a couple from the Senate. There were also some ranking members of the military scattered among the customers.

I looked across the table at Dutch, and he looked back at me. "Too bad we can't just call a meeting with all of these 'head-knockers' right here and now, and tell them just what we think of some of the crap we put up with out in the field, " he said and laughed.

"Probably too many bleeding hearts here to pay us any attention," I replied. "Besides, most of them don't know their ass from a hole-in-the-ground!"

As we were looking out over the Harbour area, a familiar voice came from behind us, "You two look like your wives just ran off with your girlfriends."

We turned and looked up into the face of Bob Walters, the Deputy Secretary of Defense. Dutch and I must have looked kind of shocked. Robert "Bob" Walters was not someone we would ordinarily be just having a pleasant dinner on the town with. Hell, we both knew him; had met him on several occasions, but never socially.

Bob said, "Let me introduce you guys to my good friend, Chip Reese. He's a good person to know if you want to speak with anybody that's close to '**the**, head-honcho.' Chip is the assistant director of the Secret Service over at the 'real' big house—the White House."

Chip laughed and said, "I'm not sure who you're talking about, Bob. I may be the assistant, but I'm not sure what I'm the assistant of. I only get to do the dirty work around there. You probably get to see the 'big' man more than I do."

Just then, Sam Drakeford, Joint Chiefs Chairman, and Mike Holder, Chief of the National Guard came up. Dutch said, "Hey guys, pardon my manners, don't keep standing there, pull up a chair and have a seat."

They each took a chair and sat down. The table was set-up for about ten people. I don't think any of us knew how many or who was going to show up for this little dinner get together. Sam and Mike no sooner got seated when two others walked up. One I had never seen before, and don't think Dutch had either.

Dave Mabry was the other, and he said, "Gentlemen let me introduce a friend and colleague, Tom Beckwith; he works over at CIA headquarters. His job is to 'lure' bright, young college graduates into the 'spy' business. You guys have nothing to fear, you're too old," he laughed.

Tom Beckwith, Director of Recruitment & Training for the CIA, was a good person to get to know; at least at the moment, with all the thoughts running around in our combined heads. In the back of my head I kept thinking, *Secret Service – CIA? Hell, I thought they were always bitter enemies, and always on opposite sides in trying to get anything accomplished. Both agencies always wanted to take credit for any good stuff that went down.*

Dave must have read our thoughts, or at least mine. He broke the spell, "You're probably wondering how the CIA and the Secret Service ever got together and agreed on something, even a place to eat," he laughed, along with both of them, "not too strange though, there are some things 'some' of them do see eye-to-eye on!"

Just then, the door to our little, "public" conference room opened. I was surprised to see Democrat Congressman, Representative Dennis Wilson, walk in.

"Good evening, gentlemen. I'm happy to see all of you here," he said.

He walked over to one of the empty seats. "I've been looking for the opportunity to come here for some good, authentic Italian food. It's been a long while since I've visited this place—used to be one of my favorites. I heard that this used to be one of President Clinton's favorite places, also."

As he sat down, he looked around and said, "Dave, I really appreciate you asking me to join ya'll tonight. We don't get the chance to see each other very often, much less to sit down and talk. There's just too much going on, up on the 'Hill'. Don't ask me what it is though; we never seem to get anything accomplished; nobody wants to agree on anything anymore. Hell, I think they would rather argue and try to make headlines than to get anything done."

Our formally dressed waiter followed the Congressman into the room to take drink orders for everyone; then left to retrieve the requests.

Dave stood and talked. "I'm really glad you came, Dennis; this is just an informal, casual, get together," he said as he walked over to the door and closed it. "You know some of the things you and I have mentioned, only briefly, and mostly in a 'gripe' session on the phone from time-to-time. Well, I think all of us here feel pretty much the same way; and most of us, at some time or other, have unloaded our thoughts on each other. If for no other reason than just to let off some steam about all the crap that's going on. Especially the crap about releasing a bunch of terrorists assholes into the U.S."

Representative Wilson said, "From the last couple of conversations we've had, Dave, I get the impression that a lot of people think it's about time to take some kind of action and do something about the situation in this country; starting right here in this town."

He slowly looked around at the others. "What do you guys think?"

"Since this is just a casual, un-official, get-together," Sam Drakeford said, "I'll tell you what I think, folks. I am fed up with all the bullshit we have been putting up with from that damn jihadist, son-of-a-bitch, sitting in that office, with his thumb up his ass, trying to run a country that he knows nothing about, and cares even less about! And if we keep sitting around complaining among ourselves, and don't take some kind of action to stop him, this country is going down the drain! I for one don't plan on letting that happen, not as long as I draw a breath!" he said.

Same continued, "My title may be Chairman of the Joint Chiefs, but under this sorry son-of-a-bitch, it doesn't mean anything. He's trying to run the show. I've had three general officers, good, combat-experienced men—who knew what to do—retire because they were not allowed to do their jobs. Because of protocol and respect for the office he holds, I have lied to defend his position on the different situations. We lost thousands of men defeating Saddam Hussain and giving the country back to the people. And what does this asshole President do? He gives it back to the enemy; the very enemy of the people we were sent in to help; by pulling all of our troops out. Now, we're back in there with more troops getting killed. You guys will have to excuse me. In case you haven't noticed, I am really pissed! I don't know what each of you think, but for me, I believe this is all planned and well thought-out—by someone bigger and more influential than that little 'piss-ant!'"

Dave stood up and kind of laughed, and said, "Sam, I believe you may be a little unhappy with all the crap."

That brought a laugh from the others; even Sam laughed.

Representative Wilson said, "Sam, I'm pretty sure you have expressed the opinion of all of us here, plus many others in both the military and up on the hill. Nobody wants to take the lead; nobody wants to step out and even verbalize what action needs to be taken. Hell, we know what it will sound like if we speak it out loud, don't we?"

The representative continued, "We all know that 'that' can't happen in the United States. It only happens in third world countries. But you know what? The founding fathers foresaw something like this happening in this government. That's why they put in a safeguard; 'But when a long train of abuses and Usurpations, pursuing invariably the same object, evinces a design to reduce them under absolute despotism, it is their right, it is their Duty, to throw off such government, and to provide new guards for their future Security. . . .' That's not all Sam, you and me, and I'm sure the others here have the same opinion; this is not some hastily devised plan. This plan has been in the making for quite some time, and it's not just the President who has been doing the planning. I personally believe that if there ever was a time to seriously consider actions that would reverse the direction the country is going, it is now. We are headed in the direction of a third world, communist-controlled government. Gentlemen, we cannot let that happen!"

A lot of murmuring started up, everybody talking at the same time to those on both sides of them. From what I could hear, everybody was agreeing with the Congressman—hell, I knew I did! That was what Dutch and I had been talking about but weren't sure how many others, if any, would see it our way.

Dutch looked across the table at me and winked; I nodded back. We were both sure we now had the backing to get some very drastic action underway, and the two of us would not be the only ones standing in front of a firing squad!

Dave rapped on the table to get everyone's attention and said, "Gentlemen, We're talking some really serious stuff here tonight, but I believe all of us are on the same page about what has to be done; otherwise, we wouldn't be here."

Dave hesitated for a moment, "You know, guys, this whole situation kind of brings to mind how the founding fathers must have felt when they got together, one of them said something to the effect, 'we mutually pledge to each other our lives, our fortunes, and our sacred honor. . .'"

There was dead silence throughout the entire room as we all, almost in sync, looked around the room at each other, some nodding, some just deep in thought.

After a few minutes, but what seemed like an hour, or more, Sam stood up and spoke.

"We all have known each other for a number of years, in various capacities and leadership roles. We have trusted each other in some pretty life-threatening situations, both on and off the battlefields, in more battles than this President has ever heard of. And I don't know how many of you feel as strongly as I do about where this nation is headed and the pace that it's going, but it will be too hard to turn around in just a little while. I, for one, certainly don't intend for my grandkids, and their kids, to have to live under the realm of some dictator, in a third-world class country," he said.

Then continuing, he added, "So, I'm telling each of you, here and now, that I am pledging to each of you, my life, my fortune, and what honor I have—that I am going to do whatever it takes, to take this sovereign nation of ours back from the strangle-hold of the cold-hearted, communist-socialist oriented group that is determined to destroy that which our forefathers struggled so hard to establish. I am damn proud to be an American and nobody is going to take that away from me!"

There was quiet throughout as everyone took in what Sam had just said.

Then there was a cacophony of "hear," "hear," from across the room. I looked out through the glass "wall" and saw a few heads turn in our direction. I guess we were louder than we thought.

Finally, Dave stood up and in a strong but humble sounding voice said, "I am with Sam! So I too am hereby pledging to each of you my life, fortune, and my honor, to do whatever it takes to protect and secure this nation from all of those who are trying to tear it down!"

Then, one-by-one, around the table each person spoke.

"I'm with Sam and Dave," I said. "They have expressed my feelings entirely. I've put my life on the line for our country a number of times, as have all of you; to add fortune and honor to that is a given!"

Paul declared, "My life, my honor, my fortune—and anything else that it takes!"

Tom Beckwith from the CIA stood up and said, "Gentlemen, you have my all! Life, fortune, honor, my service, my time, my efforts, and whatever information we may need to get the job done!"

"I know the people in my agency," Bob Walters said as he stood to speak to the group. "I also know how most of them feel about this administration; they have told me in no uncertain terms on numerous occasions—they are fed up! We have to take this action that, so far, is only implied. But we know what we are speaking about, and I'm for moving ahead. It won't be the first time my life, honor, and fortune has been on the line!"

Admiral Vince Dawkins got up, followed by Chip Reese from the White House Secret Service, and then Mike Holder; one-by-one each person made their personal pledge—"to support and defend the constitution of the United States of America from all enemies, foreign and domestic!"

Congressman Wilson, who had been sitting quietly and listening as each person in this "august" group, spoke, "Gentlemen," he said as he stood and looked slowly around the room at each person, one-by-one, eyeball-to-eyeball, "When I took the oath of office, and was sworn in as a representative of the people of my state, and the United States, like you, I swore to uphold and defend our constitution, against **ALL** enemies, foreign and **DOMESTIC**! And, like you, I seriously believe we are facing a domestic enemy right now, an enemy who is purposely trying to destroy our democracy, our Republic! Even though nothing specific has been mentioned, or verbalized, at this point, I believe we all know exactly what we are talking about. This is going to require some very careful and confidential planning. I don't believe we can do that here tonight, and in such a short time. I propose that we find a suitable date and place where we can come back together and discuss this some more, and in greater detail."

He looked toward the glass "wall" and said, "It must be a secure venue; walls tend to have ears!" Everyone nodded in agreement.

Dave announced, "You'll all be hearing from me very soon; I'll let you know when and where."

CHAPTER NINE

Dutch's Southeast Command Learjet, one of the "perks" of being a two-star general, lifted off from Andrews Air Force Base in DC at 0600 on Sunday morning and landed back at Eglin Air Force Base, Dutch's Headquarters in Florida, at 1030 hours. We grabbed our luggage and put it in the trunk of Dutch's staff car that we had left at base operations when we left on Thursday. Dutch suggested we go to the club for coffee before I headed back to Guantanamo Bay.

Before leaving Base Ops, I checked to be sure my plane and crew were ready for our return trip. We were scheduled out at 1300 hours.

At the club, we both ordered coffee and a pastry for a mid-morning snack while we talked about the weekend's events.

"Dutch," I began, "I think we have some allies who are willing to put up a fight to save the country."

"You're right, Bull, not only about 'allies,' but about a fight. We don't know how many people on up the chain feel like we do and are willing to take a stand. Our group this weekend is just a small part of what it will take to pull this off and to succeed. It's going to get very interesting. In fact, it will be interesting to see how soon we will get back together—and where!" Dutch said.

"This is going to be a busy and probably real interesting week," I said. "Senator Scott is due to arrive on Thursday; no telling what he wants to talk about. I don't think I have screwed up lately."

Dutch laughed; this was a welcome change from all the seriousness of the past few weeks. "Bull, if you haven't screwed up somewhere along the line, it will be a different Bull Miller than the one I used to know," he laughed.

"If I remember correctly, I believe you have had your share of screw-ups too," I said.

Then, laughingly, we shared a couple of "old-days'" stories. It felt good to just visit with an old friend, laugh, tell a few tales, and not get too serious.

We sat there for a bit, quiet, each of just kind of lost in our own thoughts.

"You know, Bull" Dutch began, "The good Congressman was right. I don't believe any of us, except maybe you and me, and just to each other, have come right-out and said, 'What we're talking about is taking over the government of the United States!' We're talking about a damn 'coup!'" he added.

"Sure as hell, Dutch; we're talking about the old fashioned 'coup-de-tat!' But one thing we can't let it be, and that's like some third-world country military coup," I said.

"That's for damn sure," he replied.

"Well, Dutch, this is nice, but I have to get back to the 'GITMO Country Club,' as you guys call it; for me, it's back to the 'salt mines.' I've got to figure out what the senator wants and what he is up to," I said. "Drop me at Base Ops and I'll get out of your hair until we get back together in DC."

CHAPTER TEN

Monday morning I'm back at my desk early; Penny comes in surprised to see me already in the office. She sticks her head in the door and, "You're here mighty early, Colonel Miller. Is anything wrong?"

"No, everything's fine; I just needed some time to think for a while, Penny. I've already made coffee, get your cup and come sit down for a bit," I told her.

She returned in a couple of minutes with her coffee and sat down on the small sofa next to my desk.

"You look like you're awful deep in thought," she said. "You sure everything is okay? Can I get anything for you? Did you have a bad night?"

I laughed and told her, "No, Penny; everything is alright. I've just been doing some thinking, that's all."

I looked at Penny. She was a Texas girl from the word "go," smart, knowledgeable about a lot of topics, and a hard worker to boot. She knew what was going on around the area. I guess maybe I was staring at her; she looked at me and kind of smiled.

She took a sip of her coffee, looked back at me, laughed her little laugh, and said, "Colonel Miller, are you flirting with me?"

Caught off-guard, I stammered, "No. . . no, Penny, but don't think I haven't thought about it!" We both laughed and it relieved some of the tension that I had built-up in myself.

"But speaking of flirting, how is it that a young, very attractive, young lady like you is still single, and hasn't been grabbed up by some young officer who wants to 'rescue' you and take you away from all of this?" I asked.

"Well," she responded, "that's just it; most of the attractive, young officers want to do just that—just grab! I don't go for that. Congress may tell them that they are officers and gentlemen, but some never learned how to be a gentleman."

"I'm sorry," I said, "I realize that it's only been a few years since your husband was killed in a combat operation, but you don't want to see your life just slowly drift away. You should get married again, have a couple of kids; enjoy your life," I said, and then after a moment added, "There I go again—trying to give advice about love and family, especially since all of my family is gone. I guess I married the army and still haven't gotten a divorce yet. But it could happen soon."

Penny spoke up, "What do you mean by that Colonel Miller? You aren't thinking about retiring right away, are you?"

"No. I'm not thinking of retirement, not yet at least. But others may have some different plans for me," I replied.

"Now, what do you mean? You're being pretty vague," said Penny, adding dejectedly, "Others? What others? And why on earth would any-one want to see you out?"

"Penny, how well do you know the troops here, how they feel about their jobs and being assigned to GITMO?" I asked

"I think I know them all pretty well, sir. Here, at the detention center, we're just a small cadre of personnel, and it's easy to know each other pretty well," she responded, somewhat startled at the question.

"How do you feel about your job, Penny?" I asked then.

"I love working for you, Colonel Miller; you've always been very nice to me, easy going, and easy to get along with. You're a good boss," she replied.

"I don't mean here in the office, Penny; I mean about our purpose, our assignment, keeping these detainees in prison. Are we being mean and inhumane to other humans?" I asked.

"Oh! That's a whole 'nother story Colonel," she said as she continued, and her expression changed dramatically. "I don't really know how to put it sir, but, and it's not only me, I think all the troops here feel the same as I do—we don't like the idea of sending any of these sorry bastards to the mainland, or releasing them so they can shoot at us again! I'm sure you have talked with some of the guard personnel, Colonel, or if any of them have told you about some of the crap they have to put up with from some of these asshole prisoners, or maybe I should call them 'guests' because that's the way they are treated! Colonel Miller, do you have any idea what our people have to put up with . . . because they are afraid of complaints and getting court-martialed?"

Penny was really getting worked up now; the veins in her neck stood out and her face was turning a shade of red as she kept talking. I had asked the question and she was unloading on me, getting some of her frustration out. I guess she needed it.

"These damn so-called guests piss in their cup and throw it on the guards as they pass by checking on them. Some have even shit on the floor, picked it up, and thrown that at the guards. Worse yet, some of these sorry bastards have masturbated in their hands and flung that into the guards' faces. Sick little bastards should be taken out and shot!"

Suddenly, Penny stopped talking and looked embarrassed, "I'm sorry about the language, but it gets me all worked up anytime I read or hear about the President wanting to release them, or send them to the US and treat them like some damn VIP!" she added.

I laughed out loud, "Calm down, Penny. I didn't mean to get you so 'riled' up. I believe you and I feel the same way on this, and so do a lot of other people, on up the chain of command!"

"What . . . I mean, sir? Who're you talking about, up the chain of command? That sounds pretty serious, Colonel!" she said. "I think you know a lot more about this than you're saying!"

She hesitated a moment, took a sip of coffee to help her calm down, and then asked, "Is this why the senator is coming this week?"

"I don't know why the senator is coming to this God-forsaken place. This is not exactly a paradise or vacation spot, and certainly not a 'plush' assignment post," I replied. "I guess we'll just have to wait to find out. Right now, you know as much as I do about this."

CHAPTER ELEVEN

Standing in front of the Base Operations building at the Guantanamo Bay U.S. Naval Station on Thursday afternoon, gazing up into the bright, sunny sky, I caught a glare of bright light. Must surely be the senator's plane; right on schedule. His last communication said he should arrive around 1400 hours. This was the least busy time of day at the naval station and around base ops. He was making great efforts to keep his arrival and visit quiet.

Following the senator's request, I had not notified the Naval Station Commander of his visit, as normal protocol would have it. That was the senator's responsibility, and his staff's. However, I did feel somewhat uneasy about keeping his visit quiet. I had already arranged private quarters, and a car, in case he wanted transportation to himself.

The plane touched down, and shortly after, rolled to a stop in front of the base ops building. I walked out as the crew was opening the door. Senator Lindsey Scott, Senate Majority Leader, was standing in the doorway waiting to get off.

I still hadn't figured out why he was here and the relative secrecy surrounding his visit. I had a couple of ideas running around the inside my head, however. We had met once before, several years back when I was called to testify at a senate committee hearing on the treatment of "detainees" (for some reason our liberal government never wanted to call them prisoners). Perhaps it would have been too harsh and would have hurt their feelings.

Senator Scott came down the steps; he was dressed casually—in navy colored pants and a light blue golf shirt. I greeted him as he stepped off; we shook hands and introduced ourselves and he said he remembered my appearing before his committee.

As we walked to my staff car, we made small talk about the weather and various non-committal type subjects, like "did you bring your golf clubs," about the island of Cuba, etc. As we approached the car, my driver was already out and standing with the rear-door opened. He saluted as we stepped closer, and closed the door when we got in.

I said, "Senator Scott, I thought you might like to freshen up a bit and take a short break, so I told the driver to take us directly to your quarters, unless you have plans and would like to go somewhere else first."

"That's fine with me. I can use a little break and that will give us a few minutes to talk," he replied.

As we were on the way Senator Scott,said, "Colonel Miller, I know you're wondering just what the hell I'm doing here, especially without all the usual fanfare and routine. Well, I'm not really too sure myself, but let me begin by saying that I think I know enough about you and your background, your military career, and how you feel about your country, and that I can level with you."

It was as much a question as a statement, I thought.

"I hope I have been correct in my assumption. Am I correct?" he asked.

Well shit, I thought. *That was pretty blunt and straight forward.* So I said, "Of course, Senator. I hope we can have open and honest—call it as it 'lies'—discussions. About any subject you would like to talk about."

We arrived at what was to be his quarters for the weekend—a bungalow in a quiet area of the Naval Station where he wouldn't attract a lot of attention. We got out and the driver got the senator's luggage; he only brought one small roller case, just enough clothes for a couple of days. We went inside and had a seat in the small living room area. I told the driver to wait in the car. I would be out shortly.

Senator Scott spoke up again, "I also know you don't like the way things are going here in your command, or the way these prisoners are given the red-carpet treatment, after all the crap and heart-ache they have caused. I need to know one thing before we get into any deep discussions, Colonel Miller. I need to know if we can put titles and positions aside while we visit and talk this weekend. While I am here, I am NOT a senator—I'm just Lindsey Scott, a friend whom you invited down for a round of golf. And, you're not Colonel James Miller, Commander of Gitmo Detention Center—and, I hope you don't mind—you're just 'Bull' Miller, an old friend from the states," he said.

"Senator, that suits me just fine, I mean Lindsey! It's even better. That way we can talk openly and frankly with each other," I said.

"Good; I feel much better about my visit, now. Some of the things I'd like to discuss with you is pretty extreme and could be dangerous if the word got out to the wrong people. And, Bull, the only reason that I called on you is because I think you feel as I do about the situation in our country. We have some mutual friends, Dave Mabry and Sam Drakeford, and a couple of others. But Dave and Sam and I have discussed you and your situation here at Gitmo. I know about some of the discussions you have had and I feel that I can trust you. I believe you know what I'm speaking about and the danger involved. If you don't want to get involved any further, please say so, and this get-together never happened. I'm out of here in the morning and you never saw me nor did I see you."

"It sounds like some pretty serious stuff is going on, Lindsey, but as you said, we are on the same page as far as the releasing of detainees and the current situation in the country," I replied.

Then I got up to leave and told Lindsey, "You take a break, maybe catch a nap, and I'll pick you up at seven. We'll go to the club for dinner and then we can come back here or go to my place and talk."

I walked out and got into my car and headed back to my office.

CHAPTER TWELVE

It was raining "cats and dogs" in Washington D.C. as Dave and his wife Anna climbed into their waiting car outside the exclusive Capital Club on Pennsylvania Avenue. They had attended a special retirement party, an official function for a friend who was leaving his military career after thirty-four years in the Corps. Dave was decked out in his formal "dress blues" and Anna in a very chic, long gown for the evening's events.

His driver had brought an umbrella to the door and escorted them out; he held the umbrella for them as they got in and closed the door. Then, they headed west, home to his "ranch," as Dave liked to call it.

As they got out of DC on Highway 50 West, and into the partially developed, hilly, countryside of Virginia, Dan, Dave's driver for the past two plus years, spoke up and said, "Did you see that?"

"What?" asked General Mabry.

"That car, that black Suburban; that just pulled around and cut-in right in front of us and slowed down. In fact, it has stayed on our tail all the way from the city; it doesn't have any license plates. It could even be stolen. They're driving crazy."

All of a sudden there was a hard bump from the rear, which nearly knocked their car off the road. That would be bad since they were in some hills with pretty deep drop-offs into small ravines.

"What the hell's going on?" Dave said as his wife, Anna, screamed.

"What is happening?" she yelled, just as they were bumped hard again.

"I don't know what they're trying to do," said Dave; the windows are tinted and I can't see inside. What the hell do they think they're trying to do? Be careful, Dan."

Anna screamed, crying, and yelled, "Dave, I'm scared. Who are these people and what are they trying to do to us?"

Dan tried to pull out into the left lane to go around the Suburban in front; the Suburban moved to the left so they couldn't pass.

Dan looked in the rear view mirror, and shocked, he told the General, "Sir that car behind us, it's just like the one in front; it's a black Suburban also. What the hell is going on? Who are they, and what are they trying to do, run us off the road?"

Dan moved back into the right lane; the Suburban in front slowed enough to let Dave's car pull up closer; another Suburban pulled alongside, then, the one behind them moved up close to the rear. They were boxed-in! The rear window of the Suburban on the left slowly lowered; Dan glanced and saw what he thought was an automatic weapon come out. He pressed the gas pedal and rammed the rear of the vehicle in front; as he did, a volley of automatic gunfire erupted from the weapon in the vehicle and into the back seat of the staff car. He heard the General yell as shells hit him in the side of the head and exploded! Dan felt something warm and wet hit the back of his head; he knew what it was, it was blood and brain matter. He had seen it in Afghanistan; he also knew that both the General and his wife had to be dead.

The Suburban on the left of Dan began moving to the right, into the right lane and into the side of Dave's staff car; Dan tried to brake, but the brakes wouldn't take hold.

"Oh shit," yelled Dan, "The brakes are gone!"

The big, black suburban on Dan's left suddenly made his move and crashed into the driver's side of the staff car sending Dan, Dave, and Anna careening off the road, down the deep, chasm drop-off into the wooded area below.

The last thing Dan remembered was the sound of screeching tires as the Suburbans left, speeding off into the night.

CHAPTER THIRTEEN

As I walked back into the office, Penny looked up and asked, "How did it go Colonel? Did the senator get here alright? Did he say what he wanted?"

"Whoa up there, Penny, you still know as much as I do. Hopefully, I'll find out more tonight over dinner," I said.

Penny laughed her little laugh and said, "Sorry, sir, I didn't mean to pry; I'm just a little curious about such a visit by a ranking senator, that's all."

"I'm still curious too, Penny. Maybe we'll know more a little later," I said.

I showed up at Lindsey Scott's quarters right at seven o'clock; he was at the door waiting, so we got back into the staff car and headed to the Officer's Club.

When we got into the car he said, "Jim, I would rather keep a low profile if we can. Fact is I'd rather not be recognized at all."

"You're sure making this sound very ominous, Lindsey. Since we're being totally honest and off the record about you being here, I frankly don't know what to think," I told him. "You have me quite concerned, and I'm not real sure about what!"

He thought for a moment then said, "It's something a lot of people need to be concerned about, not just you and me. For one thing, I think the country is going to hell in a handbasket and nobody's doing anything about it; I'm sick and tired of it and I am trying to figure some way something can be done!"

"That does sound pretty serious," I said. "On the surface, it sounds like some of the bullshit I'm going through and trying to figure a way to get something done."

"Jim, from some conversations I've had with a couple of our mutual friends, you and I are on the same page about this. That's exactly why I wanted to talk with you personally, and as soon as possible. And, it had to be in private."

"Oh, by the way, I believe you and Dave Mabry are friends. I hate to tell you this, but I received word, on my way down here, directly from my office, that he and his wife were killed in an accident late last evening on their way home from some function. I don't know any details yet, but I understand that his driver is in critical condition and may not live either."

"**What?**" I almost screamed! "How did it happen? Did anyone see what happened?"

I was almost in shock.

My driver looked in the rear view mirror at us and said, "What? Is something wrong, Colonel?"

"No, everything's okay," I replied. But everything sure as hell was not okay.

"I don't have any details, but you can rest assured there will be an investigation. Dave was on the Joint Chiefs as well as the Commandant of the Marine Corps," Lindsey said. "Maybe if the driver regains consciousness, he can provide some details about what happened. I'll keep you informed with any news I receive about what happened."

I was really shook-up about this. Not only was Dave a good friend, and Anna, she was one of the sweetest people I have ever known. But now, both of them dead; I could hardly picture it, hard to grasp the fact that they were gone.

Dave was to set up our next get-together in DC, or somewhere less conspicuous. I wonder who will take on that responsibility now.

Just then, my cell phone went off. I looked and saw that it was Dutch. I asked Lindsey to excuse me for a moment while I took the call.

"Bull, have you heard the news about Dave and Anna?" he asked, breathlessly.

"I just now heard it from Senator Scott; he doesn't have any details yet, other than there was an accident," I said.

"Accident, my ass, Bull, I know Dave better than that. He was always very careful; sometimes, I thought he was too careful. He never took chances," Dutch said.

"What do you mean, Dutch? Do you think there was more to it than an accident," I asked? "Find out what you can and let me know what's going on, Dutch. I'll talk with you later."

I looked over at Lindsey and said, "That was General Dutch Hall; he's the Commander of the Southeast Command based at Eglin Air Force Base. He feels like I do about the situation our country is facing; we've talked about it on occasion."

Lindsey said, "I've met Dutch a few times. I kind of thought he might feel the same, but I just wasn't sure. I . . . we . . . have to be very careful about what we say, to whomever, and wherever we say it."

We pulled up to the Officers' Club, got out, and went inside. The greeter met us as we entered and led us to our reserved table in an "out-of-the-way" place, as I had requested. We got seated and ordered drinks.

Lindsey and I both looked around the dining room, neither of us talking; I guess Lindsey was trying to get his thoughts together; I think he felt that he was in strange, new territory. Whether it was because of the location or the subject matter he wanted to discuss, I couldn't tell.

The waiter put our drinks down and we told him we would order our meal later. We were in a quiet corner of the large dining room and no one seemed to pay any special attention to us. If anybody recognized Lindsey, they didn't show it.

After a few moments, he spoke up, "Jim, I don't know any other way to put what I'm about to say, except to just be blunt and say it as I feel. As I said earlier, the only reason for my being down here is because from all I hear, you feel the same as I do, and the way many others in DC feel also. We're damn sick and tired of letting that 'dick-head' who calls himself 'President' get away virtually unchallenged with all the shit he does. And I'll tell you this; it isn't just Republicans either, many Democrats also, even though when it comes to voting on a bill or something that he is pushing, they are pressured into going along. Anyone who disagrees with him and his socialist buddies are being tabbed as 'racists' and homophobes or anything else to make them look bad to the voting public."

The Senator went on, "I realize you folks in the field know, and read about, a lot of what goes on in Washington, but I bet, I could guarantee, you would be totally shocked if you knew the whole story of what goes on behind the scenes, which the public and the press never hear about. Several of us on the 'Hill,' both Republican and Democrat, have talked among ourselves about getting something done, and getting it done now. This closing of GITMO Executive Order has kind of brought it to a head. That's one way your name came up in discussions. People know how you feel about releasing any of the detainees or sending them to a US prison. None of us want that, and we're ready for something to be done."

Then, after a momentary pause, he added, "Jim, a few of us are aware that a group of high ranking military and government officials got together in Washington, and this is what it was about. And, by the way, I caught part of your conversation with Dutch Hall in the car earlier this afternoon. I gathered that Dutch doesn't think Dave's death was an accident. Frankly, Jim, neither do I! And, as you already know, Dave was 'leading the charge' and was outspoken about getting some action on removing the so-called, President."

"How the hell did it happen, then, Lindsey?" I asked. "Who would want to kill Dave and his wife, and their driver?"

"It has to be that same bunch of assholes that are trying to take over and destroy this country, that's who," Lindsey replied. Then, he added, "After you dropped me off and left this afternoon, I made a couple of calls. I have someone I know I can trust, looking into what happened, on the quiet and personally. By the time I get back to DC, I should know a little more. This entire movement has more power than anyone may imagine, Jim. It's very surprising, not only at the number of people, but also their positions in government. They run the gamut from military leaders, to congress—both the house and senate—to the FBI, the CIA, Secret Service, to White House advisors. You name the service and there are people who want to take whatever action is necessary to get rid of this sorry excuse for a leader; a sorry excuse for a President."

Turning a little red in the face and getting his volume up a notch or two, Lindsey continued as I looked around the room to see if anyone was paying any attention to us; no one seem to notice.

"We have lost our leadership position in the world, our dignity and respect. We've become the laughing stock of the world. Russia and China laugh at us behind our back. Jim, I am damn well sick and tired of going through this day-after-day! We're getting rid of that son-of-a-bitch pretty soon now, and it won't be soon enough to suit me! Sorry, Jim, I didn't mean to get so worked up, but just thinking about what that bastard is doing gets to me," Lindsey said as he looked around.

"I know exactly how you feel, Lindsey. The feeling is also strong out here, in the field where we come face-to-face with his influence on a daily basis. These assholes that we're supposedly guarding know every detail about what the President is saying. They have nothing else to do but watch TV all day, and night," I said. "They talk among themselves and scheme."

We finished our dinner and sat for another hour, just talking about our country in general—the way things used to be. The United States was always the most liked country in the world, always ready and willing to help any other country when they had a catastrophe or some other dire need. Well respected and trusted. And we talked about the fact that as Americans we didn't take a bunch of crap off our enemies, either. If we entered an engagement, or "conflict," as some like to call them—we went in to kick ass, defeat the enemy, and get the hell out.

Finally, Lindsey decided to call it a night and "turn in" for the evening. We got up to leave and as we walked out, he asked if we had a golf course on the base. I figured he should already know what recreational facilities we had. He held the purse strings.

Anyway, I told him, "Lindsey, I'm glad you asked. I have extra clubs; I will pick you up at eight in the morning and we'll go play a quick round. I must warn you, however, it isn't the fanciest course you've ever seen. In fact, it's only nine holes, but it's all we've got."

I figured I wouldn't try to explain what the course was like, I would let him judge for himself.

I picked him up at eight, as promised, and we drove to the main part of the Guantanamo Naval Base and out to the golf course. I pulled up to a small building that serves as the clubhouse and parked, and we got out of the car.

Lindsey looked around and asked, "Where is the golf course?"

"You're looking at it!" I said with a little chuckle.

He laughed and said, "I believe you set me up on this, Bull. Is this a hint that Congress should provide funding for a real golf course here?"

We looked out over the first "fairway." No grass, just sand! About 150 yards out there was a green patch—artificial turf that served as a green; it had a flagstick in the middle. I looked over at Lindsey and said, "That's the best hole on the entire course."

He laughed and said, "I realize you didn't know I was coming down, but I think you must have had this planned for any member of congress that just happened by this place. Maybe we should include a golf course for GITMO so our 'guests' could have decent recreational facilities." And he laughed harder.

I returned the barb with, "Hell, Lindsey, do that, and we'll wind up being their caddies!"

He teed the ball up and hit it straight down the so-called fairway, and it rolled onto the fake green. I stepped up and matched his shot. We both putted in for a birdie. After playing the "best" hole on the short course, our game went downhill from there.

As we moved to the second tee box, Lindsey said, "Jim," (he alternately called me "Jim" and "Bull") "many of us in the Capitol have been discussing the fact that deep-down, we think there has been a conspiracy going on in this country for quite a long while. Some force, either from outside, or, from inside the country has been slowly trying to take over our government, one slow step by one slow step at a time. It has a lot of people very concerned. We think it has been playing in the background for years, but now the sources are getting more aggressive. It's like they seem to think they have it under control and they are no longer scared of using tactics pretty damn openly. They have been extremely successful in selling it to a lot of the general public. And, of course, the main tactic is benefits; giving everything away. Entitlements! Get certain elements of the public to believe they deserve to be taken care of without having to work for it, that it's the government's responsibility. They have effectively divided the nation and created more racism than ever before! Not just between the black and white communities, but with other ethnic groups as well."

As he talked, Lindsey stepped up to the second tee and placed his ball on the white tee, stepped back, and looked down the fairway.

"How far is this fairway?" he asked.

"You better really cream this one. The green is 350 yards and this is a par-four hole," I answered.

He stepped up and hit a long drive that "sliced" into the rough on the right. Lindsey looked at me and said, "If there were any grass out there, I might really be in the 'rough!'"

We laughed as I hit my drive straight down the middle of the fairway. "You just gotta know where to place the ball," I laughed again.

We wandered on toward the next tee box, and I could tell Lindsey was deep in thought. Since we were on a "first name" basis and being totally honest in our discussion, I asked him, "Lindsey, you look like you have an awful lot on your mind; you're mighty deep in thought. Anything you want to share?"

"I'd like to share some of these bad shots with you," he quipped and laughed.

We kept walking and talking as we took our time. There seemed to be no one else on the course this morning—can't say I blame them; it's not a real golf course.

As he stood on the tee, Lindsey said, "You know 'Bull,' Vice President Joe Bradley and I have been pretty close friends for the past twenty-five years, even though we belong to different parties politically. While he was in the senate, his office was next door to mine. We had lunch together most days and our families went out together socially. He is really from the 'old, moderate,' Democrat party thinking. We still get together frequently, even though he is vice president. I'm not sure anybody knows we do, or at least there would be very few people who know. We, Joe and I, have been having this same discussion for quite some time now. He is very frustrated. Says that he is even sorry he accepted the vice presidency and is finding it extremely hard to go along with some of the crap the President and those advisors come up with. He's not even sure just where some of those advisors came from and how they got themselves appointed to the positions. I almost believe that he is to the point that he has thought of resigning! I don't know, Bull; there is so much crap going on in DC that I don't know what to think anymore. Something is happening, something big, and it's not good for the country either."

"Lindsey, I agree; it does sound like someone is trying to take over the country—from the inside!" I said.

"That's exactly what I'm saying, and that's what I and a lot of others are thinking. You and the military leaders that got together a couple of weeks ago aren't the only ones who have held a meeting or two. Hell, Bull, we were just speaking of them and a conspiracy; I guess some of us have been thinking conspiracy ourselves. That's okay! I don't give a shit if we are planning a conspiracy, a take-over; call it what you like, but I will not let a bunch of demagogues' take over this nation as long as I'm alive! It will have to be over my dead body!"

We finished up number-nine hole and headed back to the car; we had not kept score on a scorecard, but I think both of us thought we had scored well . . . with each other. We had a "meeting of the minds" and on the right course, thinking alike. We knew where each stood in the situation.

As we got into the car, Lindsey asked, "Bull, can you spend a few days in DC in the next week or two?"

"Not a problem," I answered. "Would it be alright if General Dutch Hall came along? He is into this also; not only that, but he is my boss and I have to run it by him anyway."

"Sure. I know Dutch and how he feels; it'll be good to have him there with us," he said. "I'll head back home, to DC, first thing in the morning and get things rolling so we will be organized when you and Dutch get there. I'll also find out more details about Dave and Anna getting killed."

Then, Lindsey added thoughtfully. "I find it hard to believe that it was an accident."

I stood in front of Base Ops as US Senate Majority Leader Senator Lindsey Scott's plane rose and lifted off. After the golf yesterday, we had dinner, a couple of drinks, and more discussion before I dropped him off at his quarters for the night.

As he boarded his plane for the return trip to the Nation's Capital, he told me that he would be in touch as soon as he set up the contacts.

CHAPTER FOURTEEN

I walked into my office on Monday morning; it was eight-thirty. Penny was already at her desk and hard at work. She looked up, with a questioning smile. "How did the weekend with the senator go?" she asked as she got up and got me a cup of coffee.

"Damn, you're nosey, Penny," I laughed and said, "It was a good weekend; we played a little golf on our fine golf course, had a few drinks and dinner, and visited for several hours."

"Colonel, you know what I'm talking about. I am a little 'nosey' and want to hear what he is going to do about this closing crap. You're just putting me on. I haven't been able to sleep all weekend, wondering what the two of you were discussing and planning. It's about given me hives," she said letting out her little laugh.

I took a sip of my coffee, looked back at her. "Penny, I really don't know right now. He made it very clear that he feels as we do and plans to do something about the situation. He doesn't want to see any of these bastards released or sent to the states either. He also made it clear that he doesn't like the direction the country is headed, and he plans to something about that also. Just what, he didn't say. But he did say that he wants me to come to DC and spend several days. He didn't say doing what," I added. "I guess I'll find out when I get there."

"Do you know when you will be going, sir?" Penny asked.

"I don't know yet, but I think it will probably be next week or the week after. I expect to hear from him in a couple of days," I told her. "That reminds me; when Colonel Philips comes in, tell him that I need to talk with him. He'll need to take charge while I'm gone. I have no idea how long I'll actually be in DC."

Lt. Colonel Ron Philips was my deputy commander and actually does the day-to-day running of the detention center. When something doesn't go right, he either "fixes" it, or calls me. He would be in command while I was in DC.

Penny looked kind of perplexed. She asked, "Colonel Miller, I know it's probably none of my business, and I don't need to know everything that's going on, or even what's happening or getting ready to happen. Colonel, I don't know what you are talking about. Hell, Colonel, I don't even know what I'm talking about, but I get the feeling it's something big! Is this going to get you in trouble some way?"

I placed my hand on her shoulder, "I don't know if this will get anybody in trouble or not. It does have the potential to create some problems. But you don't have to worry, Penny, nothing's going to happen to you."

"I wasn't thinking about me, sir. I don't want you to get into any trouble with the 'powers that be,'" she said.

"Thanks, Penny. I certainly don't want trouble with anybody, either. You just don't worry your pretty little blonde head about me. I've been in scrapes before, and I have survived this long. I don't plan on giving up just yet," I said and gave her shoulder a squeeze as I turned and started back to my desk.

She laid her hand on mine and gave a slight squeeze as she blushed.

CHAPTER FIFTEEN

Democrat Congressman Dennis Wilson was leaving his house in Alexandria, VA, on his way to Sunday church services with his wife, teenage son, and one of his staff members when he dropped his keys and bent down to pick them up. Suddenly, a shot rang out from somewhere nearby. The staff member, Toby Grant fell, bleeding, to the pavement in front of the house.

Dennis Wilson yelled to his family, "Get down!" Another shot rang out and hit the wall beside Dennis' head, shattering a brick across him, his wife, and son. They heard a car speed off in a hurry. Dennis looked up and saw a large, black car racing down the street away from them, squealing the brakes as it went around the corner.

He turned to his family and saw they were not hurt. He looked at Toby and saw the blood coming from his head as he lay motionless on the sidewalk.

Dennis yelled at his wife, "Call 9-1-1, and tell them someone has been shot and to get the hell over here fast! And stay in the house; don't come out!"

Dennis' wife and son ran back into the house.

He kneeled down and looked at Toby. He could see under the other side of his head that there was no skull left. The shot had entered the left side of his head, making a small, neat, round hole. But when it entered, the bullet exploded and blew the entire right side of his head away. Mixed with the blood, Dennis could see brain matter on the sidewalk under his head. Toby was dead! Dennis had seen enough men shot and killed when he served in Desert Storm, whom he knew.

"Bastards!" he screamed. "This boy doesn't know what's going on! He is innocent! Come back and bring your shit to me and see what happens! This does it. You want a fight—I'll give you a fight you can't handle. You have just declared war on yourself; you assholes!"

Dennis turned and saw a couple of neighbors coming up, yelling, "What's happening, Dennis" What's going on? Has somebody been shot?"

"You're bleeding Dennis, did you get shot?" someone asked.

Dennis reached up and wiped his hand across his forehead and felt the wet, sticky mixture of blood and sweat, mixed with fragments of brick from the wall, next to where his head had been. He suddenly realized that if he had not dropped his keys and stooped to pick them up, it would be his head that was blown away, not Toby's.

The ambulance came screaming to a stop and two EMS guys came running over. They stopped when they saw Toby lying there. They knew it was too late. Several police cars and unmarked vehicles came tearing in and braking to a halt.

"We were nearby when we received the 9-1-1 call of a shooting," said a large man in a dark suit and tie.

Dennis looked at the man and thought he must be a plainclothes detective, or something. The man pulled out his wallet and showed Dennis his badge that read, "Washington, DC Detective."

"I'm Detective Tom Smith," he said, "And this is my partner, Detective Tim Jones. We were in the neighborhood and on the way downtown when we got the call. What happened here?"

Detective Jones spoke up and asked, "You're Congressman Dennis Wilson, aren't you? You're in the House of Representatives?"

"Yes," said Dennis. "We had just stepped out of the house on our way to church. Toby, my aide, was next to me; I dropped my keys and bent to pick them up when I heard the shot. I saw Toby fall. I heard a grunt or groan from him. I yelled for everyone to get down; I saw and heard a car take off like a bat out of hell, tires screaming as it went around the corner there. It was one of those big, black SUVs. I yelled at my wife to get in the house and call 9-1-1."

"Did you get a look at anybody in the vehicle?" asked Detective Smith.

"No, the windows were dark. Besides, looking at them wasn't first on my mind at the time," he replied.

Another car pulled up to the curb; Tom Beckwith from the CIA came up and asked, "What's going on, Dennis? I was heading to church and I heard the squelch box go off and said that Congressman Wilson had been shot. I turned around and headed straight here. Are you alright? Are Nancy and Denny okay?"

He looked over and saw Toby. The paramedics had placed a sheet over him.

"Who is that?" Tom asked.

"That is . . . was . . . one of my aides, Toby Grant. Just a young man, a friend of the family. He and Denny had become good friends. He had spent the night and was going to church with us. I sure hate to be the one to tell his parents," Dennis said, as tears welled up in his eyes.

Tom got closer to Dennis and in almost a whisper asked, "Do you think this has anything to do with our meeting and what we have been talking about? It sure as hell looks suspicious, especially after what happened to Dave; they don't give a shit whom they hurt in the process. Their mission is to destroy this country and take it over at all cost!"

Dennis was almost shocked that Tom said what he did here in public, although no one was paying any attention to them at the time.

"I'll tell you one thing, Tom. This really pisses me off and they will not get away with this!" I said, probably a little too loud. "Dave was going to set-up our next meeting; well Dave is not here any longer to do it."

Dennis and Tom stood there, watching, as the investigators took photos of the crime scene and the medics placed Toby's body into a black body bag and loaded his body into the ambulance. *He deserved better than this*, Dennis thought.

He stood there thinking, *Now I have two funerals to go to. Dave and Anna would be a double funeral; they would be buried in Arlington National Cemetery. It will be a couple of days before we would know about Toby's funeral.*

"I will be calling a meeting myself," Dennis declared. "And soon! We are going to take some kind of action and we're going to kick ass; if it's the last thing I ever do! Somebody is going down for this!"

CHAPTER SIXTEEN

It was a quiet Sunday morning on the Island of Cuba as I climbed climbed out of bed. I looked at the clock and saw it was eight o'clock; I had stayed in bed a couple of hours later than my usual getting-up time. I stretched, went into the bathroom for my usual morning routine of getting ready for another boring, weekend day.

Just then the cell phone went off. I picked it up and flipped it open, "Hello, this is Jim Miller," I answered into it.

"Jim, this is Lindsey. There has been an assassination attempt on Dennis Wilson! Someone tried to shoot him as he and his family was heading to church this morning."

"Did he get hit?" I asked.

"No. Fortunately he and his family are safe, but his son had a friend who spent the night with them, who was also an aide to Dennis; he was killed," Lindsey said. "He was only about twenty, just getting started in life when it's snuffed out by a bunch of maniacs."

"Did anyone get a look at who did it?" I asked. "Do you have any idea who or why?"

"That's all I know at this point, Jim. You can pretty well guess what group was responsible, and I guess we probably know the why. Somehow some word must have leaked out that something was going on, and they don't like the idea. But I'll tell you this; they better get used to the idea. Because a helluva lot more is going to be happening," Lindsey said emphatically.

Then after a moment's pause, he added, "The other reason for calling, Jim, is that I have already spoken with Sam Drakeford over at the Pentagon, and we would like for you and Dutch Hall to come to DC immediately. In fact, Sam said he was having orders cut right away for both of you to be placed on temporary duty (TDY) to his office in the Pentagon. I expect you will be receiving the order first thing tomorrow morning."

Then, Lindsey took a deep breath and added, "Something is going on within the administration, over at the White House. Makes me think that, somehow, word has leaked that someone is planning some kind of action or event. I also called Dennis to check on him and his family and he said that since Dave is gone, he is going to call a meeting, soon, and get the folks that he knows feel strongly about the situation together and work up a plan of action. He wants to move on it right away. He not only sounded a little scared and anxious, but I can tell you, he is really pissed about what happened. Call my private number, the one that I gave you, and let me know your schedule, when you will arrive in DC."

And then, "Oh, and by the way," added Lindsey. "I just heard that Dave's driver is slowly coming out of the coma that he's been in since that so-called accident. Maybe we can find out a little more about what happened that evening."

As an after-thought, Lindsey said, "Jim, be careful; watch your back."

"Thanks, Lindsey; you better do the same. You're closer to the action!" I replied.

After clicking off, I sat for a few moments, just thinking; reviewing all the facts and running them through my mind. I picked up my phone and dialed Dutch Hall's number.

"Good morning, Bull," he said on the first ring. "I saw it was you. I was just going to call you. I guess you have already heard about Dennis getting shot at."

"Yeah, Dutch, and I've had a few minutes to think about it, and I am really pissed about the crap that's going on. I agree with Senator Scott and Sam; we've got to get moving and get this situation settled fast! I assume that you have gotten the word also, that we, you and I, are being assigned TDY to the Pentagon, directly under Sam. Lindsey didn't say for how long, but he also told me that Dennis is so upset, he is calling a meeting right away," I told him.

Dutch added, "Bull, I believe this is a lot bigger than either of us realize. I've had some feelers out and there seems to be more people involved than we know about. I think it has been brewing for quite some time, behind the scenes. I also believe it was that meeting we attended in DC that kind of kicked thing off. Evidently, whoever is behind the killings thinks we're closer than we are."

" Lindsey said we should have orders, probably tomorrow morning," I said.

"Yeah! Dennis mentioned it, that he, Sam, and Senator Scott had already talked about it. I will call you as soon as I receive the orders here. Maybe we can meet up and go from here."

"Sounds good to me," I replied. "I'll see you in a couple of days, Dutch."

CHAPTER SEVENTEEN

I got to my office a little early on Monday morning in order to begin getting organized for however long I would be gone. I rang Ron Philips, my deputy commander, to leave a message that I wanted to see him when he came in, but he picked up on the second ring.

"Colonel Philips," he answered.

"Good morning, Ron. You're in early for a Monday too, I see."

"Yes sir. I've got a lot of little things to get done to see what these little, privileged shit-heads want, so we don't have some 'big-wig' breathing down our backs. You know, Bull, it really torques my jaws what we have to put up with to satisfy these bastards. Hell, not only them but those assholes in Washington too!" he said.

I laughed and told him, "Ron, I guess we'll have to put up with it for a while longer. That Washington bunch doesn't have to look at it day in and day out like we do. And you see it even closer than I do. Some days, Ron, when you've told me about some of the crap that has gone on, I think, I don't know how you and the guard personnel put up with it. I honestly believe the first time one of those shitheads threw some of their stuff at me, I'd stop and blow his damn head off!"

And then after a pause, I added, "I guess I would be ripe for a court martial."

Ron laughed and asked, "Did you want anything in particular, Bull?"

"Oh yes; could you drop over to my office when you get a few minutes?"

"Sure, any certain time more convenient? I'm pretty open except for a bunch of little stuff, loose ends, etc.," he said.

"I'll tell you what, Ron, let's just make it noon for lunch, at the club, it's nothing pressing," I said.

"Noon is fine with me, I'll see you there," he said and we hung up.

The door opened and Penny came in with two cups of coffee in her hands. "Good morning, Colonel Miller. I saw your light on and your cup still sitting by the coffee maker, so I thought maybe you could use a cup about now," she said with a smile that lit up the office.

"Thanks, Penny. We may have a busy day today. I'm expecting to receive orders to go TDY to Washington for a while, and we will need to be sure everything is covered around here; don't want any problems to crop up while I'm away."

"TDY, Washington; as in DC," she asked?

"That's right. I had a call from Senator Scott yesterday and he, and some others, wants me in Washington as soon as I can get there. I'll be assigned to the Pentagon, the Joint Chiefs of Staff's office," I replied.

"What will you be doing?" she asked as she sipped her coffee.

"I really don't have a clue, Penny. I'll just have to wait 'til I get there to find out," I answered.

"Does it have anything to do with the closure of this post?" she asked.

"I'm sure it does have something to do with it, but just what, I don't know. I wish I did," I answered.

We both sat quietly for a few moments, sipping on our coffee and, I guess, just thinking. To break the silence, I asked her, "How was your weekend? What did you find to do?"

She wrinkled up her nose and said, "Not much of anything; it was pretty much another boring weekend on the beautiful U.S. Guantanamo Naval Station, on the beautiful island of Cuba."

Then, she smiled real big and added, "Well, I did go over to the main part of the base, to the beach and lay out in the sun for a little while."

"I bet that brought a lot of attention and excitement to the area," I told her, "Especially if you wore your bikini."

She laughed out loud and said, "It didn't even create a small stir! Nobody even noticed!"

We heard the outer door open and she went to see who came in. It was a messenger from headquarters on the main station.

Penny came back in carrying a large envelope.

"It's marked 'TOP SECRET.' I had to sign for it," she said.

"That must be the orders I was told would be here this morning."

I slit open the envelope and pulled another out that was also marked "TOP SECRET" and slit that one open too.

The document's heading read, "DEPARTMENT OF DEFENSE" and beneath that was a sub-heading that read, "OFFICE OF THE JOINT CHIEFS OF STAFF," followed by the Pentagon address below that. In larger, bold print, centered beneath the Joint Chiefs heading, were the words, "SPECIAL ORDER NUMBER 0102."

The order instructed "Maj. General Gary Hall and Colonel James Miller to proceed immediately for temporary duty assignment, for an unspecified period of time, to the office of the Joint Chiefs of Staff, Department of Defense, at the Pentagon, Washington, DC."

"Well, Penny, I guess this is it; looks as though I am going TDY to the Pentagon. I don't know how long I will be gone, but we'll need to stay in touch, and I will try to keep you updated on what's happening. You and Ron will have to hold the fort while I'm gone. General Hall will be going also," I told her.

"Colonel Miller, this is bigger than just 'closing GITMO,' isn't it?" she asked, nervously.

"Yeah, Penny, it is. And it's probably going to get a lot bigger before it is settled, a lot bigger. Closing GITMO and releasing these detainees was just the straw that broke the proverbial camel's back," I said.

I didn't tell Penny everything or any details. I didn't want her to know too much in case the whole shooting match backfired on us. I didn't want her to get in trouble. Penny was not only a Sergeant and my secretary, but we had become closer, we were friends and I had become quite fond of her and felt the feeling was mutual. It had always been, and was, strictly on a business level; I was her commander and she was one of my subordinates; just one of my "troops," I convinced myself.

"See if you can reach General Hall at Southeast Headquarters," I asked her. "I need to coordinate our travel plans; see when he wants to leave. I'll probably be meeting him at headquarters as usual and we'll go from there together."

"Yes, sir," she said as she went out to her desk.

After about an hour, Penny rang and told me that Dutch was on the phone.

I picked up and said, "Good morning, Dutch; looks like we're being reassigned for a while."

"Looks that way, Bull. I guess we better make some plans about leaving. You want to come up here and we go together, or will you be going directly from there?" he asked.

"I kind of thought it might be better if I meet you and we go up in your plane since I don't have one at my disposal," I laughed.

Dutch came back with, "I won't have one at my disposal any longer; at least until this assignment is over. But hell, Bull, we might as well use it while we can. When do you want to leave? Although we probably don't have much choice, since the orders say 'immediately.'"

"I would like a couple of days to get things settled here so we don't have any emergencies while we're gone," I said. "How does Wednesday sound to you? Do we need to clear it with the Chief?"

"I'll follow-up with them and see if they have any objections, or if they have any particular day in mind that they want us there," Dutch said.

"That sounds great; just let me know and I'll be ready when you say," I told him.

Penny came into the office. "Sir, Senator Scott is on line two; he has been waiting for several minutes. He didn't want you to call him back; he said that he would hold. Must be something mighty important for a senator to wait on the phone for you, Colonel," she said, as she went out.

"Senator Scott, sorry to keep you waiting; I was on the line with General Dutch Hall up at Southeast Command Headquarters. What can I do for you Senator?" I asked. I kept it more formal than we had been when he was here; you never know who might be listening.

"That's quite alright, Jim, I just wanted to thank you for the hospitality while I was visiting last week. I understand that you will be coming to Washington shortly, and I wanted to invite you and Dutch Hall over to my place for dinner one evening with some other friends. When you get into town and find out what's going on and get settled, give me a call, you have my private number; let me know when it will be convenient for you and Dutch to come over."

"Thanks, Lindsey; that will be nice. We'll look forward to seeing you again. Dutch and I both got orders this morning assigning us to the Joint Chiefs' office for temporary duty; didn't say for how long, but I guess we'll find out when we get there," I said.

"Yeah, that's why I went ahead and called you. I talked with Sam Drakeford earlier this morning and he told me you were coming," he said.

We hung up and I sat back and thought about it. I believe "shit is about to hit the fan!"

I heard Ron Philips come into the outer office and speak with Penny. They knocked on my door and I yelled, "Come on in, Ron and Penny; this will involve you both."

They came on into the office and sat down in front of my desk.

Ron asked, "What's going on, Bull?"

"I just received TDY orders to the Pentagon, so I'll probably be gone for some time. I don't know yet for how long," I said. "Ron, you run the day to day operations around here anyway, so I'll depend upon you to keep me informed, and be sure to let me know if anything unusual starts happening—any strange or unfamiliar people start showing up. You too, Penny; ya'll keep your eyes and ears open for anything out of the ordinary. You should be able to reach me anytime, day or night."

CHAPTER EIGHTEEN

General Samuel Drakeford stood in front of the mirror in the bedroom of his home located on Joint Base Anacostia-Bolling; he looked slowly at himself, up and down. He checked the medals on the left chest of his dress uniform, for the third or fourth time, he couldn't remember. His wife Tammy came into the room; she too looked him up and down. They both were almost shedding tears. This was the day for the funeral of General David Mabry, a member of the Joint Chiefs of Staff, the Commandant of the United States Marine Corps, Silver-Star recipient, numerous Bronze Star medals, with a "V" for valor, and many other awards, a fellow warrior, but most of all a close friend.

Tammy spoke softly, "Sam, we have to be at the Pentagon in two hours and with the traffic we will need to leave pretty soon."

"I know, dear. It's just . . . it's just so damn hard to take, to believe. After all the wars, all the battles that Dave has fought in, only to be killed here, at home, and Anna too. It just doesn't make any sense at all. And I'll tell you something else, Tammy. I just don't believe it was an accident, and I am going to find out who it was—and they are going to pay!"

Tammy said, "I am so glad that he and Anna will be buried together, in Arlington. They both deserve the best. How are they going to get from the Pentagon to Arlington?" she asked.

"Their bodies have been lying in state in the foyer of the Pentagon since last night. I don't think it has ever been done before, but I met with the Secretary early yesterday morning and insisted, so that the procession could begin there. I believe Dave would have like that. They will be buried side by side."

"Will they transfer them from the hearse to a horse drawn caisson?" Tammy asked, adding, "I can't see them being separated prior to the burial."

"I don't know," Sam said. "I've never heard of any wife's body being transported by caisson. But in this case, I would certainly be for it; it is deserved."

Sam's aide knocked on the door and said, "General, your car is ready. The driver is waiting under the portico."

Sam and Tammy went downstairs and out to the car. The day was bright and sunny. *A perfect day to bury an old friend*, Sam thought. The driver opened the door, stood at attention, and saluted as they approached and got in the backseat of the car.

As they drove toward the Pentagon, Sam's cell phone rang; he clicked it open, saw that it was Bob Walters, the Deputy Secretary of Defense, and said, "General Drakeford, what's up, Bob?"

"Are you on the way over for the funeral?" Bob asked.

"We are on our way now and should be there in about forty minutes," Sam replied.

"Good. I just got word that Dave's driver, who has been in a coma since the accident, is awake and the doctor says we can talk with him tomorrow; I knew you would want to know," Bob said.

"Thanks, Bob. I want to talk with him. I want to find out just exactly what happened that night," Sam replied.

"He has had it pretty rough, Sam. We'll be lucky if he can remember anything about that night," Bob replied.

We arrived at the Pentagon where everyone gathered for the ride to Arlington. The Protocol Office had everything in order and was ready on schedule, and the journey began. When we arrived at Arlington, the caravan drove to the caisson area in the cemetery where everyone got out of the cars and with the help of the Protocol personnel we were arranged in ranking order behind the caisson.

The flag-draped caskets were taken from the hearse and placed on the flat bed of the caisson. The seven horses were already hooked up; sitting astride four of the horses, soldiers were sitting ramrod straight. Even the horses seemed to be standing at attention. The order was given and the horses started forward, six of them pulling the caisson with the flag draped casket on the back. The procession walked slowly behind the caisson, accompanying General Dave Mabry on his last march around the "parade ground." The solemn dignity of the ceremony was highlighted even further when the twenty-one gun salute sounded and the last notes of "Taps" faded softly away.

CHAPTER NINETEEN

As he drove out of Arlington Cemetery, Tom Beckwith decided he would stop by the George Washington University Hospital to check on Dave's driver. He had heard that he was coming out of the coma and would be able to talk with investigators in a day or so. He wanted to get a little head start on any information that the driver may have; Dave and Anna were friends, and he was going to get to the bottom of what happened.

He went in and took the elevator to the fourth floor, looked down the hall, and then went to the nurse's station and asked for the room number of Dan Johnson, Dave's driver. The nurse pointed him toward the room and told him. "He's in the room with the guard at the door. You have to have special permission to see him."

"Thanks," he said and headed down the hall to the room.

Tom stopped when he approached the guard and showed him his badge that read, "Tom Beckwith, Criminal Investigation Agency (CIA)."

"I was told not to let anyone in except doctors and nurses," the guard said.

"Yeah, I know," I told the guard, "I'm one of 'em who issued the order. We can't do much investigation unless we talk with him, now, can we?"

The uniformed guard, a member of the DC police department, let out a little laugh, "I don't believe you could. I guess that badge is permission enough."

I looked at the guard's badge and name tag and said, "Thanks, Rick." Then, I entered the room.

Dan was sleeping with his back toward the door, I approached the bed and stood there for a moment.

Dan stirred and turned, looked up at me and asked, "Who are you?"

"My name is Tom Beckwith. I was a friend of Dave and Anna Mabry. I just thought I would stop by and check on you and see how you're doing, and if you need anything," I said.

"You'll have to excuse me, Mr. Beckwith. I'm still a little groggy. I just seem to drift off to sleep without realizing it, even while I'm trying to say something. The doctors told me that General Mabry and his wife both were killed. I couldn't believe it. They were the nicest people; the General was the best boss I ever had," he said and tears welled up in his eyes, as he added, "I can't understand why anyone would want to kill them."

"Dan, do you think it wasn't an accident? That it was done on purpose?" I asked.

"It had to be, Mr. Beckwith. They kept trying to run us off the road!" Dan replied.

"Tom; call me Tom, Dan," I said. "What do you mean, 'they kept trying to run you off the road?'"

"They did. They ran us off the road on purpose; they were waiting for us. I know they must have been waiting until we got to that particular place with the deep drop-off," Dan said.

"Where were they waiting for you, Dan?" Tom went on.

"I don't mean waiting out there; the two cars followed us all the way from downtown DC, from the hotel where the function was held," Dan replied.

Then I asked kind of puzzled, "You think they followed you out of town to purposefully kill Dave and his wife? Do you have any idea who they might be?"

"No, sir; it was very strange though. The two cars were identical— two large, black SUVs, like the big Suburbans that the government uses," he said looking like he was thinking.

I asked, "And you feel pretty certain that they ran you off on purpose?"

"I'm sure of it," Dan answered. "I had noticed them following us for quite some time. After we had left the traffic behind us in DC, these two stayed fairly close on our tails until we reached the area where we lost it. One car pulled around us—you know, it's only a two-lane road at that point—slowed down a little as if they were looking into our car. Then it pulled in front of us and cut right in, close in front of us. Then they slowed a little more. I tried to pull out around them, but the car behind us moved up to the side of us, so I had to back-off. We stayed like that for a mile or two, until we reached the area with the deep drop-off; that's when the car behind us rammed us from the rear. The car in front had moved to their left; as I came up almost up to their right side, that car ran into the left side of our car and drove us down the embankment. I think we hit a tree or something; I guess I must have blacked out then.

I didn't know anything until the doctors woke me up. I think maybe it was yesterday. I don't know for sure."

Dan slowly drifted off to sleep and began snoring. I left the room, spoke to the guard and walked on down the hall thinking, *Dan will recover. Dave and Anna won't!*

Little did he know!

As Tom walked on down toward the nurses' station, he passed a nurse's assistant, pushing a medical cart toward the area he had just come from; his badge was turned backward so he wasn't able to see the photo ID or name—a common practice he had noticed before, among medical and hospital personnel. Tom looked over at him and said, "Have a great day." He was wearing a cap and gown like they wear in surgery, at least on TV.

"Yeah," he mumbled.

Tom continued on toward the exit, not thinking anymore about it.

CHAPTER TWENTY

As Tom approached his car in the parking lot and glanced around, he noticed a black SUV—a "big black Suburban"—several rows over from where he was parked. Tom got in and as he pulled out of the lot, he watched in the rearview mirror as the SUV slowly pulled out also, going in the same direction he was heading. *Well, they could just follow me all the way back to CIA headquarters at Langley, if they want*, Tom thought to himself.

He took his .38 special out of its holster and laid it on his lap, just in case the need arose. He kept a close eye on the black SUV as it stayed a few cars behind. Tom didn't try to lose them, just let them follow. *If they make any sudden moves at him, well, that would be their mistake; their last one*, he thought.

Then Tom noticed something a little familiar about the SUV. It kept "bugging" him, gnawing at his subconscious, trying to remember. Then he realized what it was. Tom already knew that it was a government vehicle. All at once it came to him; he had recognized a very small, almost un-noticeable little tag—most people would never notice it there, or have any idea what it meant, even if they saw it—Secret Service—White

House detail! The President's own "body guards." *Why are they following me?* Tom wondered.

Tom parked in his usual space and went into the building. He saw the SUV drive off as he started upstairs to his office. He checked his phone messages but nothing really important, just the usual calls from job hunters "looking for an exciting career with the CIA!" There was a voice mail from Dennis Wilson too.

"Hi, Tom, Dennis Wilson here; some of the guys are planning on getting together this evening over a couple of beers and maybe pizza or something. I wanted to see if you had any plans and maybe would like to join us. It'll just be a bunch of the guys and a lot of B-S. Give me a call when you get in and let me know; thanks," the message said.

Tom took out his private Blackberry and pulled up Dennis' number on speed dial and punched the button for his private phone and number. He picked up immediately.

"Hello, Tom, glad you got back to me. You got my message about tonight, I assume?" Dennis inquired.

"Yes. I checked my messages as soon as I was able to lose my 'tail' and get in my office," he replied, almost sure he was sounding sarcastic.

"What do you mean, 'lose your tail'? You don't mean you were followed?" Dennis asked.

"You called it right, Dennis. I stopped by the hospital to check on Dave's driver; his name is Dan Johnson. He woke up when I went into the room, although he was still a little groggy and sleepy. We had a very interesting little visit. I'll have to tell you about it tonight. They do have a uniformed guard at his door, which is a good thing, after some of the odd goings on that I'm beginning to see," Tom was saying. "Anyway, when I went to my car, I noticed a large, black SUV, a Suburban—like the government uses a lot of—parked a few rows over from my car. It looked suspicious so I kept my eye on it. When I pulled out of the lot, it followed me at a distance, all the way to Langley. It drove off when I entered the building."

Dennis said, "Tom, it looks like someone suspects something and they're keeping a close eye on all of us. We better spread the word to all to be extremely careful and to be mindful of everything around them."

Tom stayed at the office much later than usual, trying to play "catch-up" on some work that he had let slide. It was beginning to get dark as he left the building at 7:30 on his way to meet with Dennis and the others. But first he needed to make a quick trip by his house before going into town.

As he pulled out of the parking lot and out onto the highway toward McLean, Tom saw a car pull out of a side road behind him, with no headlights on, at least not at first, but they came on shortly afterward. The car kept its distance for some time. As he began to reach an area known as Turkey Run Park, an area that is pretty much deserted at dark—no people, no cars coming and going—the car began to slowly move closer toward the rear of Tom's car. Tom already had his .38 special in his belt where he could get at it quickly, but something told him he might need more than a .38.

Keeping his eye on the approaching car, Tom reached down between the front seats and pulled out his .357 Magnum. He kept it there, real handy, just in case a special need arises! Every time he took it in the house to clean it, his wife would make a comment like, "Shades of Dirty Harry," or something similar.

The car crept closer until it was less than two car lengths behind Tom. He thought of Dave, and what Dan had told him about the two cars that ran them off the road. This was a large, black SUV also. Suddenly, the car speeded up very quickly and drew up beside Tom and slowed;

the window went down and some guy leaned out the window with, what looked like an AR-15 automatic rifle in his hands. *That is his second mistake*, thought Tom.

His first mistake, thought Tom, *was that he didn't pull the trigger soon enough*. Tom's .357 hit him right between the eyes. The rifle fell out of the window and onto the road. The car started speeding off rapidly but suddenly it careened off to its left and into some bushes and trees. Tom's second shot had caught the driver in the back of his head when it went through the back window at an angle!

Tom slammed on the brakes and pulled off the road to the right; he crawled across the seat and got out on the right side of his car, just in case. He didn't see or hear any movement; with his .357 in front of him, Tom slowly approached the mangled car. He looked inside; there were two bloody bodies. They seem to have a very surprised look on their faces.

Tom dialed 9-1-1 on his official Blackberry phone so there would be a record. Next, he called Dennis Wilson and told him what had happened and explained that he would be late for our little get-together and to let the others know.

Dennis screamed in his ear! "What the hell did you say, Tom! Somebody tried to shoot you too?" he yelled.

Tom quickly explained what happened and cut it short because he had heard sirens and saw the reflection of blue lights approaching. He then told Dennis that he would talk with him later as about four or five black and whites pulled up and doors flew open.

Officers stood behind their open doors and yelled, "Down on the ground; get down on the ground!"

With all those weapons aimed directly at Tom, he complied, but he also yelled back, "I'm with the CIA, and I am armed. My badge is in my inside pocket."

Two officers approached Tom, cautiously, as the others kept close watch on him. They came up to him, with their weapons drawn, and maybe it was because he was dressed in a suit, but they told him to get up and keep his hands over his head.

Before Tom started to get up, he told them, "I am with the CIA and I have two weapons on me; my badge is inside my coat pocket."

They believed him and let him get up off the ground. Tom showed them both of his weapons and got his badge and showed that to them also.

Two of the other officers came up; they had been over to the other car, and said, "Those two won't be shooting at anybody else. What the hell happened? Do you know them? They look like foreigners to me."

"I don't have a clue who they are," Tom replied. "I just know they must be the same ones who followed me out here earlier this afternoon. Looks like the same car anyway. I don't know what their game is."

Just then, one of the other officers came up, "I can't find any ID on them and there are no tags, and the VIN has been obliterated. They didn't want anyone to know who they were."

Then after thinking a little, the officer added, "They must have thought there was a chance they wouldn't make it. I guess they should have thought about it a lot longer. What kind of weapon did you hit them with, if you don't mind my asking?"

Tom showed him the .357 Magnum, and he smiled, "Just like *Dirty Harry*! Man, if I thought somebody was after me, I would want one of those too."

A couple of ambulances pulled up at the same time as the coroner and they went over to the car with the two men still inside. After looking at the bodies for a few minutes, the coroner told the ambulance drivers to take the bodies to the morgue.

Another car approached with headlights on bright, pulled off to the side, and parked. Mel Pierson, FBI Director, and the White House Assistant Director of the Secret Service, Chip Reese, got out and came over to where the group was standing. Tom had to explain again to both Mel and Chip what had gone down. They walked over to the car as they were taking the bodies out to load into the ambulance. They looked at them closely—they were of mid-eastern descent. "Hell, maybe they were jihadist or Islamist terrorist trying to prove a point," Mel said.

"I was just thinking along those lines," Chip said, thinking aloud. "No identification on themselves, no vehicle ID information . . . . Tom, did you check the weapons for serial numbers?"

"No," Tom almost shouted in frustration. "I was so intent on checking the bodies and the vehicle, that it never occurred to me to check the weapons for serial numbers; I just kicked them out of the way until I was sure these assholes were dead and wouldn't rise again!"

Chip said, "We better get them fast before the sheriffs guys pick them up and confiscate them as evidence."

Even as Chip said it, all three moved toward where the AR-15 lay, still in the roadway. Tom picked it up carefully, wrapping a handkerchief around it just in case there were prints on it. Then, they headed to the Suburban and looked for other weapons and found two handguns—with no serial numbers!

Mel, who had been very quiet, said kind of hesitantly, "Tom, you said these two, or someone in a similar vehicle, had followed you this afternoon from the hospital to your office, and then when you left tonight, they, or someone like them, were waiting for you, and then chased you and tried to kill you. How did they know you were at the hospital . . . and why would they care?"

Tom, Chip, and Mel looked startled at each other. Tom said, "Holy shit! We better get to the hospital fast!"

They ran to the Sheriff's Department's on-scene investigator and quickly told him what was going on and that they were heading to the hospital. They also asked him to get the guard on his radio and warn him to be on the lookout, to take caution, and not let anyone in the room until they got there.

They all three jumped into Tom's car and "burned rubber" as they pealed back onto the highway.

CHAPTER TWENTY-ONE

Hospitals typically are quiet and dark in late evenings, especially on isolation floors, like the floor Dan Johnson was on; normally, there is not much activity going on, and fewer staff on duty, just enough personnel to handle emergencies.

No one noticed the "nurse" slowly pushing the medical cart down the hall toward the room with the guard at the door, carefully looking around as he walked. He was on a mission; he was nervous and anxious to get the job done and get the hell out of there.

He stopped at the coffee station behind the nurse's station and filled a cup with old, smelly, over-brewed, stale, coffee. He looked around—no nurse or anyone else in sight. He reached into his pocket and pulled out a small vial containing a liquid, and poured it into the coffee. He had no idea what the liquid was, he was just told to pour it into the cup. *My job*, he thought, *is not to ask questions—just follow instructions*.

He placed the cup on the tray and continued on down the hall toward the room with the guard at the door.

As he approached, the guard who had been sitting in a chair, stood and looked at him, and said, "You must be new on this shift; I don't believe I've seen you here before."

"Nah, new shift for me; my first starting tonight. Here, the nurse down at the station thought you could use a cup of coffee about this time," he said as he handed the cup to the guard.

"Thanks," the guard said, "I could use anything to break the boredom and keep me awake." He took the cup and took a sip of the black, hot liquid. He sat back down as the "nurse" went into the room. That was the last coffee he would ever taste!

The "nurse" went over to Dan Johnson's bedside and found him sound asleep. *Good; that would make it even easier*, he thought. Then he reached into his pocket and withdrew another vial; this one had a needle attached to it. He found the IV line that went into Dan's arm; he inserted the needle into the port in the line and slowly squeezed the liquid out of the vial and into Dan's arm until the last drop was out of the vial. He withdrew the needle, capped it and put it back into his pocket. *Job done! No problems!* He thought.

He opened the door and saw the guard slumped down in the chair, legs sprawled out and looking like he was asleep; the coffee cup lay on the floor with half the contents spilled out and running across the hall. He looked down the hall, both directions, and saw no one. He grabbed his tray and slowly went out of the room.

As he pulled the door closed, he looked to his left and saw three men in business suits turn the corner, not medical types, heading in his direction. *Damn*, he thought, *they must be police!* He quickly changed directions and started down the hall to the right.

Shit, he thought, *I'm almost out of here. I don't need a problem now!* He then started moving faster.

Tom Beckwith who was a little ahead of Chip and Mel yelled, "Hey . . . nurse! Wait up!"

The "nurse" began running toward the EXIT sign over the stairwell door, shoving the tray cart back down the hall toward the advancing men.

Tom and Chip took off running toward the stairs in pursuit of the "nurse." Tom yelled over his shoulder, "Mel, head him off downstairs."

They had four floors to descend, but so did the "nurse" and they hoped to trap him in the stairwell and quietly capture him.

As he ran past the guard, Tom slowed and took one look at him and knew he was dead. That surely also meant that poor Dan Johnson was probably dead also.

A quiet capture was not to be! Just as they made the turn half way between the fourth and third floors, they heard the echo of a familiar click, the sound of a round being chambered followed immediately by the explosion of a shot and concrete blasted behind their heads.

They could hear the sound and echo of running feet on the concrete stairs, and then the sound of a door opening and slamming closed. He had reached the first floor; Mel may not be there yet.

Just as alarms started blaring and the hospital going on lock-down, the "nurse" was heading through the outside entrance door into the parking lot, and into the night. All of a sudden, it looked as if his entire head exploded. Mel, who had been several yards behind the "nurse," had burst through the doors and fired. The shot found its mark! The "nurse" was dead before hitting the ground!

All of a sudden, all hell broke loose from all sides of the hospital. The Charge Nurse for the fourth floor had heard all the commotion of the crashing cart, looked out of her office door and saw men running down the hall—one had a gun. She stepped out of the office and saw the guard sprawled across the chair he had been sitting on, and the cup of spilled coffee. She hit the panic button that alerted the entire hospital of an emergency. She immediately punched in Security's number and told them of a possible "shooter" on the premises and explained what she had seen.

She ran down to the room where the guard lay and checked his pulse, he had none. She rushed into the room where she saw Dan Johnson, he looked like he was sleeping, she checked for a pulse and found no pulse on Dan and noticed that it looked as if his IV line had been tampered with—the little green "cap" that closed the IV port was missing, she saw it on the floor.

Just then, the door burst open and three of the men she had seen running down the hall rushed into the room. She screamed, "Who the hell are you? What do you want? You're not . . ."

"We're the good guys, ma'am. I'm with the FBI and these others are CIA and Secret Service," Mel told her. "The patient, Dan Johnson, was under our protection . . . doesn't look like we did too well though."

"Thank God," she said, "I didn't know what was going on. I was so scared I almost peed in my pants! I heard all the commotion, yelling and running, and when I looked out and saw four men running down the hall—one with a gun—I hit the panic button that set off the alarm for the entire hospital. I thought we may have a shooter here. Security notified the first responder groups."

They heard a lot of footsteps coming down the hall at a fast pace. Tom and Chip stepped into the hall; both had their weapons drawn.

The DC Police Chief and several others, some in uniforms, came up. Recognizing Mel, Tom, and Chip, the Chief asked, "What the hell is going on up here? We found a guy lying in the parking lot with his head blown off, people screaming, and security guards with their weapons drawn—some running around some others crouched behind plants and posts. One of the guards told us that the FBI was inside. We got things calmed down the best we could; our people are cordoning off the entire area and keeping an eye on the dead guy."

"Thanks, Chief," Mel said. "There are two men dead here, the one in the hall is the guard we had on the door to protect the patient—who was our only witness to what we're sure was a murder a few days ago."

"That would be the general and his wife; and supposedly an accident out on Highway 50 West of the city, I assume," the Chief said.

"Correct," Mel said, "We're going to need the coroner. We know what killed the guy in the parking lot, but we haven't the slightest idea what the asshole gave these two."

The Chief said, "The Mobile Crime Scene Lab is on the way, Mel; we'll find out as quickly as possible and I'll let you know what we find."

"Thanks," Mel replied, "And Chief, the Bureau's lab will assist you in anything you need. Just let us know and it's yours. We will have agents working with your people, also. I've already called the Bureau and they will have one of our agents here shortly to check things out as far as the Bureau's interest is concerned, and just in case there is some foreign people involved. We never know these days who is going to show up in investigations."

As Mel, Chip, and Tom walked down the hall toward the elevators several of the ambulatory patients, were standing in the hallway by their room, some holding onto their IV poles, wanting to know what was going on, what all the excitement was about. There was a half dozen uniformed police spread out through the length of the hall also. No one knew whether there was more than one person involved.

Back down in the lobby, they ran into a mob of people: more uniformed cops, plain clothes investigators, hospital staff, security guards, and some civilian types who had been there late to sit with a relative or friend.

They passed a couple of uniformed police as they went out of the hospital entrance; they were placed there to check IDs and purpose of visit of anyone who tried to enter at that late hour. They went over to the body, which was surrounded by police, medical and coroner's staff performing their routine duties before putting the body in a body bag and taking it to the morgue for autopsy and further examination, and, hopefully, identification.

The entire parking lot was cordoned off with probably a couple miles of black and yellow tape tied to and wrapped around light poles, trees, and anything else it could be attached to.

They got into Tom's car and drove back to the first 'crime' scene to get Mel's and Chip's vehicles.

CHAPTER TWENTY-TWO

Dan Black buzzed his secretary and asked, "Mary Anne, please get hold of Chip and tell him I need to talk to him. Ask him to come to the office as soon as he can. Thanks."

"Yes, sir," she replied, "He'd called earlier and said he was getting together with Tom Beckwith from the CIA and a couple of others. He wasn't sure just when he would get back. If I don't reach him, I'll leave him a message. Is it anything urgent? I can run him down if you would like."

"Nothing real pressing," Dan replied. "Just tell him I've got something on my mind that I would like to talk with him about as soon as he gets back."

Dan was the Director of the Secret Service, with his office in the White House, near the President; Chip Reese, as the Assistant Director of the Secret Service, was the number two person. They were the "head honchos" of the President's security detail and went where the President went, in addition to the hundred or more agents, all assigned to protect the President at all costs! They stayed close to the President, even in the White House. The President's personal, secret service agents were as close as his shadow; maybe even closer.

It was after seven o'clock and dark out when Dan's phone rang, "Dan Black," he said into the receiver. It was Chip.

"I just received your message," Chip said, "I've been shooting the breeze with Tom Beckwith, Mel Pierson, and Senator Scott. We're in the bar at the City Club. What's up, Dan?"

"Chip, I've got something on my mind that's bugging the hell out of me, and it's driving me up a wall. It is super-sensitive and I can't talk with just anybody about it," Dan replied.

"Can you tell me what it's concerning? Have I screwed up somewhere along the line?" Chip asked jokingly.

Dan responded with, "No, nothing that simple; I wish it was as easy as that. I'm afraid it's more complicated, much more! To be honest, it has me pretty upset and worried; I haven't slept very well the past few nights."

"Damn, Dan; you really sound upset; is it something personal, our jobs, the staff, or something on that order?" Chip asked.

"No, it's even more serious than any of that, Chip," Dan said.

Chip thought carefully and said, "Dan, why don't you come on down here and have a drink with Tom, Mel, Lindsey, and me? We're talking some pretty serious stuff that has been bothering us for quite some time too. These are the guys we can talk to and it want go any further than the four of us. We will just sit back and wait for you; it will take a load off your shoulders, give you the opportunity to relax a little."

"You're on," replied Dan, "I'll be right there; I'm leaving the office now."

Chip had been watching and saw Dan come through the door and got up to go meet him. He led Dan to their booth in back corner of the bar where the others sat waiting on him to arrive. Due to the nature of their jobs, the men already knew each other, both on an official level and social level. Their wives were friends also.

Dan greeted the others. "There must be some high-level 'crap' going down here, with so many VIPs getting together," he remarked and laughed.

Mel spoke up and said, "Chip was just telling us that you were pretty uptight and upset about something, Dan. Come on, sit down and have a drink." Then, he motioned for the waiter who came and took their order for another round and the first for Dan. He thought that Dan may need more than a couple tonight.

Chip looked at Dan and said, "You sounded pretty tense and anxious on the phone; you mentioned that it was serious and complicated and had been keeping you awake at night. That's not good, Dan. Is there anything I can do? Or any of these guys? They're always ready to help a friend. We've all known each other too long to let something drag out; get it off your chest and talk about it."

Dan looked around at the others; then, he slowly looked around the room and then back at his friends. "I probably should swear you all to secrecy, but you were sworn in when you accepted your positions. You swore to protect our country from all enemies, foreign and **'domestic.'** With that in mind, I want to show you something—and this is just between us here tonight—until I or maybe WE, can decide what must be done."

Tom, Mel, Lindsey, and Chip looked at each other. Then, Lindsey said, "Dan, this is sounding like something more serious. I was thinking it was something personal, like family problems, medical, or something like that. But if this is heading along the lines of where I'm thinking it's going, we better keep our voices real low and not get too involved in discussion tonight, but get together tomorrow, or real soon, and talk some more."

Mel asked, "What is it that you want to show us, Dan?"

Dan reached into the inside pocket of his coat and pulled out a greeting card-size envelope. He opened it and pulled out a couple of photos; the first was a photo of what looked to be a rug rolled up, or piece of colorful carpet. The second photo was of the same rug or carpet unrolled, and looked like it was laid out on the floor of a small room, on a light colored tile floor.

"What the hell is that?" asked Lindsey Scott; "It looks like somebody's doormat!"

"If you say that in the wrong place, you would get your head chopped off," said Dan.

"What does that mean?" asked Lindsey

Tom Beckwith looked at the photos closely and remarked, "That looks a lot like one of those Islam or Muslim prayer rugs; you know, where they lay the carpet out, kneel on it, face Mecca, and pray—I believe three times a day."

"Where did you get the photos, Dan? Who took them, and where was this 'prayer' rug?" Chip asked, adding, "And why would a couple of rugs or pieces of carpet upset you?"

Dan looked at Chip and asked, "Chip, you know Johnny Miller and Cathy Wilson, I believe they are assigned to the President's personal detail. Anyway, they both came into the office the other day and wanted to talk confidentially. As part of the President's personal detail, they are charged with keeping a close eye on him; they are like a 'shadow' of the President—where he goes, they go; pretty much what he sees, they see! They are very loyal to the President, but more loyal to their country! I could see that they were visibly upset."

Then after a little pause, Dan said, "After a few minutes of chit-chat, I asked them how things were going in the 'big' office and how they liked working directly for the 'Big Boss.' They said that's what they came to talk with me about. Cathy said they liked their assignment and were happy with the job and the risks that came with it. Both said they would not hesitate to "take a bullet" for the President. Johnny then pulled these photos out of his pocket and handed them to me and said 'this is what we're concerned about!' I knew immediately what it was a photo of, but I asked them what it was and where they got the photos. Cathy said, 'I took them myself, about two weeks ago; they were in a small room just off the tunnel leading to the East gate. It is someone's prayer rug—a damn Muslim or Islam prayer rug! And it was here in White House!'

"Johnny spoke up and added, 'It is used frequently, we believe, by someone here in the White House. We figure we must have one or more practicing Islamic or Muslims on the President's staff. We started keeping an eye on the area and have seen two top-ranking staff members enter the room. And to make matters or our thoughts jump even more, we saw the President and his wife in the hall, just outside the room and it looked as if they had just come out!'"

Dan hesitated and looked at his startled audience.

Mel asked, "What in the hell is going on over there?"

"Well . . . it looks kind of like the shit is going to hit the fan sooner than I, or we, expected," Tom replied. "We have been digging into some rumors and information that has been slowly coming into the office."

Everyone got quiet for a while, all deep in thought about what exactly was going on and how could they explain what was happening—not only to others—but mostly to themselves! The four investigative-type leaders sat quietly, nursing their drinks, slowly.

Finally, Dan broke the silence, "Tom do you remember a couple of weeks ago when I mentioned to you that one of our agents was clearing up some mess; something that the President had dropped. And he asked the agent if he would put it in the wastebasket by the desk. This was in the Oval Office. The President left the office and headed down the hall. The agent decided he should empty the basket; when he did, he kind of 'glanced' through the stuff as he was throwing it into the larger trash bin. Then, he realized that most of the President's wastebasket material is usually taken to be shredded or burned. If you recall he was quite upset at a couple of the notes he saw. Also, if you recall, the President's Chief of Staff, Susan Brice, is a devout Muslim and makes no bones about it. She had given the President a couple of notes—for his eyes only—that are pretty damn telling and puts a new sense of urgency on this whole situation!

"One note said, 'Too many people are beginning to ask questions. We can't wait much longer to take some action; several events have taken place, creating suspicion!' Another note said, 'Our leaders sent word that if you, or we, couldn't get moving, they would send in a specially trained group who could get the job done. We can't keep waiting! You have to get something going or we're all in real trouble!' Not only that, I think it is common knowledge that his Intel Chief, John Beaman, is Muslim also; he converted from Christianity to Muslim while he was station chief in Iran. Hell, I'm sure there are several more in the administration that we don't know about. For all we know, at this point, this administration is likely saturated with Muslim fanatics who are determined to take over the government. They are biding their time; waiting for orders from who in hell knows. Shit, we don't even have any idea how far along they are with their plans; we're just certain they have plans."

After a pause, Dan continued, "One of the things that have my guys so uptight is a list they found when going through the wastebasket. It was a list of quotes taken from that socialist asshole, Paul Skalinsky's book on changing a democracy to a socialist society. Items such as increase poverty level—poor people are easier to control and will support the government—because the government gives them everything. Other items include gun control, increase the national debt, healthcare, education, religion, create class warfare and several other items."

Chip, startled, said, "Damn, Dan, I remember talking about Johnny and Cathy finding some bad crap in the President's trash, but I didn't realize it was to this extent. Damn! This is pretty damn dangerous stuff we're dealing with; we better find a way to resolve this situation before it's too late to do anything! But just what in the hell we can do about it, and how quickly? That's going to present one helluva problem!"

"Tom and I have discussed some of this over the past several months, based on pure rumors that we had picked up on from different sources," Mel said, adding, "I opened a file; kind of a 'personal' file, just to put notes in when I heard bits and pieces of information concerning this subject."

Lindsey said, "I'm going to call Sam Drakeford as soon as I get home. I don't care how late it is; Sam was in the process of setting up a meeting for all of us to get together again to prepare a plan of action to "nip this in the bud" before all hell breaks loose and we find ourselves fighting a shooting war right here, on our own dirt!"

Chip spoke up and responded with, "Gentlemen, **WE ARE AT WAR!** Just the actual shooting of ammunition hasn't begun—yet!"

Dan said, "Chip, if we stop to think about it for a bit, we can see where this started and where it's going. As a nation, we have kind of had our heads in the sand—the Mid-East sands most likely! Think about some of the things these ultra-liberals have been saying and doing; in fact, the President himself said, in the state of the union message, as President, ". . . I have a telephone and a pen . . .," indicating that he could make his own laws. Others, leaders on a national level, have espoused ideas such as establish mosques throughout the country. Guess what, they have already done that! They have encouraged people to resist national authorities."

Chip interrupted, "They sure as hell have done that, too! Look at all the protests going on; attacking and killing the police and any law enforcement that gets in their way!"

Dan continued, "They want to create an enclave; grow the population among the poor people because they are more easily controlled, the government feeds them. Hell, they even push to institute Sharia law within their own community! I think they even introduced a bill in their state legislature in Michigan or Minnesota to establish their own laws, the Sharia Laws. It's all part of the world-wide plot to establish a 'One World Order' government! No borders, no control, except by the government. Their goal is to weaken the United States globally, and then they can take complete control, destroying the U.S., as we know it! You know something else, Chip? This didn't just begin with this President; I think it started a long time ago. There are people out there who are providing the money to pay for all this to happen!"

CHAPTER TWENTY-THREE

Dutch and I had arrived in DC early on Wednesday afternoon, checked in, and had lunch and a drink in the restaurant at the JW Marriott Hotel, our "home away from home" when in DC. We were ready to leave for the meeting that Dennis had called but had stopped by the lounge to kill a little more time; we didn't want to be too early. Also, we would have to report for duty tomorrow at the Pentagon. We were now officially working directly for General Sam Drakeford.

My phone buzzed and I picked up. It was Senator Scott.

"Hello, Lindsey, glad you called. Dutch and I were getting ready to go the meeting that Dennis has planned. What? It was called off? Cancelled? What's going on, I thought this was pretty important! You're kidding me! Someone tried to ambush Tom Beckwith," I asked? "Who would have the balls to try to gun down the CIA Chief?"

I asked Lindsey when the meeting would be rescheduled but he wasn't sure.

When I flipped my phone closed, Dutch asked, "What's going on? Who is shooting at whom?"

"It seems a couple of guys tried to kill Tom Beckwith, the CIA Director of Recruitment, whom we met at the last meeting. They had an AR-15; I guess they were planning to really blow him away. They must not have known that those guys are usually prepared for emergencies and know, not only how to protect themselves, but also how to take care of any situation they may be faced with. Tom shot them both, and the coroner said that both were DOA—dead on his arrival at the scene. Sounds as if he 'bout blew their entire heads off," I told Dutch.

"Well, so much for our meeting for tonight," Dutch said. "Now what do we do?"

"I know just the thing Dutch," I said, "Let's order another drink, sit back, and relax. I guess somebody will contact us when they get reorganized and figure out what we have to do."

"Sounds good to me," he replied. So, we ordered another drink and sat back.

About thirty minutes later, a gentleman walked up to our table and introduced himself.

"I'm Congressman Bill Winters, representative from South Carolina. I've just come from Senator Scott's office over in the Russell Building. He and Congressman Dennis Wilson asked if I would see if you were here and if you were available to stop over there with me for a visit," he said.

"Of course," said Dutch. "Would you like a drink first?"

"Thanks, I could use one about now. It's been one of those days when you're busy all day and it ends with you feeling that you've accomplished absolutely nothing," he answered.

Dutch and I introduced ourselves to Bill and we just passed some small talk, about nothing in particular. We finished our drinks and walked out of the hotel.

Bill pointed out his car and said, "I'm not high enough in the hierarchy to rate a government vehicle and driver, so if you gentlemen don't mind riding with an amateur, climb on in."

Bill took us in the official senator's entrance. It didn't dawn on us as to why a young, fairly new congressman was doing an errand for a senator and another member of the house. He took us up to the second floor and into Senator Lindsey Scott's office.

Senator Scott got up and welcomed us and said, "I see you have met Bill. He has been helping Dennis and me with some research and other stuff. By the way, he knows what we know; Bill wants to turn this country around too, and kick ass of those who are determined to destroy it."

Dennis had also gotten up and came to greet us. "Come on in and have a seat. We were just talking about both of you and your assignment to the Pentagon," he said. "That's going to come in very handy; the two of you here, close by. We need all the guts and brains we can get to resolve this situation."

"You guys sound kind of serious," Dutch said, "Scott, you're Republican, and Dennis you're Democrat. How in hell did you two ever get together and agree on something?" he added laughing.

"You don't know just how serious we are, and how serious the whole damn situation is," replied Lindsey. "Right now, we have to locate a meeting place, something private and quiet, where we can have a rather large group of people, where they all can have the opportunity for input, without a lot of confusion and everybody talking at the same time," he added.

Dennis spoke up and said, "I'm working on that now, and it's top priority; especially since we have had to cancel tonight's get-together. I guess you two heard what happened to Tom Beckwith earlier this evening?"

I said, "Yeah, from what we heard, Tom blew their heads off. Good for him. And you Dennis, you had a close call also, I hear."

"Yes, but what scared me the most was my family, and Toby, my new, young aide. If I could get my hands on them, I would gladly pull them apart, piece by piece, and shove it 'where the sun don't shine,'" he said. "I didn't have my .9 mm on me, or I might have taken a shot at that car when it took off. Better yet, I think I'll do like Tom—I'll get me a .357 Magnum, something that will do some damage when it hits!"

The outer door opened, so we dropped the level of our voices. Lindsey's secretary knocked, opened the door, and said that Admiral Dawkins was in the outer office.

"Tell him to come on in," Lindsey told her.

The Chief of Naval Operations came through the door as they stood and greeted him.

"Glad you could make it, Vince," Lindsey said.

"Come on in, neighbor," I said, explaining to the others that Vince and I had grown up together in the same neighborhood back in South Carolina.

Vince said, "I have located a place where we could get together, a pretty good size group anyway, in private and not have to worry that 'uninvited' guests would show up. You remember when we met at Dave's house and he had the dinner catered. Well, as soon as I thought of it, I contacted his friend, Bubba Roberts, and he said that he would be more than happy to have us come out. In fact, he said if we let him know how many, he would close the place that night and feed the whole group. He and Dave were pretty close friends. I know Dave and Anna used to eat there very often."

Dutch spoke up and asked, "How many will it accommodate?"

"Not sure," Vince replied, "But it will handle over a hundred; that should be large enough for us, I would think."

"Bubba is usually closed on Mondays," Dennis said, "So why don't we set next Friday? That will give Bubba extra time to prepare for a large group, and it gives us a week to notify everybody."

Turning toward the Senator, he asked, "How does that suit your schedule, Lindsey? I would say around eight o'clock?"

Lindsey checked his calendar and said, "It's okay with me. How about you other fellows?"

Everybody acknowledged the meeting time and place and got up to leave Lindsey's office.

Just then, Bill spoke up, asking, "Speaking of notifying everybody, just who IS everybody? Do we even have a real idea of who we can count on? Who we can trust at this point?"

"Good point, Bill," said Dennis, "I'm not sure who all we should let know about this, either."

Lindsey said, "I have been talking with a number of people who have very strong feelings, and several of them have mentioned that they have been approached about getting something done —along the same lines that we have been thinking."

Then, lowering his voice, Lindsey added, "Everybody I've spoken with lately, and I mean on both sides of the aisle, say we have to get this President out before he does irreparable damage to the office and to the entire country!"

Dennis also spoke up, "I've had the same experience. I have been approached on numerous occasions, also from both sides of the aisle, about doing something about the President, asking how in the hell can we get him out of that office without shooting him."

"Gentlemen, I'm not one-hundred percent sure yet, but we may be in for a very important, and unprecedented surprise when we get together next week," Lindsey announced. Then he added, "I don't know if I believe it myself. I'll only believe it when I see and hear it for myself! I'm not at liberty to disclose what it may be, or even give a hint; sorry, but I'm sworn to secrecy."

CHAPTER TWENTY-FOUR

Senate Majority Leader Lindsey Scott was at his desk early, 7:30 in the morning, reading the *Wall Street Journal*, when his secretary buzzed him. He answered, and she told him that Senator Harold Reed was on the line. Senator Reed was the ranking Democrat in the Senate and pulled a lot of weight. Before the Republicans took over, he was the majority leader. He had also been the strongest supporter of the President since the President took office. He had pushed every bill the President wanted and stonewalled everything the Republicans tried to accomplish.

"Good morning, Harold, what brings you out so early?" Lindsey asked being as friendly as he could.

"Lindsey, I need to get with you as soon as you can spare a couple of minutes," he sounded kind of anxious.

"Sure, Harold, I don't have anything pressing today; you say when and where," he replied.

"How about within the hour; let's meet out back, in Union Station. It's noisy and we can't be overheard when we talk. Let's meet at the East Street Café. Our drivers can drop us off and we don't have to worry about parking, if that suits you," Harold returned.

"That sounds fine, I'll see you there in thirty minutes," said Lindsey. He sat back in his chair and thought about what Harold had said, "It'll be noisy and we won't be overheard." That sounded mighty strange and got his curiosity up for sure.

Lindsey got out of his car and walked into Union Station and turned right, toward the East Street Café, located at the end of the station. Senator Reed was already there, seated and waiting.

"Good morning, Harold, you sounded kind of anxious for so early in the morning; you must not have had your coffee yet," he remarked.

"Good morning, Lindsey. I am anxious; I'm anxious as hell!" he exclaimed and spoke again. "Lindsey, you know how hard and how often I have put my reputation on the line to protect that lying son-of-a-bitch we call 'President!'"

Harold then looked around to see if anyone was watching them. "I've taken a lot of abuse; I've been called every name in the book and then some; I've alienated almost every friend in both the house and senate. Hell, I've even alienated most of my friends back home!" he exclaimed.

"Whoa up a bit, Harold, You're going to have a heart attack right here, right now if you don't calm down a little," Lindsey told him. "Slow down and start at the beginning. What has happened? What has changed your mind and your feelings about the President?"

"Lindsey, I think you know Dan Black and Mel Pierson?"

"Yeah," he replied. "Dan is the head of the White House Secret Service; he's the Director, and everyone knows that Mel is the FBI Director. But what has that got to do with you being so anxious and uptight, and I might add, about to have a coronary?"

"Well, Mel called me last night, late—it was after eleven o'clock; Mel and I have been good friends for many years, since long before he rose up the ranks to be Director. Dan and I have been friends for a long time also," Harold was saying. "Lindsey, you'll have to pardon my rambling so much, but I'm not quite sure how to explain what I'm about to tell you. Mel asked if he could come by to see me, right then, last night, at that hour. He sounded upset, so I told him to come on over; I was still up. Mel told me that he had dinner with Dan, and Dan was really disturbed, and very upset. He was hesitant to talk about it, so I pressed him on it. What he told me then is unbelievable. He said that it began sometime back, months ago. Dan had picked up on bits of a conversation between the President and his top advisor, Alisha Jackson, something about the Muslim faith, Kenya, Hawaii, and stuff that has floated around the Internet for years."

Lindsey broke in and said, "You do know that Alisha Jackson is of the Muslim faith, and that she was born in Iran? In fact, her parents still live there, and she visits them periodically."

"I know, Lindsey," Harold said, "but what had Mel so upset was, Dan told him that when he first heard the remarks between the two, it reminded him of all the rumors going around the Internet. That, just on a 'lark,' he was playing around on the Internet, just for the heck of it, when he came across something that really clicked his interest in the whole story. So he began checking further, and further; the further he dug into the story, the more variations he found, so he got really serious. So he decided he was going to 'de-bunk' the rumors, once and for all. Dan called some friends of his, who he trusted, and who are also investigators, and work for the FBI. He told Mel that he swore them to secrecy, even though they were old drinking buddies anyway, and asked them to look into it, unofficially of course. Well, it seems as if these friends got more interested in it than he or they intended. In fact, the deeper they got into it, the more interested they got! They put out the word and talked with some of their covert friends, operatives, over at CIA who have secret, undercover and double agents in different parts of the world.

They say they have verifiable evidence that the President was not born in Hawaii, Indonesia, California, or even close. He was actually born in Kenya and they can prove it beyond any doubt. He was, and is a Kenyan citizen, born Muslim, and even though he has attended other churches, he remains Muslim. There is no evidence that he has ever converted to Christianity either!"

Lindsey was shocked; he was right—it was unbelievable!

"Harold, do you realize what you're saying? What they are saying? Hell, this can turn this entire country into a panic-stricken, torn-apart nation filled with mayhem from coast to coast," Lindsey said.

"I know," Harold said. That's what has me so upset. I don't know what to do! What do you think it will mean, Lindsey?"

"Well, first of all, if what you say is actually true, it means we have had a President for these seven years who is not a natural born citizen, and is not eligible to be in the office. Let's keep this quiet for the time being, just between you and me. Let's stay calm; let me do some thinking and I'll talk with some people who will know how to handle this," I said. Then I asked him, "Can you make a meeting next Friday evening about eight o'clock?"

"What kind of a meeting, and where?" he asked.

"I'll have to let you know; I don't have the details yet," Lindsey replied.

"If it has anything to do with this, I will certainly be available, no matter what," Harold replied.

Lindsey decided not to tell him the meeting had indeed everything to do with this. After Harold left, he put in a call to Mel Pierson, sat back, and ordered another cup of coffee. He needed to think quietly for a few moments before going back to the office. There were some other items that Mel and he had already discussed and were going to talk about when they had a meeting. It wasn't only the President's fault; it went a lot deeper than that! *So deep*, thought Lindsey, *most will not believe it; it could never happen in the United States of America! No, Sir! Not in our country. No one in this nation would try to convert our country into a socialist, communist, or Islamic nation. Basically, make it a third world country! By damn, not on my watch!*

But it was happening right before their eyes! The hardest part for Lindsey to understand was that it had been going on for many years, one tiny step at a time! It sort of reminded him of that child's game that he used to play as a small kid: "Johnny, take one baby step." The answer had to be "May I?" If you failed to say "May I" you would get the answer back, "No you may not." Remembering kind of brought a smile to Lindsey face. *Thank goodness, because there hadn't been a whole lot to smile about lately*, Lindsey thought.

Mel finally returned his call.

"Lindsey, we have a lot to talk about and I'd like to get with you for a half hour or so, before the meeting next Friday. There is some big stuff that we need to discuss, just between the two of us, before we lay it out to the rest," Mel said. "You and I have discussed conspiracies before, but, Lindsey, you won't believe all the shit in this one!" he added. "Worse yet, from everything I can tell, at least at this time, this one is true, and some of our own people have uncovered the evidence to back it up. When can we get together? Somewhere private?"

"I think we better make it soon; it's getting more serious each day," Lindsey replied. "How is your schedule for tomorrow?"

"I will clear my schedule. This has become 'priority one'. Morning or evening, and where; either time suits me, you pick the place," Mel said.

"Well, I am sitting in Union Station, at the East Street Café, I just had lunch with Harold Reed, and even though it's a busy and noisy place, it's probably as private as we can find in DC. The noise drowns out any conversation that goes on. I doubt anybody could hear anything that we say anyway. There are so many people coming and going I don't believe we would attract any attention. Besides, I think you and I have had lunch here before, so there would be nothing unusual about our getting together for lunch," Lindsey said.

Mel answered, "That's fine with me. How about 1:30? We'll have a late lunch. I'll clear my schedule and we can take as long as necessary."

"I'll see you tomorrow," Lindsey replied, and headed back to his office to clear his schedule for tomorrow.

CHAPTER TWENTY-FIVE

Democrat Congresswoman Nancy Patrick, Speaker of the U.S. House of Representatives; the most powerful woman in the country, perhaps even the world—three heartbeats away from the presidency of the U.S., sat at her desk in the Rayburn House Office Building. It was late night—almost twelve, midnight—and she couldn't stop crying. She was upset, not just at the President, but mostly at herself. How could she have been so stupid? So stupid to believe that he was going to change the country for the better! He lied!

He had lied to her, to Congress, and to the American people! What could she do? How could she face her friends, her fellow congressmen, her constituents, her family? He had ruined her reputation, literally destroyed her. She was completely humiliated.

She cried and cried until she couldn't cry anymore.

Patrolling the perimeter around the Rayburn Office Building, Patrolman Sergeant Guy Spence of the Capital Police Department checked his watch, ten minutes after one o'clock. It was a long, quiet shift so far. He glanced up at the second floor and saw a light in one of the windows. That's unusual, he thought as he looked at his watch again, then called the inside security team to check it out. He continued his tour around the building, a slow walk that normally took him about thirty minutes or more, where he checked the outside doors and any kind of unusual movement on the grounds.

As Patrolman Spence turned the corner of the building, completing his round, he was shocked to see flashing blue and red lights coming from several black and white police cars and the ambulance sitting there. He had not heard any sirens so they must have come up quietly. The security team leader was standing with the door open talking with a police officer. Several of the officers were standing behind their open car doors, with weapons drawn.

Several other cars began pulling up to the building, large, black SUVs, Suburbans like the FBI, CIA, and other government agencies use. People in coats and ties got out and headed for the door, and went inside.

Patrolman Spence went up to his team leader and asked, "What's going on? Why the black and whites, and ambulance?"

The team leader replied, "Congresswoman Patrick, the Speaker of the House was just found dead in her office. That's the office you called in about seeing the light on."

"My God! What happened to her? Did she have a heart attack or something?" Spence asked.

"We can't tell right now; I guess it might have been. There are no physical signs to indicate any type of violence," the team leader replied. "After you called, I went to check it out. I knocked on the door and got no answer, so I figured she had just left the light on when she left. I opened the door to turn off the lights and saw her slumped over her desk, like she was sleeping. I tried to wake her and she didn't respond; I called 9-1-1."

All of a sudden, the place was swarming with FBI agents, CIA, and DC detectives. The Crime Scene van pulled up and the crew got out and rushed inside followed by the coroner and a half dozen other people. Then, the Minority Leader of the House of Representatives drove up and went inside. The local DC police formed a perimeter around the building. Nobody seemed to really know what was going on, or for that matter what they were doing. There was just a lot of confusion.

Patrolman Spence stood by and watched, thinking, *She was high profile, the 'stuff' is really going to hit the fan now.*

More important people started showing up. A few, those Spence assumed were important enough, were allowed to go in the building; the rest had to wait outside. *Hell, it was three o'clock in the morning, for God's sake,* he thought. *Is the whole city awake?* Then, all hell broke loose; the word leaked out. TV news crews with their satellite hook-up dishes on top of the vans, news anchors, and camera people, from every national network, plus local and foreign correspondents, all were on the scene!

The local DC police added barriers and broadened the perimeter around the entire building and grounds; no one could get within fifty yards of the building.

After another couple of hours or so, Spence could see the ambulance crew bringing the gurney out with the body on it and put it in the ambulance. They sat for a few minutes longer and then slowly pulled away.

As he walked close to the barricades, reporters would shout questions, "What happened? Who are they taking away?" *I guess they were just doing their jobs, trying to be the first with the "scoop" and information for their station's audience. Can't blame them, I guess,* Spence thought.

He then went up to his team leader and asked, "Tim, did they determine what happened to the Congresswoman? Did she have a heart attack?"

Tim replied, "We don't know anything yet. The medics said they could see no signs of a heart attack or stroke, but wouldn't really know until they got the body to the hospital or morgue and the coroner could check more closely. I'm sure they'll do an autopsy to make certain."

Spence stood there watching the ambulance, with the body of U.S. Congresswoman Patrick, pull away. He wondered what was going on; there was something very ominous about this.

He looked around and realized the whole area was swarming with investigators, police, FBI, CIA, probably Secret Service too. No one seemed to know where they were all from. Just looking on, it didn't look like any of them knew what they were doing either! Then a Mobile Crime Scene Lab van pulled up and a team got out and entered the building.

His shift over, Spence went home and went to bed—the twelve-hour shifts were tough. He had hardly gotten to sleep when his phone rang; it was the DC Police Department. The FBI and the DC Police Investigators wanted him to come down to the station for an interview. Grudgingly, he dressed, got in his car and drove back downtown to precinct headquarters near the senate office building.

He was taken into a small room. He assumed it must be an interrogation room, where they take hardened criminals for questioning. A well-dressed man in his mid- to late-forties introduced himself and let him know that he wasn't under investigation but that they needed some information that he may or may not have. That sounded reasonable to him.

After maybe a half hour of asking about any strangers or visitors that he may have seen wandering around, they asked if he had been on duty inside the building, on the floor where Congresswoman Patrick's office was located; if he had been inside the office.

Since his primary duty that day was to check and secure the grounds around the building, they finally decided he knew little or nothing, so they let him go back home. All the exercise accomplished was to get his curiosity up again. He could feel in his bones that something very sinister had happened in that building, in that Congresswoman's office.

CHAPTER TWENTY-SIX

Dutch and I were sitting in the restaurant of the hotel having breakfast before heading over to the Pentagon for our first day of duty, doing what we didn't have the slightest idea. We both were engrossed in the news on the screen of the restaurant TV. It was blasting over and over, "Breaking News!" "Breaking News! Congresswoman Nancy Patrick found dead in her office early this morning. Congresswoman Patrick is the Speaker of the U. S. House of Representatives, the Majority Leader, and one of the President's strongest supporters. There are no details available at this time; according to authorities on the scene, foul play is not suspected, but we will keep you informed as we receive more. All we know right now is that the body was taken to the Medical Examiner's office for an autopsy to determine the cause of death."

Dutch looked across the table and said, "There is something real 'fishy' going on around here, Bull. That woman was one of the strongest proponents of closing GITMO and turning those shitheads loose on the world."

"I do know that she was a pain in the ass for the military, and anything that the conservatives tried to get through Congress," I replied. "You think we better get on over to the Pentagon before we both get fired?"

"I guess you're right; however, it might be a good thing if we got fired. Before this thing is over, we may be faced with something a whole lot worse than being fired," Dutch added.

Even though we were in uniform, we still had to work our way through the maze of complicated security check-points to gain entry into the inner sections of the Pentagon where Sam Drakeford's office was located. We entered and were greeted by the secretary, who asked us to have a seat and said that the General was on the phone. She asked if we would like a cup of coffee, which we accepted. After about five minutes, the secretary's phone buzzed and she listened and for a moment then told us the General would see us.

We entered General Sam Drakeford's office and Sam met us as we came in. "I assume you've heard the latest news, about Congresswoman Patrick?" he asked "Both the FBI and CIA are investigating, and probably every other agency, so we should know something pretty soon about how she died although the word is that there was nothing amiss and they don't suspect foul play. Dutch, Bull, I don't know what all in hell is going on right now, but I'm telling you there is something new every minute; shit is hitting the fan from all different directions. I have retirement papers on my desk right now from three general officers—long time guys, battle hardened, and trained, great leaders throughout their service. I know them personally and I also know that they were not ready, or even thinking about retiring yet."

Then after a moment's pause, Sam added, "The problem is they are not allowed to do their jobs. They have been micro-managed ever since that sorry, that SOB, took office and started withdrawing troops from Iraq and letting the terrorists and Jihadist take over again. They are really pissed and say they can't put up with the crap any longer."

"But, Sam," Dutch interjected, "If we keep losing our best leaders, the very people who we have trusted, and who have done the job all these years, what the hell is going to happen to the country and to the overall military complex? I think there is something very sinister going on; somewhere in the current national leadership, someone is purposely attempting to bring down the military and the entire government."

Sam replied, "That's exactly why you guys are here and we are meeting with a group, I think it will be a pretty large group, to determine what to do and our next step to prevent a take-over from happening."

Just then, Sam's secretary buzzed him and said that Admiral Dawkins was in the outer office. Sam told her to send him on in. Vince came in; Sam had told him earlier that Dutch and I would be there.

"Has the boss told you what you would be doing while you're here?" he asked.

"Not yet," I answered; "And I'm almost afraid to ask!"

Sam laughed and said, "I haven't given them an assignment yet." Then, after hesitating for a moment, he added, "Hell, I don't have the slightest idea what to put them on as they're on a bogus assignment. We'll probably call it 'Special Assistant' to something, unless one of ya'll have a better thought or title, for the time-being anyway."

Sam's phone buzzed again. He picked-up then said into the phone, "Good morning, Senator Lindsey, how are you?"

"What? Dave's driver is dead? Before he could be questioned? What happened; how did he die?"

Sam listened intently for a few minutes, and then asked, "Did they see anyone else? I thought there was a guard at the door to let only nurses and doctors in. Something in the IV; who the hell, besides a nurse or doctor, could have put something in the IV?"

Vince, Dutch, and I looked at each other. Finally, Sam put down the phone. "Dave's driver, Sergeant Dan Johnson, is dead!" he said softly.

We all kind of stammered, but I managed to get out, "Where was the guard? There was supposed to be a 24-hour guard at his door to be sure something like this didn't happen, especially since the manner in which the accident occurred!"

"Did anyone ever talk with him, question him about the accident?" Vince asked.

"From what I could gather from Lindsey, just now," Sam replied, "All hell broke loose on the fourth floor of the 'GW' hospital late last evening. It all started, it seems, when Tom Beckwith stopped by the room yesterday to check on Sergeant Johnson, and was followed when he left. Whoever it was followed Tom back to his office, then drove off. Tom worked late last night and when he left, he noticed the same car, or one like it, pull in behind him as he got onto the highway; the ones in the car started shooting. Anyway, as you already know, Tom took them out—permanently! In all the excitement at the scene, Mel Pierson and Chip Reese drove up. As Tom was telling them what was going on, they suddenly realized that if Tom had been followed from the hospital and someone had tried to kill him, they were probably going to hit the hospital as well, so they took off to the hospital. That's when shit hit the fan."

Sam continued. "As the three ran down the hall toward the room, they could see the guard sprawled out and, what looked like a 'nurse,' come out of the room. When the 'nurse' saw the three men she, or he, or whoever it was, took off running toward the exit. He made it out of the hospital entrance—that was as far as he got. Mel, who was in pursuit put a round in the back of the 'nurse's' head! Tom Beckwith stopped by and saw Johnson shortly after Dave and Anna's funeral. Tom said Dan was groggy and sleepy but was able to talk and told him what had happened. They were murdered. The FBI boys were waiting until he was a little better before they were going to begin the investigation by questioning him."

"It looks as if someone doesn't want him, or for that matter, anyone else to be questioned," Dutch said.

"Sure looks that way," Sam added. "I'm anxious to talk with Tom to see what Sergeant Dan was able to tell him. That may shed some light on the cause."

Sam looked over at Dutch and me and said, "By the way, fellows, I did make arrangements for the two of you. You will share a couple of adjoining offices a few doors down the hall while you're here. I believe they are already set up and ready for you. The personnel office will send you a couple of people to interview as temporary secretaries while here also. If you need anything else just let me know and we'll see what we can do."

"Sam," I said, "If it's all the same to you, with your permission of course, I would rather bring my secretary from GITMO up on TDY while we're here."

Sam looked over at Dutch, smiled and asked, "Dutch, does Bull have a little something going on the side?"

"Beats the hell out of me, Sam; but then, he is single and probably 'horny.' I also know his secretary, but I don't think she would drop to his level," he laughed. "But she is good looking. I wouldn't blame him."

Sam, Vince, and Dutch stood there laughing.

I felt a little blush cross my face, but I told them, "If you had an efficient secretary, you would do the same; besides, I'm old enough to be her daddy! I'm sure she's not interested."

"Is she married or single?" asked Sam smiling.

"Her husband was killed in Afghanistan three years ago; got caught with an IED and they never found all the parts," I replied.

They all muttered a "Sorry, I didn't know that."

Then Sam added, "That's terrible. Did they have any kids?"

"No, they were both army and didn't want to put kids through the kind of life where they would have to pull up and move, or be without one of the parents half the time," I answered.

"Go ahead and have orders cut putting her on TDY to your office; it is fine with me," Sam said, and then laughed and added, "Dutch, I guess you'll have to find your own secretary."

CHAPTER TWENTY-SEVEN

Mel Pierson and Senator Lindsey Scott met each other as both were arriving at Union Station for their 1:30 afternoon meeting and Mel said, "Good timing, Lindsey, glad you were able to clear your calendar so we could get together."

"Me too, Mel; there seems to be a lot of crap happening, and happening fast," Lindsey replied.

"Lindsey, we—and I mean not only you and I, but also the whole group of us who have met and have implied that the President was guilty of treason—are wrong! Hell, I'm not really sure right now exactly what he is guilty of, but I sure as hell know that he is guilty of much more!" Mel said.

"I'm sure of that also, Mel, but what do you have in mind, or think that he is guilty of, beyond treason, that is?" I asked.

"When you called yesterday, you said you had lunch with Senator Harold Reed. Did he tell you anything about what he and I had talked about?" Mel asked.

"Well, he kind of unloaded a bunch of serious stuff. He was so nervous, I was afraid that he would have a heart attack or stroke sitting here. He was telling me that someone had real proof that some of the rumors that floated around the Internet for the past seven or eight years is actually true. That, that sorry son-of-a-bitch was never even eligible to run for the office of President. You know, Mel; that really has me pissed!" Lindsey said.

"Me, too," said Mel. "But the problem becomes even bigger, I think. I don't know just how to handle it, not yet anyway. I'm not sure that it would be wise for the people of this country to know the real truth. If it was me, and I found out by some announcement, I would want blood! Don't tell me that he has been arrested and will be given a hearing and trial. I know I wouldn't believe it, I would be sure that some kind of 'fix' was in, and he would get off. I figured Harold probably told you about it, but I have a bit of other news too. Ever since the guys at the White House Secret Service began their 'unofficial' investigation, they have been watching every move the President and his closest associates have made. They have even been checking the trash! One of the Secret Service guys usually takes the trash can from the President's desk to the incinerator to be burned; they have been going through the paper notes and items in the trash. One of them found a list that the President had made check marks on. You know what the list was? It was a list of items that Paul Skalinsky had outlined in his book for the take-over from democracy to a socialist society! Top on his list was poverty, with the quote: 'Increase the poverty level as high as possible; poor people are easier to control and will back the government, because the government provides everything for them.' He had this checked as done. Next, he had listed, and checked off, the national debt; increase the national debt to an unsustainable level, increasing taxes, thus producing more poverty; then, he had gun control, but it was not checked off, but it had a note in the margin that said, 'almost,' 'working on it'; then it went on from there. I'm supposed to get a copy of the note; I think others in the Secret Service, as well as the CIA, and by now the FBI has heard about it. The note went on to list other items like healthcare, welfare, education, religion, and even class warfare. Some were checked and others were noted, 'Almost there.'"

Mel was exasperated when he finished telling Lindsey all of this, and obviously extremely mad!

"Do you know what this reminds me of, Mel," Lindsey asked? Do you recall what Krushchev said when he spoke before the United Nations; the time when he banged his shoe on the podium?

He said that our children's children will live under communism. 'You Americans are so gullible. No, you won't accept Communism outright; but we'll keep feeding you small doses of Socialism until you will finally wake up and find that you already have Communism. We won't have to fight you; we'll so weaken your economy, until you fall like overripe fruit into our hands.'"

After a pause, Lindsey added, "He said that back in 1959 when JFK was President. Well, it looks as if he was almost right. If we don't get this situation corrected right now, he will be right!"

Then, emphatically, Lindsey went on, "I remember seeing him on TV banging his shoe, and I've never forgotten his words."

"I do recall that," Mel said solemnly. He sat quietly for a few moments, and then after some thinking, in a manner more than a statement, he said, "After what happened to Nancy Patrick, I'm some-what concerned about Harold. He was visibly upset and shaken when we talked."

"So am I; I don't think he would do anything that drastic, like taking his own life. But there have been others stronger than Harold that have done so," Lindsey replied.

Just then, Lindsey's cell phone went off and he touched the button to receive the call; it was Harold. He sounded upset again.

"Hello, Harold, what's up?" He asked

"Can we get together tomorrow morning, say around 7:30 at the same place in Union Station?" he asked. "I need to discuss something with you."

"Sure," Lindsey replied. "The East Street Café in Union Station at 7:30. I'll see you there."

Mel asked, "Is he still upset and nervous?"

"Yeah, he sounds as anxious as he did the last time," Lindsey answered. Then he had another thought.

"Mel, would you be available to meet with Harold and me at 7:30 tomorrow morning, here?" he asked.

Mel thought for a moment before answering, "I can be available, sure, but what about Harold? He would not be expecting me."

"I will give him a call and clear it with him although I feel sure he would agree. In fact it will probably help him, knowing that you also know what's going on," Lindsey said.

----- Senator Harold Reed sat nervously in the East Street Café at 7:30 am waiting on Senator Lindsey Scott and FBI Director Mel Pierson to show up. He kept looking around to see if anyone he knew was there, and maybe watching him. He couldn't keep from twitching and turning in every direction, like he was expecting to be jumped any minute. He kept thinking about Nancy, how she had come to him, upset, and wanted to talk. She was going to resign from Congress and was thinking about announcing that the reason for retiring was because the President had lied to her and the nation. That she no longer trusted him; that she was embarrassed and sorry that she had supported his policies. To help make up for it to the public, she was resigning her seat in Congress.

Now, she was dead!

He was still deep in thought when Lindsey Scott and Mel Pierson came in and sat down at the table.

"You look like you've lost your best friend, or your wife. You're so deep in thought; you look very nervous, too. Are you expecting somebody else also?" Lindsey asked.

Senator Reed replied, "Oh no, but I have been doing a lot of deep thinking, however. I can't fathom all the crap that I find going on in this administration, and the damage it has already caused. How we could have been so gullible? You won't believe some of the stuff I'm about to tell you."

"Harold, you sound awfully serious; have you found out something new?" Lindsey asked.

"I'm glad that you called yesterday and asked Mel to come, and briefed him on some of our concerns. He and I have talked about it before also, and I'm happy that you're here, Mel. Eventually all of this will fall into your lap anyway. I know you and Mel have heard all of the conspiracy theories that have floated around for years, especially on the internet and social media; well it seems that more of them are true than not," Harold said.

Then, he looked over at Mel and said, "Mel, you probably know a lot more about this than I do; you probably have a file on it. Most likely you have had a file for quite some time."

"We've got a lot of files, Harold; some based on a lot of that internet and social media crap that goes around. Which particular rumor or file are you talking about?" Mel asked.

"Have you seen, or are you aware of the investigation into the President's birthplace?" he asked Mel.

"Yeah, Harold, I now have a file on that and we are kind of sitting on it for the time being. Frankly, we don't know just how in hell we're supposed to handle it!" Mel said. "So for the time being, if anyone asks, we're just saying that we are investigating it. We can't even go to the Attorney General about it. She is in his hip pocket and would stop any kind of investigation or discussion concerning the issue."

Lindsey spoke and said, "I thought that was pretty drastic; I mean the information about where he was born, but you sound like you have something new to add. I think you're about to throw another log on the fire, Harold."

"Probably so, and it's bigger than just another log; it's the whole damn tree this time!" he said.

Mel spoke up and said, "By the way, speaking of throwing another log on the fire, I just received a report that Speaker Nancy Patrick didn't have a heart attack or anything medical that caused her death."

"What!" exclaimed Harold!

"Mel, what the hell happened to her then?" Lindsey asked.

"This is just between the three of us, at least for now," Mel stated. "The Medical Examiner finished his autopsy and found traces of arsenic in her blood. A couple of my investigators went through her desk thoroughly and picked up some medication that she kept there. It was all clear. However, they did find a very small trace, actually just dust particles, of arsenic in one of the bottles, probably from a pill that was put in the same bottle with her other pills."

"Why would she put arsenic in the same bottle with other pills?" Harold asked.

"We don't think she did. We think someone else put the arsenic in the bottle when she wasn't near her desk," Mel said.

"You're talking murder!" exclaimed Harold.

"Exactly!" Mel said

"But, Mel," Lindsey interjected, "Why in hell would anybody want to murder Nancy Patrick? She has been the darling of this administration, doing anything they wanted done. As the House Majority leader, she pushes bills through the House without reading them."

"Herein lies the problem, gentlemen," Mel began. "Harold, this should sound very familiar to you. You have told us that you are upset and disappointed in the administration, the congress, and the President because they are going against the Constitution and everything this nation stands for. You even said that it took some time before you actually realized it."

"But what does that have to do with Nancy Patrick?" Harold asked.

"Well, you're not the only one that was disappointed and saddened by what has been going on around here." Mel said. "In fact about two weeks ago, Nancy called and asked to meet with me in her office as soon as I could. So I met with her a little over a week ago, as she requested, and I got the shock of my professional lifetime. When we went into her private office and she began talking, she teared up. I didn't know what to think! I asked her if she was not feeling well, that we could meet another time. She assured me that, health-wise, she was fine. Then, she asked if we could talk 'off the record,' in confidence. And of course I assured her she could and it would go no further."

Then after a pause, Mel added, "Well, since she is no longer among us, I'm sure she wouldn't mind me telling you what she had on her mind. The first thing she said was that she was planning to resign from Congress. I didn't respond. I just let her talk without interrupting. She told me that she had compromised her principles, her beliefs and thought the President was violating the Constitution. She talked at length about all she had done, thinking that she was helping the country in its time of need for leadership. We talked—actually, she talked—for almost an hour, and she repeated herself, that 'she was going to resign, go back home, take a much-needed rest,' and that then she was going to work against the current leadership of the administration. Then she mentioned something that really shocked me further! She told me that she had heard some 'rumblings' about a group of elected officials, military leaders and even agency heads that were planning to take the matter in their own hands and try to get the government back on the right track, to straighten it out and get back to following the Constitution. Then, she said that if she had known, she would like to join with them and help."

Harold and Lindsey looked at each other and back at Mel. Then, Lindsey said, "I wonder if she really knew what was going on and who all was, or is involved."

"I don't know for sure," Mel replied, "I don't think so. But if she mentioned it to the wrong people, it might explain what happened to her, and how she had arsenic in her pill bottle!"

Then, Harold said he had to get back to the office—he had several appointments that he had to keep. He got up to leave and Lindsey reminded him of the meeting on Friday evening. He told Harold he still didn't know where, or the time, for sure but that he would let him know as soon as he found out.

"I will make time whenever it's scheduled," Harold said as he walked away.

"Mel," Lindsey said, "I'm concerned about Harold. He is frightened. And now with what happened to Nancy Patrick, I'm afraid something might happen to him. He has even mentioned that he might resign and retire and go back home to Nevada."

Mel answered, "Lindsey, I'm a little concerned about Harold also. There are too many mysterious things happening; and it's going to get worse before it gets better. I'll see if I can keep an eye on him for a while."

As we got up to leave also, Mel said, "Lindsey, that goes for you too. You watch your back; be careful, and be aware of everything and everybody around you. If you run into any of the others whom we have spoken to about any of this, warn them also. Tell them to be especially careful and keep watch; tell them not to talk with anyone about what's going on, whom they're not sure about."

"Thanks, Mel, but remember, that goes for you too!" Lindsey told him.

CHAPTER TWENTY-EIGHT

It was Friday morning, I was sitting at my desk in my new office in the Pentagon; the sign on the door said, "Assistant Director." There was a knock on the door and I said, "Come in."

The door opened and my heart skipped a beat! The prettiest sight I had seen in a week walked in; Sergeant Penny Fulbright came through the door with a big smile on her face. She walked straight to the front of my desk, snapped to attention, saluted, and said in her most formal, military voice, "Sergeant Fulbright reporting for duty, as ordered, sir!" The smile never left her face.

"Damn, I'm glad to see you, Penny!" I said and walked around to the front of the desk.

"Me too, sir," she said, still smiling.

We both stood there, looking at each other, just smiling. We shook hands and held on for an extended period of time, for a handshake. Then, I guess because of the way we were looking at each other, we hugged, military protocol be damned!

Penny, with a little blush showing up around her cheeks pointed to the door and said, "Assistant Director; Assistant Director of what, Colonel?"

"Beats the hell out of me, Penny! General Drakeford hasn't told me yet. In fact, he isn't sure what to do with me, or what my job title is," I said and laughed.

Penny asked in jest, "So what do we do? Do we just sit around all day?"

"I'm sure Sam will come up with something for both of us and for General Hall, too. You do know that Dutch was assigned here also, don't you?"

"As close as you guys are I figured he would be, and that something pretty big was going down," Penny said.

Just then, the door to the outer office, where Penny would be, opened and Dutch walked in and called out, "Anybody home?"

"Back here," I answered, "Come on in."

Dutch entered and stopped short when he saw Penny standing there. "Oh, excuse me; I didn't know someone was with you."

"Come on in, Dutch and meet Sergeant Penny Fulbright, my secretary while we're here," I said. "She came up from GITMO on TDY. As she already knows my operating style, she won't need any training."

Dutch walked over to Penny, "I'm glad to meet you Sergeant Fulbright. Colonel Miller has spoken of you often and told me how efficient you are."

"Thank you, General Hall. Colonel Miller has spoken of you often also, of how close you have been through the years. You two have been through a lot together," Penny replied.

Dutch looked at Penny and said, "We have been through a lot together and somehow we still survived, Sergeant . . . ."

Then hesitating, Dutch looked over at Bull and back at Penny and continued, "You know, I believe we're going to be working pretty close together while we're here on this job, whatever it may be . . . that we can be a little less formal. If that's alright with the two of you. When it's just the three of us and no one else around, how about first name basis? I believe we all would be more comfortable."

"That's good with me," I said. "Penny, how about you?"

Penny looked quite nervous. "It's fine with me, sir, if that's how you would like it. But I will have to say that it may take some time getting used to. I'm not used to calling Colonels and Generals by their first names," she said.

Dutch and I laughed, and Dutch said, "Don't worry about that, Penny, you'll get used to it. Like I said before, we don't really know exactly, or I should say, officially, just why we're here. I have a hunch that, in the long run, it will involve something that probably has nothing to do with us being military. I don't know if Bull has told you anything that's going on in our minds or not, but it's pretty damn serious."

Penny looked over to me.

"We have had a couple of conversations about what's going on, about the closing of GITMO and the situation with the Executive Order; she's familiar with some of that. We think alike on the crap that's going on," I said.

"I think it's a shame and the overall situation is terrible and has our country in a very untenable situation; the whole darn country is going to hell in a handbasket!" Penny replied. "In fact, sir, I have worried myself about it—that we have gone so far down, I don't how in the world we are going to get back up to a level of national confidence and pride that we have always been used to."

"Well said, Penny, but if we're going to be on first names, you can drop the "sir" stuff also. I know Bull and I are a lot older, but we're still just "soldiers" like you," Dutch said.

I looked at my watch and told them, "Well, 'troops,' it's about lunch time. What do you say we go down to the cafeteria and see just what kind of 'chow' they serve here in the big city?"

"Suits me," said Dutch, "Penny?"

"Fine with me General . . . err . . . Dutch? Ahh, sir?" Penny stammered.

Dutch and I both laughed out loud. "Dutch it is, Penny. You'll get used to it, don't be nervous," he said.

"I told you it will take getting used to," Penny replied as we walked out of the office.

We went into the cafeteria and got into the buffet line and loaded up on the "specials of the day"—baked chicken with dressing, cranberry sauce, green beans, sweet potatoes, and anything else that would go on the tray.

As we were eating, I looked up and saw a familiar face coming into the dining room. He was an old-time friend from earlier days in the army. He was now retired but was still doing the same thing he did in the military, only now he was getting paid twice as much, "double dipping" they called it!

He was an electronics communications expert and the last I had heard from him he was assigned to the White House Communications Agency (WHCA). He had designed the system down in the inner bowels of the White House and the Executive Office buildings so that the

President could have instant contact with anyone, anywhere in the world. He was there during and after the administration of the first President Bush. If anyone needed to know anything about any form of communication, Rick Winstead was the "go-to" guy. I mentioned this to Dutch and Penny and said that he just may come in handy at some point in our investigation.

CHAPTER TWENTY-NINE

Senator Harold Reed was deep in thought as he drove back to his office in the Rayburn Building. He never noticed the large, black SUV that was following him. He decided to change course and swing by his house, just over the Maryland line in Bethesda, to pick up some items that he might need for a meeting in his office later in the day. Bethesda is one of the finer neighborhoods in all of the suburbs around Washington.

As he drove up into the front drive, he decided not to pull into the garage; he was only going to be a few minutes. He went into the house, saw a note his wife had left that said she would be back early evening; she was at her bridge club with the other ladies. He went into his office, spent several minutes clearing some much needed paperwork, picked up his second briefcase, and started back out to his car. As he was locking the house door, he turned toward the car and pushed the "Auto Start" button on his key fob. He heard the engine start, followed by an earth shattering explosion that almost knocked him off his feet. Pieces of metal flew past his head as he ducked down.

"What the hell," he stammered; "My damn car just blew up! What in hell is happening around here? Some-damn-body is trying to kill me!"

He grabbed his cell phone and hit the 9-1-1 button and told the dispatcher what had happened. The dispatcher told Harold that someone was on the way, to stand by and wait for them to arrive. Harold quickly dialed Mel.

"Hello, Harold, that was quick, what's going on?" Mel asked.

"Mel, my car just exploded, right in my front yard. It's a good thing I wasn't in it. I would be dead now!" Harold told Mel, almost yelling.

"Calm down, Harold, and tell me what happened," Mel told him.

"My damn car just blew up, that's what happened! Some body killed Dave and Anna, and now they are trying to kill me!" Harold yelled into the phone. "What am I going to do?"

"I'll be right over, Harold, where are you?" Mel asked.

"I am at my house. My car was sitting in the drive. I was locking the door and I pushed the Auto Start button on my key remote and the whole damn car blew up! Flying pieces almost hit me in the head!" Harold was speaking rapidly, in a shrill, scared voice.

Mel was already on his way out the door while talking with Harold. As soon as Harold hung up, Mel called his assistant director and told him about the bombing and asked him to send agents to Harold's house, along with a couple of bomb experts and try to find out what kind of explosives was involved. He then called Tom Beckwith at CIA and told him about the bombing.

"I'm on my way," Tom said, adding, "I wonder who is next?"

Mel replied, "No telling, Tom; but I'll tell you one thing, somebody knows every step we take and every move we make. They seem to know our thoughts. Somebody knows we have had 'secret' meetings and know what has been discussed. Either somebody has spoken out of turn or, maybe some of us have been 'bugged,' and the phones tapped."

Tom said, "Either way, we better be extra careful; we also need to speed up the process. Get everybody together if need be and do something! Whoever the hell is behind this is getting real serious and they don't give a damn about the country or who they have to kill to finish their takeover. I believe this was further along than any of us thought."

Mel and Tom pulled up at Harold's house within a minute or so of each other and parked just outside the perimeter that had been set-up. They stepped under the yellow and black tape barricade and into the chaos and mass confusion of police, FBI, firefighters, bomb squads, and who knows all that were on the scene.

Mel led the way over to his lead investigator; a rather large man of about forty who had been in the explosive business for twenty years—first in the military and then for the FBI.

"Donny, can you tell me what happened? Have you had the chance to get a handle on things yet?" Mel asked.

"Not for sure, Mel," Donny replied. "Not yet anyway. The senator said he was locking the house and that he turned and pushed the remote to start the car's engine and the damn thing blew up! It kind of looks like someone, at some point, someone fairly close to him, inserted a small "chip" in his car remote, then planted the explosives underneath the car after he arrived here. Otherwise, the explosion could, or would have, gone off in some other location. Just imagine if he was parked in the Congressional parking deck and it had gone off. No telling how many could have been killed. Whoever did this was only interested in taking out the senator."

Mel looked at Tom, and they nodded at each other, knowing what the other was thinking.

"Somebody seems to know everything that's going on," Tom said.

"You got that right," Mel answered. "I think someone must be listening in on our conversations."

"Let me check with my people; they have everything under control for now, I believe," Tom said. "I want to stop by the Pentagon. Bull Miller and Dutch Hall are in town on temporary assignment to Sam Drakeford's office, and I want to welcome them to the rat-race of Washington!"

Mel laughed, "Yeah, tell them that they will love it here in the big city with the quiet, peaceful atmosphere and friendly neighbors."

"I'll talk with you later, Mel. We've got to pull this thing together before anyone else gets hurt, or killed. I'll give you a call if I find out anymore. You do the same, okay?" Tom said.

As Tom drove off, Mel headed to his car and back to the office.

CHAPTER THIRTY

Tom spoke into his cell phone mounted on the dashboard of his car, "Call the Pentagon; General Hall's office," he said.

"General Hall," the voice said, as the call was answered.

"Dutch Hall, this is Tom Beckwith; just wanted to check-in with you. I heard that you and Bull had arrived in the 'big-city,' so I thought I might stop by, if your schedule permits, and say welcome; I might even offer to buy dinner this evening," he laughed.

"Anytime I can get a free dinner I always have time, and to hell with the schedule," Dutch laughed, adding, "although it might cost you twice as much. Bull Miller is here also and has the office next to mine."

Tom said, "That's great; tell Bull to get the coffee on, I'll be there in about thirty minutes."

Dutch hung up the phone and called Bull. "Bull, we have company on the way over; Tom Beckwith just called and is stopping by."

"Great," I said. "He is just the person we need to see; we've got to get to the bottom of what-all-is-going-on around here!"

"He said to tell you to put the coffee on. And as you're the only one with a personal secretary around here, we'll meet in your office. Besides,

I'm not sure you know how to make the coffee, that's probably Penny's job anyway," Dutch said.

About forty-five minutes later, Tom stuck his head in Dutch's office and called out, "Dutch are you in?"

Dutch came from the back office and as they shook hands, Dutch said, "We're going next door to Bull's office. He has the coffee maker and the secretary who makes the coffee."

"Secretary? How does he rate to have a secretary so quickly?" Tom replied.

Dutch laughed and said, "Bull had her brought up from GITMO on TDY also; since she already knew his methods and he wouldn't have to train somebody new. Sam gave the okay but not without giving Bull some razzing about Penny being his 'personal' secretary. She is a Sergeant and lost her husband to an IED in Iraq about three years ago. She's not only a good soldier, but a nice lady as well."

The duo walked next door to Bull's office and entered the outer office where Penny sat at her desk looking busy. She stood as they came in and said, "May I help you, sir?"

Dutch responded, "We're here to officially inspect the coffee."

Penny looked surprised, "The coffee?"

Dutch and Tom laughed and Dutch said, "At ease, Penny. We were told you probably had some coffee ready; and by the way, what were you so busy doing when we came in? I didn't know we had anything in particular to do yet."

Penny looked from one to the other, paused and said, "When you knocked, I figured I better at least look busy, like I know what I'm doing. I don't want to get fired before I even get started," she grinned at the two men.

I heard the commotion and yelled out, "You guys leave my secretary alone and come on in."

Dutch and Tom walked inside and sat on the leather sofa; Bull pulled up a matching chair.

Penny came in and asked, "Would anyone like some coffee? It's freshly made and strong."

All three indicated they would have coffee and Penny left the office.

Dutch asked, "Tom, to what do we owe this visit from the CIA Director? Is it official or is it a friendly visit?"

"Yes!" Tom replied.

"Well, that's pretty much a short answer," I said.

"I guess you could say it's an 'off the record' official, but mostly a personal friend visit," Tom responded. "It's off the record, but officially, I'm looking for some information and I can't just go to anybody to find out; that's why I thought a couple of friends would be the best choice."

"Hell, Tom," I said, "I don't know what kind of information we could give you, what with us being the new boys on the block."

"I know," said Tom. "But here is my predicament; first, have you heard about Senator Harold Reed's car being blown up? At his house, for Pete's sake! While he was locking the door to the house, before getting into the car, the damn car blew up! Somebody was trying to kill him!"

A shocked Dutch said, "What the hell is going on, Tom?"

"There are too many people getting killed and shot at, to suit me," I added.

"You're damn right," said Tom. "And we've got to do something about it, and fast! Anyway, the other thing is, I believe that some, or most, of us have been 'bugged,' by whom I don't know. But I believe with all that's going on, the shootings, the killings, and who knows what else, we have to be 'bugged.' Whoever is doing it knows every move any of us make. I need a clean, electronic sweep of all who are involved. Maybe we can find out just who is 'bugging' us, and maybe stop someone else from getting killed. My problem, I don't know who at the agency I can trust, at this point, to do a sweep. I've got to find somebody else, an expert in electronics."

I spoke up, "I know just the guy that can handle it and never be noticed! And he works right here in the Pentagon."

Tom and Dutch looked over at Bull, and Tom asked, "Who?"

"Rick Winstead," I said. "Dutch, remember when we were having lunch the other day, down in the cafeteria and I saw Rick come in and mentioned that he was an electronics whiz? I know he would check this out and we can depend on him to keep it quiet."

"How soon can you reach him," Tom asked?

"How about right now?" I replied.

I spoke a little louder and called Penny in. "Penny, please see if you can find out where a Mr. Rick Winstead is located here in the Pentagon, and try to get him on the phone; he is a retired 'old time' sergeant, too."

"Yes, sir," Penny answered as she went back to her office.

The three sat there in silence, sipping on their coffee for several minutes, deep in thought. The silence was deafening until Bull spoke up and asked, more in thought than questioning, "What the hell are we going to do? The shit is getting deeper and people are getting hurt. I began by trying to find a way to keep from turning a bunch of terrorist assholes loose on the streets of the country; now, I'm beginning to find out that my 'guests' at GITMO aren't the only 'terrorist assholes' I've got to worry about. It seems like maybe we've got more of them here in the good old 'U-S of A' than I've ever had at GITMO at any one time."

"You've got that right, Bull," said Tom. "The only difference is that I believe the ones here are much more dangerous than your 'guests!' Your 'friends' will kill a few people and move on to the next target. The ones here are willing, and are trying to kill an entire culture!"

"You are right there, Tom," said Dutch. "It looks as if the Muslims, especially the Radical Islam branch, already have a pretty good foothold on the government now. Just take a look at the people in 'high' places in our government; I mean in Congress, agency heads, advisors, and the like. I sure as hell don't like the idea of so many "foreign" cultures in those positions and running things; right here in Washington at that!"

I grinned and said with a laugh, "I thought I was just getting involved in a 'little war,' a minor skirmish, something simple like, trying to take a President down."

Tom chuckled and said, "Better be careful what you say, Bull. I'm beginning to believe some of these walls have 'ears.'"

The phone on Bull's desk buzzed and he picked up and told Penny to put the call through.

"Rick Winstead, you old son-of-a gun, how the heck are you?" I said.

"Colonel Miller, this is a surprise," Rick replied. "I haven't heard anything from you in ages. Where are you and what have you been up to?"

"Rick, I am right here in the Pentagon on TDY. I saw you from a distance the other day down in the cafeteria, but didn't get the chance to speak. But I need to speak with you now, in fact, as soon as possible. What does your schedule look like?"

"Hell, Colonel, ever since I got my walking papers, my schedule is pretty much what I make it. How soon do you want to get together?

Since you're here in the Pentagon, I can probably be in your office in the next half hour, if you like," Rick replied.

"That's great! I'm in office 5A210. I think that's still in the Pentagon. It's so far from anything that I believe the 'powers-that-be' don't want anybody to know we're here," I responded with a grin. "Come on up, Rick, I've got some friends I want you to meet."

About thirty minutes later, Penny stuck her head in the door and said, "There is a Mr. Winstead here to see you Colonel."

"Send him on in, Penny."

CHAPTER THIRTY-ONE

I started toward the door as Rick Winstead walked in.

"Hello, Rick!" I said. "It's been a long time since we ran into each other; in fact I can't even remember the last time we crossed paths."

"It has been a while, Colonel. What brings you up here? I thought you were vacationing down in Cuba or someplace; I thought you were too smart to get duty in this big palace!" Rick said, laughingly.

"You're a civilian now, Rick, and I'm just plain Bull Miller. You outrank me, so let's drop the Colonel stuff. Let me introduce a couple of friends: this is General Dutch Hall, the commander of the Southeast Command down in Florida, and this is Tom Beckwith. Tom is Director of Recruitment for the CIA. You guys come on and have a seat. Would anyone like coffee? I think Penny has a fresh pot ready."

I buzzed Penny and she came in with the pot and cups for everyone and placed them on a small table in the back of the office.

"So, you hung it up and retired," Dutch remarked.

"Yes, sir, General; at least I thought that was what I did. I got my papers, went home, received a call from Lockheed-Martin, changed clothes, and came right back, making a little more than before, I might add," Rick replied.

Dutch grinned and said, "Rick, we're not wearing any rank among us, let's drop the general and colonel stuff. As a friend of Bull, you're automatically a friend of mine, and I'm sure Tom feels the same. Although after you hear why you were called and asked to come here, you may decide you don't want to be friends with a bunch of outsiders and misfits!"

"Damn, General . . , ah, Dutch, you make it sound pretty ominous; like some pretty serious shit is about to happen!" Rick said.

The four of them looked at each other for a few moments before anyone spoke.

Finally, Tom said, "Bull, why don't you bring Rick up to speed about what's going on and what we need?"

"Sure," I said. "I don't know how much you know about some of the President's executive orders, Rick, but I guess that's the place to begin. My involvement began with Executive Order Number 13492."

"Is that the stupid, idiotic order about closing GITMO?" Rick asked.

"That's the one," I continued. "I vowed that I would not release any of the detainees upon the public of the United States by putting them into some 'country club' stateside prison facility or release them to fight against us again. They have killed enough of our troops. I first talked with Dutch about my feelings and discovered he felt the same. Then, together, we spoke with several folks in high places, here in DC and found that we weren't by ourselves—most everybody we know seems to feel as we do. But that's not the crux of the problem, Rick, it goes much deeper. With that said, you need to stop me at whatever point that you think I'm just 'blowing smoke' and don't want to hear anymore, Rick. I probably have already said too much without knowing for sure your feelings on the matter, although I think I know you well enough to have a good idea of how you think about turning our country over to some misfits who got themselves elected, or perhaps I should say were 'placed' into the offices they now hold."

Rick nodded his head in agreement saying, "I believe I know what you're getting at. You wouldn't believe some of the 'scuttlebutt' that goes on down in the very bowels of this place. People from the lowest rank, military and civilian, to the very top of the 'totem pole' think that the guy sitting over in the oval office is a traitor and should be removed, one way or the other! If that's what you guys are thinking, count me in, although I'm not sure what I can do down in the basement."

Tom said, "That's exactly where you come in, Rick. There is a rather sizeable group who are trying to get something done. However, someone seems to know every move we make, and almost every thought any of us have. In fact, five have already been killed and several others have been either shot at or an attempt made to blow them up. We need to know how these other guys are finding out what we are doing; personally, I believe we have been 'bugged' and they are listening to everything we say. Hell, for all I know they may even have this office 'bugged.' That's where Bull thought you might come in; since you're a communications expert, perhaps you could do a 'bug' sweep in some of our offices and maybe even our cars. You never know how far they have gone with this."

Rick said, "Doing a clean sweep is not a problem. I've got the equipment. All I need to know is who, where, and when. Just let me know when you would like it done, and which offices and cars."

"Hell, it could even be in some of our homes and wives' cars," Tom said. "Probably the biggest problem we have is, we don't know who we can trust, even in my shop, the CIA, for heaven's sake. We have so many agents running around, I'm not sure who feels the way we do or whom I can trust."

Tom continued, "Rick, we don't want to put you in any danger of losing your job or physical danger either; we want you to understand exactly what you're getting into by helping us on this 'little' project, so be sure this is something that you want to get involved in."

"Tom, don't worry about me! However, it seems like you guys need to better be extra careful and keep one eye on your back. I would recommend that you carry a weapon, if you don't already carry one," Rick said and started for the door.

Then, he stopped, turned, and asked, "How soon can you get me a list of who you think needs the sweep? Also, will they be aware we will be checking their office or home, car, or where ever? I've got a couple of guys working for me whom we can trust. We can get started ASAP."

As he passed Penny's desk, he sat his cup on her desk on the way out.

CHAPTER THIRTY-TWO

Back in his office in the "pits" of the Pentagon, Rick sat behind his desk and smiled; he thought, *This is right down my alley! I haven't had any excitement since Desert Storm. All the rumors that float around this place about this and that, and nothing ever happens. Everybody's afraid of the next person; they're too damn rank-conscious! No wonder the country's in the mess it's in.*

He went to the door and looked out into the electronics lab where they did their communication designs and layouts prior to installing new systems. He spotted Pete and Paul, two young, twenty-something employees who he knew he could trust and count on to do a confidential job, "off-the-cuff" and not talk about it. He was always cutting-up with them and asking, "Where's Mary?" They were too young and had never heard of "Peter, Paul and Mary" from the sixties music era.

They would usually respond with some smart-ass wise-crack like, "She's probably 'down under the boardwalk' where you old farts hang-out when you're not working."

"I've got a special job for you two," he said. "And, it's top secret and un-official . . . understand?"

Paul spoke up, "Un-official—Top Secret? It sounds like trouble is heading our way; I believe we're getting ready to catch some crap—'big-time!'"

"Is this something off the record, boss? That if we screw up it's our ass in the sling, and nobody-else-ever-heard-of-it type of 'un-official?'" Pete said.

"You've got the picture!" Rick said in reply. Then he "swore" them to secrecy and leveled with them about the situation. He had known them well enough to know they were in total agreement with anything that might help straighten the country out and get it back on the right track.

"What do you want us to do?" Pete asked.

"Well, the first thing is to get some equipment together that is sensitive enough to pick up any type of 'bug' that has been placed within a hundred feet or more—the smallest equipment possible, so it won't be so easily noticed," Rick replied.

"Who and where are we going to sweep?" Paul asked.

"I don't know just yet, but we should be finding out in a day or two," Rick answered.

"I think we've got just what the doctor ordered," Paul said, more thinking out loud than replying. "We recently received a dozen small detectors that are supposed to be the latest thing in finding 'bugs,' of any type."

Pete added, "Yeah, we haven't even had the opportunity to check them out yet. I didn't see a particular need for them at the time. Well, I guess the time has arrived!"

"Hold on a minute," Paul said, "Let me grab one and show you."

About five minutes later, Paul returned with a gadget in his hand, no bigger than one of those small, outdated, "flip phones."

Peter, Paul, and Rick went through all the memoranda and instructions that came in the box—it was a "James Bond" kind of thing they were holding in their hands.

Rick smiled and said, "Damn guys, you are really on the ball. I thought it would take a month to get what we needed, and here you 'got 'er' done in minutes! This is one of the newest detection devices out, and it does about everything. According to the instructions, you can set it to vibrate, just like a cellphone and no one will hear it or notice it; and it's small enough to go into a shirt or coat pocket."

Then he added, "I've got to go upstairs and show these babies off. How about get me half a dozen more and I'll sign them out? I've got a couple of friends that need these now!"

While Pete and Paul went to get additional detectors, Rick took out his phone and punched in the number of my office.

After a couple of rings Penny picked up and said, "Colonel Miller's office."

"Hi, Penny. Rick Winstead here, is the Colonel still in?"

"All three are still here, but General Hall and Mr. Beckwith look like they're getting ready to leave," Penny told him.

"Hold them there, Penny; tell them I'm bringing something to them that will help them in their 'travels' around town." Rick held his phone down as Pete came through the door carrying a box.

Pete handed Rick a small box with the de-buggers in it, and said, "Tell whoever is going to use these, they better watch their ass. It sounds like they're onto some dangerous stuff."

Rick headed out of the door and upstairs to my office.

"Hi, Penny; are they still in there?" Rick asked her as he came through the door.

"They're waiting for you," she replied.

Rick walked into my office with the small boxes in his hand and said, "Gentlemen, I've got just what you need right here in the palm of my little hand!"

"What took you so long?" I wisecracked.

"Well, Bull, you know how it is with the government. However, in *my* department, we do the hard stuff immediately. Sometimes, the impossible takes a little longer!" Rick responded.

Everyone laughed and Dutch asked, "What do you have there?"

Rick then opened one of the boxes, removed the detector, held it up, and said, "This little device is known as an MCD-22, the very latest gadget for detecting 'bugs.' This is truly a space-age eavesdropping item; it's also known as the Hook-Switch Bypass, Third Wire Tap, and other names. It will even monitor your conversations with your telephone still on-the-hook! Now, the thing is, everybody knows this, so nobody discusses sensitive stuff on the phone any longer. But we've got that whipped, too; this little bugger, pardon the pun, detects the latest technology used by eavesdroppers. The more sophisticated folks use the device known as 'The Infinity.'"

Tom spoke up and said, "I've heard of that; in fact, I believe my folks are using that, or at least a version of it. It's unbelievable what these things can do."

Rick continued, "This is probably what someone is using on you guys. They don't have to be anywhere close, all they do is dial your number, and using different electronic methods, they prevent your phone from ringing. Then, he turns your phone into a super-sensitive listening device. They can hear even the slightest whisper from anywhere in the room, with the phone still on the hook! But here's the catch, for your guys. Now, you will be able to hear what they hear—and what they say!"

"Damn!" Dutch said. "Nobody is safe anymore! Hell, now I'm even afraid to think; some-damn-body is probably reading my mind!"

They all laughed, and then I said, "It would probably be X-rated if they did!"

Dutch asked, "How many of these toys do you have available, Rick? We need at least half a dozen more, right now."

"I have six right here and six more down in the shop. I'll check with my guys and find out how long it takes to get more, I'll give you a call back within an hour. In the meantime, figure how many you might need and if I don't have them I'll get more," Rick told them. He gave each of the guys one of the "buggers" and then went over the instructions with them. He gave the extra to me and headed toward the door and back to his *office.*

He stopped at the door, turned and spoke, in a loud voice, "Bull, you might want to give the other device to Penny. She's in a prime position to be 'bugged' and would probably have more information someone would be interest in than all of you others, put together."

He winked at Penny as he walked out; as he closed the door behind him, he came face-to-face with a four-star general who was reaching for the door to open it.

"Good afternoon, General," Rick said as he walked off.

I turned my MCD-22 device on but heard nothing; it was not emitting a vibration. I told the others, "It looks as if my office is clear, at least for the moment, but I think we are going to need a couple dozen more of these. I'll have Rick go ahead and acquire them as quickly as possible."

The door opened and General Sam Drakeford walked in; neither Dutch nor Bull was expecting him. However, as Chairman of the Joint

Chiefs, it was his building, at least for the time being anyway, so he could just walk into any office he decided to.

Tom Beckwith was speaking very solemnly, "I suggest we all keep these devices on beginning right now—in our vehicles, our offices, and, our homes. In fact, we should keep it active anytime we're in a different environment; this little gadget could be a tremendous help in resolving some situations and answering some bothersome questions. If you should get a 'hit' and it buzzes or whatever, let me know immediately, and I will put an agent on it ASAP!"

Virtually at the same time, Dutch and I looked up and said, "Sam, what brings you down here?"

"Would you like some coffee? I think Penny has a fresh pot," I added.

"That sounds good," said Sam, "I need something to 'pick me up' about this time of day."

I buzzed Penny and asked her to bring in the coffee pot and another cup. A couple of minutes later, Penny brought in the coffee and sat the pot on the table and handed the cup to General Sam Drakeford; she looked nervously at the glittering, four stars on his shoulders, wondering just who he was and what he was doing here in my, a Colonel's, office.

Sam took the cup and held it while Penny poured the coffee. He smiled and said, "You must be Penny; Sergeant Fulbright. Thank you for serving your country, Sergeant. I understand you served in Desert Storm, lost your husband to an IED . . . and were wounded yourself. I am sorry about your husband—and I salute you for your bravery and for 'carrying on.' Bull told me your background and I certainly understand why he wanted you here also. Welcome to Washington and the 'big' house."

"Thank you, sir. It is my pleasure to be here, and to serve among real warriors!" Penny replied.

It was Dutch who spoke next. "Penny, let me introduce you to General Sam Drakeford. Sam is Chairman of the Joint Chiefs of Staff; he is the reason we are here."

"I'm very pleased to meet you, sir; forgive me if I seem a bit nervous. I've met a lot of people—officers of most ranks—but you're the first four-star general I've ever even seen! I'm a little out of my league—sir," Penny said, hesitantly.

Sam and the others laughed. "You'll probably be seeing a lot of 'stars' walking around this place while you're here, Penny. Don't take them too seriously though; they take themselves seriously enough!"

Then, turning to Dutch and me he asked, "Where are you guys staying?"

"We're still checked in at the J W Marriott, downtown. You know—in the high-rent district," Dutch replied.

"I'll call you sometime later in the morning. I'll have the Command Sergeant Major set you up with more 'permanent' 'temporary' quarters. He has connections in all the right places and will fix you up with something nice; probably over at Fort Meyer, home of the 'Old Guard' outfit. Hell, the Sergeant Major has so much pull he just may have you pulling a tour as an honor guard at the Unknown Tomb," Sam said and laughed.

"Yeah, with my luck it would be during a snow storm!" Dutch shot back.

Then Tom spoke up and said, "Sam, you need to take one of these gadgets—a 'debugger'—or at least a 'bugger' detector, and keep it on, and on you, all the time. We have reason to believe that some or maybe all of us have been 'bugged'; our offices, probably our vehicles, and, most likely, even our homes!"

He then explained to Sam how the device worked and what to watch for.

When Sam stood up to leave, he looked a little perplexed. He said, "Damn; I'm glad you guys are here! I believe shit is about to hit the fan—sooner than later—and in more ways than we may expect. We've got to head it off before it happens. I'll check in with you tomorrow."

He then turned around to Penny, and said, "Thanks for the coffee, Penny," and walked out the door and into the long hall on the fifth floor of the massive Pentagon Building.

The others got up to leave and agreed to keep each other posted. As they left, I called Penny into my office and explained the situation and the listening device to her and handed her the device I was holding.

"Colonel Miller, should I start wearing my sidearm?" she asked, only half-jokingly.

"No . . . not just yet anyway. Just stay very alert and keep your device on; be aware of it if it should go off. Also, be very aware of your surroundings at all times. We don't know who or just what we're dealing with yet."

CHAPTER THIRTY-THREE

"Any calls while I was out?" Sam asked Sarah, his secretary, as he entered his office.

"It has been a quiet afternoon," Sarah replied and said laughingly, "No calls, no visitors, not even an emergency today."

Sam grinned and said, "That's good news—for a change! Maybe the 'powers that be' have forgotten I'm here and will leave us alone."

"I doubt that, sir!" she said.

"Sarah, I'm going to be working a little late, before you leave please call my driver and have him pick me up at the front entrance at seven o'clock."

"Will do, sir; seven o'clock at the front entrance," she confirmed.

Sam walked into his office and as he approached his desk, he became aware of a strange 'buzzing or vibration' feeling in his pocket. It wasn't his cell phone; all of a sudden it hit him . . . it was the "bug" detector in his pocket!

"Shit!" he said out loud. "My office is . . .!"

He didn't finish what he was thinking. He walked back out to Sarah's desk, motioned her to be quiet and come with him out into the hall.

"Sarah, has anyone been in my office recently, perhaps to do some type of maintenance work or updating lines, or such?" he asked

"Not that I know of," she stated. Then, she thought for a moment and said, "About three weeks ago a couple of guys came in and told me they were here to update your modem and phone system. Why, General; is something wrong?"

Sam said, "Keep your voice low. I think our office has been bugged! Whoever it is has been listening to everything we've been saying."

"What? Our office is 'bugged?' You mean like someone has put something in the office to hear what we talk about?" Sarah asked with a startled look.

"We will have to be very careful what we talk about and who we talk with, until we can get this thing fixed. If you have something important, write it on a note and pass it to me without saying anything. I'll do the same," Sam told her, adding, "We have to find out who in the hell is 'bugging' us – no pun intended. Meanwhile, we need to be sure to keep our *normal or usual* conversation, the same as always. We don't want whoever it is to know, that we know, we're being 'bugged!'"

Still in the hallway, Sam took out his cell phone and punched in Tom Beckwith's number. Getting no answer he left a message asking him to return his call, on his secure cell number, and use *his* secure line as well.

Since it was already after five-thirty, and Sarah was looking a little bewildered at the idea of the phones being 'bugged,' Sam said, "Go ahead and leave Sarah, I've got everything under control. Don't worry; just have a pleasant evening with the family and I'll see you tomorrow morning. Be careful what you say in the office when you get your purse and stuff."

"Thank you, General Drakeford. I think I will do just that," Sarah said as she went back into the office.

Sam punched in General Dutch Hall's cell number; after a few rings, the voice of Dutch Hall came on the line, "General Hall here."

"Dutch, Sam Drakeford, I'm still in my office here in the Pentagon and I've been 'hit,'" he told Dutch.

"Hit? What the hell are you talking about Sam? What do you mean you've been hit?!" Dutch asked.

"Our little 'debugger' device picked up a signal in my office this afternoon, in fact, just a few minutes ago. I had been out and when I walked back into my office, with the device in my pocket, it went off—vibrating; shook me up until I realized what it was. I'm standing in the hall just outside my office, on my cell phone, since the office is 'bugged.' Don't know who might be listening in the office."

"Damn," said Dutch. "I guess we better really start watching our ass!"

"Where are you and Bull?" Sam asked.

"We just got back to the hotel, Bull Miller and me. We plan to go down to the restaurant, have a drink and dinner. Why don't you come down and join us?" Dutch asked.

"I think I will take you up on that, Dutch. We've got a lot to talk about. I'll give my wife a call so she won't worry. I'll be there, say around eight to eight-thirty, if that's not too late," Sam said.

"That's good—sounds like a plan to me," Dutch replied.

Sam gathered his material and placed it in his briefcase and walked out of the office. In the hallway, he stopped and called his wife, Tammy, and told her that he would be home late, that he was meeting with 'some of the guys' for a drink and dinner. He then headed for the elevator.

On ground level, as Sam started for the main entrance, he could see his car and his driver, Sergeant George Smith, already there and waiting. The driver opened the door as he approached and greeted Sam, "Evening, General, you've had a long day. I guess you're ready to get home and relax for a while."

Sam said, "Evening, George. It has been a long day and I think I am going to relax a little—before going home, that is!"

Then, Sam climbed in the backseat on the driver's side, and as George got into the driver's seat Sam told him, "George, I'm going to meet a few friends for dinner at the J W Marriott hotel downtown. You can just drop me off there, and I'll get one of them to drive me home."

"Not a problem, General; I don't mind waiting. I'll just sit and catch-up on some reading and whenever you're ready, you can just give me a call and I'll be right there," said George, adding, "Anytime you're ready to head home, just yell,"

George closed the door , put the car in gear, and started forward. As he approached the first turn lane, heading toward the exit of the VIP parking, he noticed movement out of the corner of his eye; turning his head he saw this vehicle, with no lights on, speeding down the lane directly toward them, to the intersection of the two lanes.

"What the hell!" he yelled, jamming on the brakes as hard as he could! The staff car wouldn't stop that quickly and went sliding into the intersection just as the larger vehicle with no lights, T-boned the lighter-weight staff car on the passenger side knocking it side-ways into a tree on the sidewalk.

Just as George slammed on the brakes, Sam yelled, "George, what's going . . . "

He didn't get to finish the question—the big car hit with a loud crash—Sam was slammed against the side of the car that hit the tree, and lost consciousness. George was slammed against the side of the car also, his head hitting the window hard enough to break the glass! Before losing consciousness, he saw the large, black vehicle back-up and take-off as fast as it would go, tires screeching and vehicle fish-tailing, as whoever was driving gained control.

General Sam Drakeford woke up in the Walter Reed Military Hospital the next morning with a broken shoulder, and his left arm in a sling, also broken, plus a humongous headache. He looked around the room trying to acclimate himself to his surroundings and figure just where he was. Then, he saw the nurse coming to check on him.

"Where the hell am I and what happened?" he asked.

The nurse said, "Good morning, General. You were in an accident last night. You and your driver, Sergeant George Smith, were brought here by ambulance. You both were 'repaired' down in ER, sedated, and slept soundly all night."

"How is Sergeant Smith?" Sam asked.

"He is much better this morning; he had a busted skull where his head hit the side window, and he also has a broken left arm, like yours, from hitting the side of the car door with such force," she replied, "You're both very lucky not to have much more serious injuries."

She checked his vital signs and told him all was normal, and then said, "Your wife is here, and has been all night. She has been looking in on you every few minutes; she is very anxious to see you. I think she managed to catch a few minutes of sleep during the night. There are several men waiting to see you also, if, and when you're up to it."

"I'm good," said Sam smiling, "Send my wife in and tell the others I will see them shortly; oh, and find out who they are and let me know before you send them in."

"Yes, sir," the nurse replied as she left the room.

A few minutes later, the door opened and Tammy came in with a nervous smile on her face; she rushed to the bedside, bent over and gave Sam a big kiss and told him, "You scared me half to death last night! I got a call about ten o'clock that you were in an accident and in the hospital; you had called me just a couple of hours earlier and told me that you were going downtown to have dinner with friends. Thank goodness your aide, Major Johnson, was in his quarters. I called him and he brought me here and stayed with me until we knew you were alright. The doctors told me I should go home and get some rest and come back today, that they had fixed your broken arm and sedated you, and that you would sleep the rest of the night. Major Johnson wanted to take me back home, but I couldn't leave; I spent the night in a recliner in the waiting room. I called him this morning and he's in the waiting room."

Sam smiled at her and said, "Don't you worry; I'm too tough to let something like a 'little' broken arm and shoulder keep me down. It seems that some half-wit clown was speeding in the parking lot and hit us broad-side and then took off without stopping—a hit and run."

Sam didn't tell Tammy that he didn't think it was an accident, that it was on purpose, and someone was out to kill him like they did Dave Mabry and his wife.

After about thirty minutes, Tammy said, "Oh, Sam, I almost forgot, General Hall, Colonel Miller, and a Tom Beckwith are in the waiting room also. They came up late last night, or I should say, earlier this morning, as soon as they found out about the accident. When you didn't show up at the restaurant, they started looking for you. They came back about thirty minutes ago; they're very anxious to find out first-hand what happened. General Hall knows that Major Johnson is your aide, so he was able to reach him on his cellphone; in fact, he called while we were still in the Emergency Room, waiting for the results last night, when they brought you and George in. They were trying to find out what had happened."

"Tammy, I'm fine; and I'm going to be better—when I get out of here," Sam said jokingly. "You look tired. Why don't you go home and get some sleep and food, and just relax for a bit? With no more injuries than I have, I don't think I will be here more than a day or two at the most."

"I think I will," Tammy said, "I am a little tired; besides you have people waiting to see you; they look kind of 'official' too."

Tammy leaned over the bed and kissed Sam on the forehead, and then started for the door. "I'll be back later this afternoon, or early evening," she said as she opened the door.

Sam said, "Those guys in the waiting room are the ones I was to have dinner with last night; tell them to come on in."

"Okay, but don't get too involved. You have to get some rest, too. You may think the shoulder and arm is just something small, but don't take it too lightly; it could be worse and could have been much worse last night," Tammy said as she went out.

A few minutes later, Dutch Hall, Tom Beckwith, and I walked into his room.

"What the hell is going on, Sam?" Dutch asked. "We've just come from Sergeant Smith's room; we thought we would check on him while we were waiting to see you."

"How is he doing? Sam asked, "Was he hurt very badly; is he going to be okay"?

"He's going to be fine—busted skull and broken arm, "Dutch said, "But that's not all; he said that he wasn't too sure that it was an accident! He said before losing consciousness, he saw a 'large, black car' back-up, turn, and speed off like a bat out of hell! He also said that as he was thinking about what happened, it occurred to him that he pulled in to pick you-up at the door of the Pentagon, where he normally does, except that he came in from the opposite direction this time since he was parked in a different spot than usual. Had he driven in as he usually does, you would have been right in the center of the crash-spot on the passenger-side, where you normally sit. Instead, this time you got in on the driver's side, in the back-seat. He seems to think you were targeted, Sam!"

Tom Beckwith spoke up and said, "I've got a couple of my agents on it already; they're checking out your car and looking for a large black car with damage to the front! Mel Pierson has a couple of his agents on it also. We're going to nail it down, Sam; we're going to get the sorry SOBs, one way or the 'other'!

"In the meantime, I'm sending out a special notice to everybody that we've had any discussion with, or is aware of, what we have been working on. I'm telling them they better watch their ass and their back at the same time. I'm also telling them to pay attention to the little debugging devices that Rick gave us to determine whether we're being bugged or not."

"Hell yes!" Sam exclaimed. "That's how they knew I was leaving the office late! When I called Dutch and Bull, I told them that my device had gone off, and I was sure my office was bugged. Before that, I told my secretary to call Sergeant Smith and let him know what time and just where to pick me up! Shit. I set my own self up for an ambush!"

The door opened and Senator Lindsey Scott walked in. "I heard about the accident, so I thought I better come over and check on the 'sick, lame, and lazy,' General," he laughed. "How are you doing? The nurse told me your injuries were not life threatening; that you and your driver got banged up somewhat. How did an accident happen in the Pentagon parking lot, that time of night anyway?"

I said, "Lindsey, we're about to believe this was no accident! We're beginning to believe, and Sam's driver, Sergeant Smith, thinks so too, Sam was targeted and someone was sent to take him out!"

Lindsey looked around the room and greeted Tom, Dutch, and me. "That's some pretty heavy stuff, Bull. What makes you think so?"

I told him about Sam discovering that his office was bugged, and his secretary notifying the driver with new pick-up instructions.

Lindsey, looking very solemn as he spoke. "Gentlemen, as we have talked during the past few weeks, things are getting tougher and about to get out of hand; we've got to get it under control—NOW! This can't keep waiting for the 'right moment!' I spoke with Vince yesterday about the meeting we have scheduled; he has already arranged everything with Bubba and his bar-b-que place. We now have to notify everybody who we know, or who we think we know, who has been discussing the national situation and get them to this meeting. But," he emphasized, "We have to be certain knowledge of this doesn't get into the wrong hands!"

I spoke up, saying, "Lindsey, we have come up with a 'debugging' detector, each of us has one; that's how Sam knew his office was bugged."

Then I reached in my pocket and pulled my device out and handed it to Lindsey. "This will make you feel a little like James Bond; it's what told Sam about his office. You keep that one, I've got a couple more at the office and we're getting enough for several others."

The door opened and the doctor who had been treating Sam came into the room, greeted everybody and said, "General, you and Sergeant Smith were extremely lucky last evening. Had either of you been sitting on the side of the impact . . . well, most likely neither of you would be here this morning. I just saw a picture of your car; if you didn't know better, you would never guess it had been a car!"

Then he checked Sam over and said, "We want to keep you and Sergeant Smith here one more night for observation; if everything stays the same, you'll be released and going home tomorrow morning."

As he started out the door he stopped, turned, and, with a soulful look on his face said, "Very lucky; God was with you!" Then, he closed the door.

Sam, Dutch, Tom and I just looked at each other, neither of us speaking.

CHAPTER THIRTY-FOUR

Vice President Joe Bradley and his wife, Cille, short for Lucille, were relaxing in the back seat of their official, 'Vice Presidential Sedan,' heading home after a late Friday night official function at the White House. They were discussing plans for a quiet, non-working, relaxing weekend. Their 'now' home was located on the grounds of the U.S. Naval Observatory in Washington, DC. Number One Observatory Circle is an old house, built in 1893, originally for its superintendent, and then "acquired" by the Chief of Naval Operations for his residence. For security purposes, it was designated as the official residence of the vice-president in 1966.

Like the President, the vice president's vehicle travels in a convoy of at least three similar vehicles, in varying positions in the convoy, for security purposes. As the vice president's entourage turned off Massachusetts Avenue onto Observatory Circle, the front car exploded in a ball of fire that shook the ground and lifted the vehicle, flipping it upside down! In less than a heartbeat, Joe's driver jerked the steering wheel to the side, but not quite fast enough, as another explosion shook the earth surrounding Vice President Joe Bradley's car; the force of the explosion was so great it lifted the vehicle off the ground; it landed with a terrifying crash and jolt on its side. The heavy, bullet-proof windows were blown out; fortunately for Joe, and his wife, they had their seat belts fastened but, they were left hanging from the belts, both unconscious. Knocked out by the force of the explosion!

Neither Joe nor Cille knew when the Secret Service agents, from the third car, swarmed around the vehicle to provide immediate protection, in case there were gunmen nearby; nor did they know that other agents were trying to get the doors open. They did not also know when the paramedics, police, other enforcement agencies and rescue teams finally extracted them from the destroyed vehicle and loaded them into a waiting Med-Evac helicopter!

They couldn't hear the wailing, screaming, blaring of the sirens from all the emergency vehicles that were rushing to the scene; and those that were leaving, carrying the wounded to the nearest medical facility for emergency treatment.

As the Med-Evac departed, Joe couldn't see the teams of rescue, law enforcement, FBI, Secret Service people that had descended upon the scene; it looked more like a war zone than part of Northwest Washington, DC; in the United States of America! It wasn't something that Vice President Joe, or any other American, would want to see; not here, on our own "dirt!"

The entire area had been cordoned off for a hundred yards in all directions. In less than thirty minutes after the explosion, there were at least a hundred uniformed DC law enforcement troops on the scene manning the perimeter to keep everyone out. And that everybody in who were already in! Was it a bomb of some sort, a hand grenade, an RPG (rocket propelled grenade)? No one knew; it could be anyone of these weapons. It would take a thorough investigation to determine just what it was—and who was responsible. The culprit could still be inside the perimeter and could be armed with assault weapons waiting to gun down any survivors; after all, this was the Vice President of the United States of America! War had definitely arrived on the mainland of the USA.

Among those who had arrived on the scene amidst the frantic scurry of activity was Dan Black the Director of the Secret Service in the White House, and his assistant, Chip Reese. Also spotted in the crowd of high ranking investigative officials were: Mel Pierson, Director of the FBI, and Tom Beckwith, the director of the CIA's training unit, and former field agent.

Arriving separately, the four were not aware of the others presence on the scene. As they spotted one another, they merged away from the crowd so they could discuss the situation privately, with no one listening in. A second Mobile Crime Scene Investigation Unit arrived on site and parked just inside the perimeter fence as the four stood looking around the area and talking, trying to make some sense of the situation. A moment later, another mobile investigation unit, a large van, pulled into the area; this one was marked, "ATF" *Alcohol, Tobacco, Firearms, Mobile Investigation Lab,* in large letters.

Tom said, "I've already had a dozen calls asking what happened and who did it. No one even mentions that it could have been an accident. Senator Lindsey Scott called a moment ago, as I arrived; he wanted to know the condition of the vice president and his wife. Although from different political parties, the two families were close friends. He said that the vice president was supposed to attend the meeting we have scheduled at Bubba's Bar-B-Que next week. He also said that we need to postpone the meeting, **but** we are running out of time! Something has to be done immediately—that this is no outside, terrorist attack; he is convinced that it is all planned right here in this country, most likely within the walls of the White House itself!"

"It sure as hell is being planned within the White House," Dan Black said. "That creepy, son-of-a bitch President, his Islamic Chief of Staff, and Islamic Chief of Intelligence, and the rest of his sorry, asshole, 'personal' assistants, who 'advise' him on foreign affairs and intel activities, have to be removed, somehow, someway!"

Mel Pierson said, "Gentlemen, I believe we have just about run out of time to take some type of action. In recent discussions with Lindsey Scott, and with the vice president himself, both believe we have to act now! But just what; the timing is extremely crucial—not just to this operation, but the entire country!" he emphasized. "That is the question. Tom, you were telling me the other day that General Hall and Colonel Miller had come up with some 'bugging' detectors; I think we need to get one in the hands of anyone who knows what's going on, as quickly as we can. In fact, it looks as though we are going to be here for a little while; maybe you can reach them on a secure phone, and if they are available, ask them to come on down here. I think they are located pretty close. Also, if Rick Winstead, the guy who came up with the devices, is available, see if he can come down also. We're going to need all the advice and help we can get."

Two of Mel's special agents came up. The lead agent said, "Mel, I hate to bother you, but I think you want to take a look at the area where one of the explosions took place; we are sure that there were two separate explosions close together. Whether it was a timed explosion or some other means, we can't tell right now, but we sure as hell will find out. It looks a lot like some I have seen before—but not here in the US—on home territory! This shit can't happen here, not if I can do anything about it."

"You can, and we will!" Mel said, as all five special investigative types followed the lead agent.

About half an hour later our military staff car pulled into the perimeter; me, Dutch Hall, and Rick Winstead got out and found our way to the explosion site where the others were gathered, looking it over, ever so closely and carefully; not touching anything that might disturb any evidence or trail as to who, what and why this had occurred.

As we approached the area and saw some of the debris, and the crater in the ground, where the first explosion had occurred, Rick said, "This has signs of a roadside bomb—an IED! I've seen those in Iraq and Afghanistan. How in hell did something like these, wind up here in the US—in the vice president's driveway? Guys, there is some really serious crap going down around here tonight!"

Chuck Westwood, Mel's leading investigative agent, came up to Mel and said, "Mel, you're going to want to take a look at this area where we think the second explosion occurred." The group followed Chuck back a ways, closer to the entrance, but still just inside the secure compound of the vice president's residence, onto Observatory Circle, several yards behind where they figured the first explosion took place.

"We're pretty sure this is the explosion that got the vice president's vehicle," Chuck told them. "This is all speculation right now, but from what we can tell, the vice president's vehicle did not get the full effects of the explosion; although, it was enough to take the armored vehicle out of operation and do a lot of damage to the exterior; however, the interior provided some protection for the occupants; in fact, it may have saved their lives, we will know that later when we hear from Walter Reed Military Hospital; I'm told that is where they Med-Evac-ed him and his wife."

Chuck continued, "We think, and again, this is just speculation at this point, the first explosion took place, and in a split second the second vehicle's driver instinctively jerked the wheel to the opposite side of the street from the blast, preventing the vehicle from taking the full force of the explosion. The driver and the two agents that escort and ride with the vice president were not killed, but one is seriously wounded. First responders tell me that all of the occupants had their seat belts on and were actually hanging, unconscious, by the belts! They had to be cut down and lowered to get them out and onto the gurney. The fast reaction of the driver probably saved their lives."

And then Chuck added softly, "Not so for the driver and three agents who were in the lead, decoy vehicle. They were all killed! Dammit! They were my agents; one of them was a female. They were my friends!"

Mel was trying to comfort his lead agent, but Chuck said, "Mel, I'll tell you one thing, if I can get my hands on these 'sons-of-bitches' they will never see the inside of a courtroom! I may go to jail, but they won't; I'll send them straight to hell!"

"We all feel the same as you, Chuck, and most likely we would do the same if we had the opportunity; but for the record—we didn't hear you say that!"

Congressman Dennis Wilson and Senate Majority Leader Lindsey Scott came up to the group as Chuck was blasting away at the "whoever" was responsible for all of the carnage they were witnessing.

The Congressman asked, "What in hell is going on here? I was listening to media reports on the way here and they were saying everything from a gas leak to rockets, to roadside bombs. If the media doesn't tone it down a couple of notches, we'll have all kinds of rumors running the gamut throughout the entire nation."

"I heard the same thing, including that there are reports of armed men in the area with rocket propelled grenades—RPGs—or weapons of that kind," Senator Scott replied.

"Follow me," Chuck said. Then, he took them to the site of the first explosion, where the lead vehicle took the full blast. There was a crater in the ground two feet deep where the force turned upward to completely demolish the armored vehicle; the explosive was intended to kill and destroy—not to injure or demobilize!

Chuck explained to the group, "We're not sure about anything yet, but we are fairly certain that this was the work of some terrorist group, organization, or local individuals who have been radicalized. Whoever it is knows enough about bomb making to give us a shit load of trouble, and they have targets in mind that they are going after. Gentlemen, we are pretty sure these were IEDs—or roadside bombs—with tremendous killing capacity. They can be made up of conventional explosives, military explosives or such. And they can be detonated by different triggering mechanisms, or timed. This type of explosive is generally used in unconventional warfare activities such as guerrilla units. They were used extensively in the second Iraq War."

It was Mel's turn to speak. He said, "Our lab experts are already here and will be spending whatever time and effort necessary to get to the bottom of this. The field investigative lab has been set-up and they will be working very closely with the primary labs back at headquarters. You can rest assured that every piece of shrapnel, no matter how small, will be thoroughly analyzed."

CHAPTER THIRTY-FIVE

Senator Scott looked around at the group gathered around the bomb site and motioned them in to a closer circle and he began talking, in a lowered voice, "Gentlemen, we've got a problem that has to be resolved immediately. I spoke with Tom just the other day, about the meeting we have set-up for next week; we may have to postpone it for a few days or a week, but no longer!

"In fact, I would like for us, the nine of us here now, to get together on Wednesday evening to talk over a few things. Where we meet can't be at an office or anyplace where we may be overheard or any place that might be bugged, which brings to mind, we need to get a couple dozen or so of those 'debugging' devices you were telling me about, Bull."

Rick said, "I have them already. They came in a couple of days ago, and they are charged and ready to go. I can get them to you tomorrow if I know where you will be."

"I'll come by your place in the morning and pick them up," I said.

Dutch added, "I'll go with you and we can distribute them to those we know who need them immediately."

"Dennis and I are going to head out," Lindsey said, as he and Dennis turned to walk away, "There's nothing that we can do here. Mel, if you will keep me posted on any developments, I will appreciate it. And if any of you run into anything more, anything that's unusual, be very careful; watch your back. Let me know, and the rest of us also, so we can stay aware of everything what's going on."

It was seven-thirty on Saturday morning when the nerve-racking, never-ending chatter of my cellphone slowly brought me back to the real world. Forcing the sleep from my eyes and the cloudy mist from my brain, I fumbled for my phone wondering just who in hell would be calling me this early, and on a Saturday at that.

"Colonel Miller," I spoke into the phone.

"Colonel Miller, this is Penny, Sergeant Fulbright."

"Oh, good morning, Penny," I said. You're up and about early for a Saturday morning. Dutch and I were talking about you last evening, wondering where you were billeted, and if you got nice, comfortable quarters, and, if you had gotten settled in."

"Yes sir; I'm pretty much settled in and trying to get my bearings; this place is kind of confusing for a new comer," Penny replied.

"Where are you located? You are on Fort Myers, aren't you?"

"Oh yes, sir; in fact, I'm just around the corner from where you and General Hall are staying; less than a block away. The reason for my call Colonel. . ."

"It's 'Bull,' Penny. You, Dutch, and I are together on this little venture up here, whatever in hell that is. Perhaps we will find out more about what we are supposed to be doing on Monday or at least sometime this week!" I said.

"Yes, sir; sorry about that, Col . . . I mean, Bull. The reason for my call, Rick Winstead called me a few minutes ago wanting to know where you were staying and your secure cellphone number. Then he asked me to give you a call instead and to ask you to call him back as soon as you could. He said that it was very important. He sounded pretty serious. Is there anything you would like me to do, or check on?" she asked.

"I don't know what it would be at this point, Penny, but stand by and let me get hold of Rick and see what he has cooking that is so urgent on a Saturday morning. I'll call you back in a few minutes," I responded.

Then I punched the numbers for Rick into my phone, and waited a couple of moments.

"Rick Winstead," the voice on the other end said.

"Rick, Bull Miller here; Penny said you were trying to reach me, and that it sounded pretty urgent. What's up?"

"Well," began Rick hesitantly, "I just thought that since you and Dutch were the new cowboys in town, you might like to grab some breakfast. There's a nice restaurant a few blocks from where your quarters are located, and they serve a great breakfast 'from what I hear'! And bring Penny too; she's new on the block also."

"That sounds like a great idea, Rick. I'll wake Dutch up and get him moving; give us an hour and we'll meet you there," I said.

"Great," Rick said, and then added, "You guys be careful!"

I thought that a little strange, *You guys be careful.* Also, Rick had sounded a little different when he said *"from what I hear" about the great breakfast they served!"* I called Dutch's number, two doors down on the same floor.

"General Hall," said a sleepy voice.

"Dutch, this is Bull; Rick Winstead just called and invited us 'newcomers' to breakfast at that fancy restaurant just outside the post. I told him we would meet him in an hour. I told Penny also; it'll just be the four of us, unless Rick brings his wife or has invited someone else, but I don't think so."

I called Penny back and told her the plans and that we would pick her up in about forty-five minutes. As we turned the corner, we spotted Penny waiting near the curb; as we came to a stop, Penny opened the door and stepped in.

"Good morning, gentlemen," she greeted us; "What's for breakfast?"

"Morning, Penny," we answered, and then I said, "We don't know just what they serve, but it's supposed to be a good little breakfast place, according to Rick, that is. It's called the 'CRAVE' or something like that. Rick said it is located in a strip mall just off McGregor Blvd. and that it is pretty popular and sometimes there's a wait for a table. He also added that it would be a good place to visit and talk about the old days . . . without being interrupted."

"That sounds kind of ominous," Dutch said. "Does that sound like the Rick Winstead you know, Bull?"

"Hell, no! He must have run into something and doesn't trust the phones to tell us about it!" I replied.

Penny spoke up and asked, "Would ya'll let me know what's going on?"

"Ya'll?" I asked. "What is this 'ya'll' speak?" we laughed.

"That is 'Southern" for you, or both of you, or anyone else who is in listening distance!" she told us.

All three laughed as we pulled into the mall parking lot and a spot near the door of the "CRAVE."

Rick spotted us as we entered and stood up so we could see him; he motioned us over. He had a table in the far, back corner of the restaurant, not too conspicuous but one where we could talk without being interrupted, or overheard easily. It was about as private as you could find in the greater DC area nowadays. After greetings, we sat down and the waitress came over; we each ordered coffee.

I emphasized, "Be sure it is fresh, strong and not decaf; at least mine anyway—the stronger, the better!" And then I added, "Be sure to warm the cup before you pour the coffee!"

I turned to Rick and asked, "What's up, Rick? What's going on? Especially on a weekend?"

"Well," Rick began. "You recall I told you that you better watch your back; well, I think you better watch your 'front' also! In fact I'm damn sure you're going to have to watch yourselves 360 degrees, 24/7 from now on! Especially while you are here in this 'swamp,' doing whatever in hell you're doing. That goes for all of you, and the other guys, too. First, I know that Mel, Tom, Chip, Senator Scott, Dan Black, and Dennis Wilson are 'bugged!' I don't know how long they have been bugged, but someone has been listening in on them for a while—not only in their offices, but also in their cars and their homes!"

"Damn," Dutch said, "This is about to get out of hand and pretty shitty, too. How about Bull, Penny, and myself? Are any of us bugged?"

"Not yet; that we know of," Rick replied. "However, that is probably because you three are the 'new kids on the block'; I'm sure it's just a matter of time and someone will be listening to everything you guys say in your office, and in your quarters, too. You best keep a sharp eye on anybody, maintenance personnel, maids, etc., that are in and out of your building and quarters. The others are the only ones we know of so far."

"How did you find all that out," Penny asked.

"I think I mentioned the two guys that work for me, down in the basement of the Pentagon, Pete and Paul; they design and install systems of various sorts. They like excitement; and when I first mentioned to them about doing a sweep of certain offices, they thought that would be something different from the day-to-day grind. They also figured it would be more exciting than just sitting in the shop and working.

"They also knew I had been in contact with you guys and had provided you with the detectors; and I had originally mentioned to them about possibly doing a clean sweep of several different people; so, on their own they began doing a little checking. And, BINGO! Right off the bat they hit pay-dirt! Congressman Dennis Wilson!"

"Dennis? Dennis Wilson, the Congressman? Why would someone want to 'bug' him; and why," Dutch asked?

I spoke up and said, "Power! Someone is trying to get to the people who have power in this city! As the Majority Whip in the House of Representatives, Dennis has a lot of power; keep in mind that he could be third in line for the presidency of the United States!"

"That's right," said Rick, "Look at who is President right now; and where is the Vice President right now? If Vice President Joe Bradley doesn't make it, who gets to select his replacement? Think about it; the control of this country can shift, as they say, 'in a heartbeat'!

"With Nancy Patrick, as Speaker of the House, dead, that's one 'heartbeat' out of the way. Dennis is most likely the next Speaker of the House. Someone is trying to kill him already; if they succeed that's another 'heartbeat' out of the way! Who would be the next speaker, and probably be named vice president? I feel certain that whoever is running this 'show,' don't want Dennis; they know he is a conservative Democrat. That wouldn't fit into their plans very well. Next in line would be Lindsey Scott, a Republican and President Pro Tempore of the Senate; and that sure as hell would not work out for their plans. In fact, we better warn Lindsey to be extra careful; I really think he should consider having a security detail with him at all times. I spoke with Dennis as soon as I found out that he was bugged; I wanted him to be aware. He asked us to do a sweep of his house, office and cars—all were bugged!"

The four of us sat sipping our coffee, thinking, not talking for several minutes. The waitress came to the table for the third time to see if we were ready to order, we had waved her off each time. This time, though, we all ordered the breakfast special and just sat back, still not talking for several minutes.

My phone beeped; I answered and the familiar voice of Mel Pierson said, "Bull, I'm glad I was able to reach you. I just had a call from, I think, your hometown friend, Admiral Vince Dawkins; if you recall, he was arranging a meeting next week out at Bubba's Bar-b-que, the place, where we met before; just a little distance West of DC."

"Yeah, I remember he was setting up the meeting for next week, but also last night at the site of the explosion you were going to set up something for the smaller group of us, right way," I said.

Mel said, "I'm going to come up with a place sometime today; but in the meantime, we have to find another venue for the meeting next week – Bubba's place was fire bombed last night! While we were at the Vice President's place looking at the site of the explosion, some-damn-body, or I should say a group of 'somebodies', in large black vans, stormed into the parking lot, which was empty since Bubba's was closed, and tossed Molotov cocktails through the windows; they didn't get away real clean though, Bubba was inside doing some paperwork. He heard the vehicles speeding down the gravel road leading to the restaurant and got up to see what was going on. When he saw the two black vans he grabbed his twelve gage pump shotgun and when the first bomb was thrown, he blasted the vehicle and pumped several rounds through the window, hitting both the driver and the one who threw the bomb; the vehicle went out of control hit a tree, crashed and burned. The first responders got there in just a few minutes and were able to pull the two bodies out, they were pretty burned. They have temporarily identified them as of mid-eastern descent. The second vehicle got the hell out of there!"

I said, "Damn, Mel, we better get a move on. We can't wait any longer. I'm with Dutch, Rick and Penny now, having breakfast. I'll let them know what happened. Let me know as soon as you find out where and when we will be meeting."

"Will do," replied Mel.

I explained the whole scenario of what went down at Bubba's, shocking the others, especially Penny, who wasn't in on all the events that had been taking place the past few months. She only knew sketchy parts that she had gleaned from talking with me, and other information that she had heard mentioned, and added it all together.

"This is why I called you guys," Rick said. "Whatever is going to go down, we best make it soon; from what we already have learned, someone is listening in on everything we say. When I say 'we' I mean everybody who has had any connection with you guys and all your contacts. We can't sweep and debug everybody who works for the government; first off, it would be impossible, illegal, and not practical. Besides, it wouldn't tell us anything that we don't already know. The best solution, for the moment anyway, is to tell everyone to assume that they are bugged and proceed accordingly. You might also remind everyone that this is a dangerous situation we are facing. At least a dozen or more people have already been killed; they won't hesitate to kill again. Matter of fact, I kind of believe they already have plans to kill several others who they believe are in their way!"

The waitress arrived with our breakfast specials, labeled 3x3x6: three eggs over, three spicy sausage patties, and a stack of six pancakes, plus a bowl of Southern grits! It was enough to make any cholesterol-laden artery shout for joy! We each looked at the four plates of food, looked at each other and laughed.

Still laughing, I commented, "I haven't had a breakfast like this in twenty years, since I was stationed at Fort Jackson in South Carolina."

"I don't recall ever having so much greasy food at one time," Dutch said.

"Me neither," Penny chuckled.

Rick laughed at the others and said, "Hell, this is just a standard breakfast for a working man to start his day on, down in South Carolina. It gets his blood flowing and muscles and joints loosened up and moving."

We all laughed and began eating.

CHAPTER THIRTY-SIX

I noticed a man sitting at the counter who glanced our way, and had looked over his shoulder at us several times while he was eating also. He had some type of foreign look about him; then it struck me; it was a 'mid-eastern' look—complexion, hair, and features. I didn't say anything to the others; I just chatted and kept watch out of the corner of my eye, without looking up.

Then I said, "Let me ask you guys a question. If I were to tell you that I think we have been found, would you be able to keep your head down and not look around? Keep looking at your plate or each other as we talk?"

"What the hell are you talking about, Bull?" Dutch asked.

Penny asked, "Are we being watched?"

"I think maybe we have been watching the same asshole," Rick said. "I saw him pick up on us shortly after we got seated and I have kept an eye on him. I don't think he is carrying a weapon, from the way he is dressed; if he had a weapon the bulge would show through the tight shirt he's wearing. I didn't want to say anything in case I was wrong, didn't want to shake you guys up. I'll tell you something else—even though Virginia has a weapons ban, if that shithead pulled a weapon I'd have blown his head off, right here in this restaurant. Virginia may have a weapons ban, but I sure as hell don't!" Rick was pretty pissed.

He then turned to Penny and told her, "Penny, I apologize for the language, but I have no patience for the way we, as a country, are giving these terrorists the VIP treatment!"

"My feelings exactly!" said Penny.

I asked, "Rick, do you carry a weapon?"

"I wouldn't leave home without it!" Rick replied.

As we finished our 'greasy' but delicious breakfast, we saw the guy from the counter get up, pay his bill, and leave.

Rick asked, "Do either of you have a weapon on you?"

We all replied no.

"I would suggest you get one and keep it on you at all times," Rick said. "I agree with Bull, you **and** I, have been found, and they have started keeping a watch on us. No telling what they might attempt; remember, they don't mind shooting someone."

Then looking at Penny Rick added, "Anyone! Ya'll be especially careful of everything around you, keep your eyes moving, taking in your surroundings—don't take any chances."

Penny chuckled.

Rick asked her, "What's so funny?"

Dutch and I laughed, and said, "The 'Ya'll' speak. We gave her a hard time coming over here this morning, about saying 'ya'll'! She said it's Southern for one or more people at the same time."

Rick laughed and said, "She's right; don't 'ya'll go giving her a bad time for using proper English."

The four of us got up and headed for the register when Rick said, "This is on me; you guys can get it next time, when I order a big steak!"

When we got to the door, Rick told us to wait a minute while he took a look around outside. We watched as Rick slowly opened the door, looking at the parking lot, making a 180 degree, slow sweep of the lot, and checking out the different vehicles parked there. He saw a large black vehicle parked at the rear of the lot with the running lights on; he motioned for us to take a look.

I glanced at Rick and asked, "What do think, Rick? You think that's the guy from in here, and he's waiting for us to come out?"

"Hard to say," Rick replied. "But that vehicle is like those used in all the other attacks. They look a hell of a lot like government vehicles; a few years older perhaps. But it seems strange that from all the reports I've seen, or heard about, it's always that same type vehicle. You guys wait right here for a couple of minutes; I'm going to step outside and to the left toward the river, where those trees are. Ya'll wait two minutes and come out slowly, as if everything is normal, just talking and grinning, but stay close to the wall and behind those bushes. If it's someone waiting for us, maybe they'll show their hand."

"And if they do?" asked Dutch.

"Then they're mine! If they try something like the others, that is," Rick said.

As Rick started out the door, out of the corner of his eye, he saw the vehicle begin to inch forward.

The restaurant door opened, I came out first with the others following closely, looking around with 'make-believe' smiles and conversation. We actually heard the sudden roar of the engine before we saw the movement of the vehicle.

I yelled, "Duck; get behind those bushes, fast!" I could see the window was open and a hand was outside; it had a gun in it!

Rick saw the same thing. He had knelt behind one of the trees; as the vehicle roared closer, he stood and raised his arm, outstretched, with a .357 magnum in his hand. He fired once and the windshield blew out taking with it the head of someone in the passenger seat; he fired twice and the head of the driver disappeared; the vehicle veered sharply to the right into the entrance lane of the parking lot; bounced across McGregor Blvd; crashed through a barrier and landed in the river.

Fifteen minutes later, the area was swarming with police black and whites and dozens of officers. Rick had already gotten back together with me, Dutch, and Penny.

Dutch said, "That was pretty scary, Rick. I'm sure glad you picked up on whoever it was. They would be putting us in body bags by now if you hadn't."

Penny asked, "Are we sure we're in the States and not in Afghanistan, Iraq, or some other place?"

"It sure as hell is getting harder to tell anymore," I replied.

Rick said, "One of you call Mel and let him know what's happened and ask him to come down if he can. I'm going to find out who is in charge of this operation and let them know what happened."

I punched Mel's number into my cellphone. When Mel answered, I briefed him on the breakfast get-together, shooting, and crash. All Mel could say was, "Shit! I'm on my way."

Before Mel arrived, Tom Beckwith showed up and looked the scene over. Mel came rushing up about five minutes later and immediately began walking and checking the entire area. He called Tom over to where he was looking at the vehicle 'drowning' in the river. After a few minutes, he and Tom came over to where Dutch, Penny and I were standing.

Mel looked at us and said, "There is something that Tom and I thought you three should probably know; it's highly secretive and only a very small handful of people know. So I need you guys to be sure not to breathe a word of this conversation."

He looked over at Tom, who spoke up, "Because you three are so involved in this situation, whatever it is, and your necks are stuck out so far, Mel and I thought you ought to know that Rick is a special operative agent for the two agencies we represent—that's one reason he had a weapon on him, a pretty significant weapon at that! He is in a rather unique situation in that he does work for the Department of Defense as a contractor, but he works for us at CIA, and for Mel and the FBI. In his position, he can provide us with an inside look into critical areas, especially at the Pentagon, which we would not have access to without jumping through a dozen hoops first," Tom said.

CHAPTER THIRTY-SEVEN

From within a heavily guarded "room for two" hospital suite, Vice President Joe Bradley and his wife Lucille, sat and discussed the explosion with Senator Lindsey Scott, Dan Black, the Director of the Secret Service in the White House, and the Assistant Director, Chip Reese.

The Vice President asked, "Tell me why we are still alive and all those are dead? In the split second before our car went airborne, I saw the huge ball of flame lift skyward with the car and then we went airborne and I guess we both lost consciousness, probably when we hit the ground again. Tell me why 'Cille and I are sitting here talking with you and a dozen or more agents are dead and their families will never see them again—tell me WHY?!"

Dan and Chip looked at each other for a moment and then at the Vice President. Dan began speaking slowly, "Mr. Vice President, we really don't know; at least not yet. However, according to some of the investigators who were on the scene very early after the explosions, they think that because of the quick action of your driver, your vehicle didn't take the brunt of the explosion like the other vehicle did. "Had you taken the full impact of the explosion, we wouldn't be sitting here having this conversation. The investigators believe the heavy armor on your vehicle saved you and your wife. Because of the way the driver turned the wheel, you got more of a 'glancing' blow instead of the full impact. Either way, we are very happy that you are here."

'Cille spoke up and said, "Well, we're certainly glad that we're still here also; it's down-right scary as hell! I'm really surprised that we're still alive and with no more serious injuries than we have. In fact, the doctors are talking of releasing us tomorrow, or in a couple of days at the most. I certainly hope so!"

VP Joe spoke softly, "We lost some good people last night; as Secret Service Agents, they not only protected us on a day-to-day basis, but they had become our friends also. They worked for you, Dan. You know how good they were."

"They were some of our top agents," Dan replied, "Well trained, best of the lot; that's one reason they were assigned to you, Mr. Vice President."

"Thanks, Dan," the VP said. "Now, Lindsey and I need to talk with Senator Reed and Representative Dennis Wilson as soon as I can. Can that be arranged quickly and quietly? Also in a secure place; we can probably arrange to meet here in the hospital, one of their small conference rooms or something similar."

Senator Lindsey Scott, who had been sitting quietly during the discussion, spoke up and said, "I suggest that wherever we meet, we have a debugging sweep done prior to meeting; just to be sure, Mr. Vice President. We know a number of people who have their offices, homes, and cars bugged with listening devices. We must be very careful!" he added.

Chip said, "We are checking every possible angle and reviewing our procedures to be sure we have all the bases covered. We already have two of our special agents stationed outside this door twenty-four/seven;

plus, we have two others stationed at each end of the hall and one by the elevator door. No one comes on this floor without special permission and credentials."

"That's a good idea," the Vice President said, "We don't want another Sergeant Dan Johnson scenario, especially involving me and 'Cille. We appreciate the protection!"

Dan and Chip stepped out of the room into the hall between the two special agents, one on each side of the door. Nobody was going to get through these guys easily.

Dan asked them, "You guys have everything covered and know what you're here for?"

"You bet your ass, sir," the bigger agent said. "Nobody gets inside until we have completely cleared them, and they have full authorization—not even doctors or nurses. We heard what happened at Walter Reed a couple of weeks ago. It ain't going to happen on our watch!"

Dan looked at the other agent; he wasn't really any smaller. Then, he and Chip walked down the hall toward the elevator, stopped at the nurse's station, and asked directions to the administrator's office.

Suddenly Chip broke into a laugh and said, "I pity anyone who tried to force their way into that room. Those two guys must be six-four and weigh at least two-fifty. I believe they would go looking for a fight, just for entertainment."

"I'm sorry to say I don't even know their names, but I'll tell you this, they are my good friends—whether they know it or not!" Dan chuckled.

They entered the Hospital Administrator's office and were greeted by the secretary. They asked to see the Administrator. "Do you have an appointment?" the secretary asked.

"No," said Dan, as he showed her his Secret Service badge. "But it is very important that we talk with the Administrator immediately."

"Yes, sir, please have a seat, and I'll let Mr. Smith know you're here," she said as she entered the inner office.

A moment later, she returned and said, "Please come in. could I get you some refreshments? Coffee, water, or a soft drink?"

"No thanks," Dan said, "We will only be a few minutes."

The inner office door opened and a man, probably around sixty maybe sixty-two; looking to be in excellent physical health, stepped out. He reached out to shake hands and introduced himself.

"Please come in," he said; "I'm George Smith, the Administrator of this 'haven' of healing. To what do I owe the pleasure? We usually don't see the Secret Service around here. I assume it's because we have the Vice President with us. How can I be of service?"

Dan and Chip introduced themselves and chatted for a few moments about security, protecting the Vice President and other government officials.

Smith said, "Oh yes; my people told me that there are several guards on duty around the clock, stationed at the entrance to the floor where the Vice President is located, plus two more stationed at his door. That's pretty heavy security, if you don't mind my saying so. Are you expecting trouble or an attempt on his life? I am aware of what happened over at Walter Reed recently. I certainly hope nothing like that happens here."

Chip said, "That's exactly why we have those agents here—to prevent any repeat of the other incident."

Then, Dan added, "We need to borrow a small meeting or conference room for the Vice President and a couple of other officials. "Nothing special—just quiet, confidential, and secure—and we need it right away, if that can be arranged."

"That's no problem at all," said Smith. "In fact, there is a small room on the same floor as the Vice President; sometimes, we hold a staff meeting there. How soon do you want it?"

"Right now wouldn't be too soon!" Dan said half-jokingly. "But seriously, as soon as it can be isolated so no one could get in. We would appreciate it. We will have a team come in to double check it for possible listening devices, or anything out of the ordinary. This is routine, nothing out of the ordinary for us. It's just protocol; we're required to double check every point of contact for any of the upper level officials we provide security for."

"I see no reason why we can't block it off right now; let me call our facilities manager and have him take care of it. It should be cleared and turned over to you within the hour," Smith said, and added, "Just let me know when you are through with it. Any idea how long you will need the room?" Smith then punched in the secretary's number and told her to have the key to the small conference room brought up.

"Possibly a couple of days, at the most, I think," Dan replied; "The Vice President said his doctor told him that he would probably release him and his wife in a couple of days."

Within a couple of minutes, the secretary opened the door and handed Smith the key, which he passed on to Dan.

Dan and Chip left the Administrator's office. When they got in the hall, Dan told Chip, "I'll call Congressman Wilson and Senator Reed and set up the meeting; in the meantime, you can call Rick Winstead and see how quickly he can have a clean sweep done of the meeting room. Tell him its top priority and must be done immediately. You take the key and meet with him when he and his team get here."

"I'm on it now!" Chip replied and took out his phone and punched in Rick's number; Rick answered on the third ring.

"Rick, Chip Reese here, I'm glad you picked up. We need your help and we need it fast! ASAP! Or sooner!" Then, Chip explained the situation and why the rush.

"We'll be over in a couple of hours and do a clean sweep of the room and any adjoining rooms that might have thin walls," Rick said. "I would also recommend that if they don't meet today, we do another sweep about an hour before they do get-together, even though the room will be locked down in between."

Chip said, "Good idea, Rick. We'll leave that up to you and your team; handle it as you see fit."

Then Chip made his way back to the Vice President's room; Dan was already back. "Rick and his team will be here in a couple of hours; they will clear the conference room and any adjoining rooms, and lock them down until you're ready for your meeting, Mr. Vice President," Chip reported.

"Dan tells me Congressman Wilson and Senator Reed will be here at 9:00 in the morning. There may be a couple of others here also; I haven't decided yet; but I don't want this little get together to grow into something unmanageable and attract any more attention than necessary," the Vice President said.

It was about four in the afternoon when Dan's phone beeped; he answered it. "Come on up, it's on this floor and I already have the key. You will need your IDs to get on the floor. Chip and I will meet you in the hall," Then he told the Vice President, "That was Rick Winstead. He is our communications man. He and his team are going to do a clean sweep of the conference room you will be using tomorrow morning. When I spoke with him on the phone earlier, he said they would do another sweep before your meeting in the morning, also."

Dan and Chip had met Rick and his team—Pete and Paul—in the hall; they were each carrying a small back pack, slung over a shoulder, like you would ordinarily see a first grader carrying to school. But then, first graders don't carry a lot of books!

Rick introduced his guys to Dan and Chip and jokingly told them they better watch their backsides, that Dan and Chip were Secret Service and could haul them in for farting too loud!

Pete said, "Now I know we're in big trouble!"

Pete and Paul opened their backpack and took out a small instrument; he held it up for Dan and Chip to see. "If there is any type of 'bug' in this place, these guys will let us know in a nano-second," Pete told them, and then added, "Where is this room you want us to check?"

"It's down next to the nurse's station," Dan said. "Come on, follow me. I've got the key, and I will leave it with you Rick, until the Vice President has completed his meeting; I suppose he may even have more than one meeting before he and his wife are discharged."

As they started down the hall, both Pete and Paul clicked their devices on. As they passed the nurse's station the devices started vibrating, it also had a quiet buzzing sound also. They all stopped in their tracks.

"Shit!" said Dan very softly. "Don't tell me they already have this place bugged." He motioned the others to follow him further down the hall; when the vibrating and buzzing quit, they stopped.

"Well, that certainly answers a lot of questions," Chip said. He looked over at Pete and said, "I guess this is where you guys start earning your pay."

They went into the nurse's station, startling the ones who were there. Pete and Paul held their devices in front of themselves as they went in and moved around the area. The vibrating and buzzing increased when they got to the section where patient records were, and where doctors usually discussed each patient with the attending nurse on duty.

Rick asked the Charge Nurse, "Has anyone been in here recently to update your phones or IT system, or anyone to do maintenance of any kind in this area?"

The Charge Nurse was watching Pete and Paul, and the devices they were holding. She could hear the faint buzzing sound.

"Actually, yes," she replied, "A couple of telephone maintenance men came in to check the phones. One of them said they had to be sure we had secure lines since the Vice President was here. I didn't think anything more about it; it sounded logical to me, after all, he is the Vice President."

Pete went down one side of the station scanning the area, while Paul scanned the other side. They motioned for Rick and the others to go outside the nurse's station and followed them out into the hall.

Paul said, "There are five phone instruments in there and everyone has a tap, or bug on it; we could even use the devices we gave you earlier to listen in on this entire area ourselves."

"Somebody wants to know, and keep track of, the Vice President's condition," Chip said.

"That must mean they don't know his condition right now," Dan added. "Well, let's just keep that our little secret for now. We will have to let the Vice President and Senator Scott know, of course. We'll brief them when we get back to the room. But for right now, let's go check the conference room and clear it," he said.

Rick spoke up and told them that his guys could disable the devices in the nurse's station, and anywhere else they found bugged, whoever did it would never know, until they began wondering why they were not hearing any conversation going on.

"Do it!" Dan said.

They went into the conference room and found it clean, no bugs.

Dan said, "This kind of confirms that they don't know the Vice President's condition; they wouldn't expect him to be using a conference room while in the hospital. Let's get back to the room and see what he wants to do."

As they were heading out the door of the conference room, Rick told Pete and Paul to do a sweep of the entire floor, just to be sure there were no other 'bugs' hiding out somewhere. Rick, Dan and Chip went back to the Vice President's room to report.

CHAPTER THIRTY-EIGHT

Dan briefed the Vice President on their findings, that the nurse's station, the conference room, and the entire floor was clear with no other 'bugs'. That they had deactivated the ones they had found.

'Cille, who had been sitting in a chair beside her bed listening to all the talk, spoke up, "What about our house? Is that 'bugged', as you call it? Has someone been listening in on me and Joe and heard every word we have said?"

"We're sending the team over to check your residence very thoroughly," Dan said.

Chip started for the door and said, "I'll get the com team on it right now; incidentally, I called for another agent to be place on duty at the door to the conference room, just to be sure nobody—nobody—but one of us goes in."

"Good," said the Vice President, "We can't be too careful at this point."

The Vice President looked over at Senator Scott and asked, "Lindsey, will you get hold of Mel Pierson and Admiral Vince Dawkins and see if they can meet with you, Dennis, Harold, and me here in the conference room, say, about eight-thirty tomorrow morning. Oh, and ask Vince to not wear his uniform; we don't want this to be conspicuous."

"That's going to be kind of hard to do, Joe," Lindsey said. "That many people, of some importance and reputation will cause some eyes to widen and ears to prick up."

"I realize that, but this is important, and I think they should be here for their input. Can you work out a plan to stagger their arrival times and come in individually, not in a group?" the Vice President asked. "I would also like for Mike Holder to come; if you think that is too many, then maybe Mike could stop by on his own."

"I'll give him a call when I leave, I doubt there would be any problem," Lindsey said.

Dan said, "Rick and I are going to leave now also, but we'll stay in touch; you have my secure number, call me any time if you have any questions or concerns. I will see you back here for tomorrow morning's meeting."

As they walked toward the elevator, Chip asked Rick, "What the hell happened to Bull Miller and Dutch Hall Saturday. I haven't seen a report or anything on it, but I understand someone took a shot at them and tried to run them down in the parking lot of a restaurant."

Rick responded, "Yeah, somebody was waiting for us to finish breakfast, but didn't want to give us time to digest it."

Dan chuckled and said, "You didn't let them digest theirs either, you pulled your .357 Mag and blew the heads off both the driver and the gunman; sent their vehicle careening across the street into the river. I think the DC Police are still trying to lift it out."

"Were any of our guys hurt?" Chip asked.

"No, not physically anyway, but it surely scared the shit out of Penny. Have you met her, Chip? She is a Sergeant, army gal, and I believe can be pretty tough if she gets riled up; she is Bull Miller's secretary at the Pentagon. She came up from GITMO with Bull," replied Rick.

"I haven't met her yet, but I heard her husband was killed in Iraq a while back, also that she got hit while in Afghanistan, or somewhere over there," Chip answered.

"You guys know what?" Rick asked suddenly. "I just had a thought." But then Rick stopped in mid-sentence.

"What?" Dan asked. "Something must have just crossed your mind."

"I don't why I didn't think of it before," Rick said, sounding somewhat dumb-founded. "There has to be a connection between all these vehicles that have been involved in every incident that has occurred so far."

"Damn," said Dan all of a sudden! "You're right! All of the vehicles have been alike, large, black Suburbans, or Suburban type—similar to what the government, at least some of the government agencies use—especially in covert operations!"

Rick said, "Hell, they must have their own motor-pool; we, or some of our folks have destroyed almost a dozen. Just think about it for a moment; none of these were brand new, they were a little older, but only by a couple of years or more. The government buys new vehicles for intel operations and similar agencies each year."

"Then, they must really have their own motor-pool to operate from," added Chip.

"Right you are," said Dan! "We better let the others know to keep watch out for large, black, suburban type vehicles."

Rick said, "I'll give Dutch a call and see how they are doing after that little incident Saturday morning. I hope they have picked up a weapon of some sort by now. I think their 'Carry Permits' have already been sent to them. I encouraged them to stay armed at all times. We're all going to have to be prepared until this crap is settled."

Me, Sergeant Penny Fulbright and Major General Dutch Hall—all in civilian clothing—came out of the Ft. Meyer Post Exchange, near the Hatfield Main Gate. We walked over to some benches and sat down, no one talking—we just sat, looking over the quiet of the Post, each in his or her own thoughts about the events of the previous day.

After several minutes, Penny broke the silence, "We're in some pretty serious stuff, aren't we? I mean, those guys yesterday were out to kill all of us! They didn't even seem to care that it was in broad daylight, with a lot of other people around. If Rick had not been with us and alerted us, we would be dead right now, probably several other people too!"

Dutch said, "I guess this brings back some pretty nasty memories, for all three of us, of some of the scrapes we've been in—only not here on home ground. I know you've seen action before also, Penny. Bull has told me about your husband, and about you being wounded in Afghanistan. I spoke with Mel, the FBI Director about getting concealed carry permits for Virginia and military authorization for us to be armed at all times."

"Great!" I said, "I packed my old M1911 .45 in my bag; I never leave home without it! I'm not sure the best way to keep it on me, so it's not too conspicuous; it is bulky and heavy but it is made to stop somebody in their tracks. Penny, do you have a weapon that you can carry with you at all times?"

"Who would have thought I would need one here?" she said. "No, I don't even own one of my own. Back at GITMO, I went to the range pretty often, but I always used one of the range firearms."

I said, "Not a problem. I'll get you one tomorrow. What would you like? A .9 mm with a couple of magazines, or a .38 revolver, something like the police carry? Take your choice." I asked.

"I think I would rather have the .38, it is smaller, less noticeable, and lightweight. But you don't have to get it, I'll go to the PX and see what they . . . . . ." Penny was saying, but her comments were interrupted by a loud blast; the explosion shook the ground around them. We jumped to our feet, looked back toward the PX, and then beyond the PX where we saw a cloud of smoke and flames from whatever had just blown up.

"What in hell was that?" I asked.

"Somebody just blew something sky high," replied Dutch.

"That's over in the area of our quarters!" said Penny, with a stammer, "Where we are living right now! Do you think . . . could that have been meant for us too? Since they failed yesterday?"

I said, "Don't go jumping to conclusions, Penny. We don't know what happened; besides, if it was a hit job on us, they didn't succeed!"

All of a sudden the streets were filled with fire engines, military police vehicles, and crash-rescue trucks, all with sirens screaming at top volume!

Dutch said, "Maybe we should get over there and see what's going on, just how close it is to our quarters."

We picked up the pace, walking as fast as we could, in the direction of our billets.

As we turned the corner of the street where Dutch and I were staying, we stopped; me and Dutch looked at each other while Penny just stared in disbelief.

I said in a haltingly voice, "I guess we'll have to find another place to sleep tonight, Dutch."

Penny said, "Me too! I'm certainly not going to stay in my quarters, not in this area, knowing that some damn body is trying to kill me—trying to kill all three of us!"

We walked closer to the scene of the explosion, where we were stopped by one of the uniformed police. Several other uniformed officers were stringing yellow **"POLICE LINE DO NOT CROSS"** tape around the entire area.

Dutch spotted a uniformed fireman, a lieutenant, who seemed to be in charge of the nearest crew of fire-fighters. He approached the lieutenant and said, "Pardon me, lieutenant, I'm General Hall; I'm assigned here to the Pentagon and this is, or was, my temporary quarters. What the hell happened here?"

The lieutenant introduced himself as the Battalion Chief and told Dutch, "Sorry, sir; we don't know right now—possibly a gas leak. The fire investigators are already on the scene and will be taking a close look at everything. It will take them some time though it's pretty hot in there. In fact we are trying to determine if anyone was inside; we have guys trying to work their way in as they get the blaze under control."

Dutch walked back over to where me and Penny were standing.

"What's the news?" I asked.

"It's too early to tell; the lieutenant said maybe a gas leak or something of that nature. But you and I know that's bullshit," Dutch replied.

"You think it wasn't an accident? That it was on purpose, and maybe you guys were the target?" asked Penny.

"I feel sure of it," said Dutch. "And, I'll tell you two something else: we need to find other facilities to stay, without anyone else knowing. Also, I think we should stay close together, within hollering distance. Perhaps we can find a hotel with adjoining rooms. That is, if you're comfortable with it, Penny. I don't feel good about you staying someplace separate from us, not at this point anyway."

Penny replied, "That's fine with me; I know I'll be more comfortable with you guys close."

Just then, Dutch's phone beeped. It was Mel Pierson, "Dutch, I just received a report about an explosion on Ft. Myers, in the visiting officer's quarters. I figured someone had targeted you and Bull; I'm enroute there now. I should be there in about ten minutes. Where are you guys? Are you okay?" he asked.

"We're fine, Mel! We just want to get our hands on the bastards who are doing this. Penny is with us; we were over at the PX when the explosion occurred so we headed back to the VOQ and we are outside the perimeter on the PX side right now."

"By the way, Dutch, as soon as I got the report, I dispatched a couple of agents and a bomb expert to Penny's quarters to check it out. We can't afford to take any chances," Mel said.

"Thanks, Mel, that will make Penny feel a lot better knowing that we're looking out for her too," Dutch replied. "We've got to watch each other's backside," he added.

"Who is going to be watching whose 'backside'? Penny said with a blushing smile on her face, the first in several hours.

After about ten minutes, we saw Mel drive up, followed by two other unmarked cars with two people in each; obviously FBI agents.

Three men and one female dressed in business attire. They got out of their vehicles and came over to where Dutch, Penny and I were standing, watching the fire raging around our quarters, our beds, the place where in just a few hours we would have been laying down our heads—only to have them blown off!

"I'm sure glad you folks decided to go shopping instead of back to your quarters," Mel said as he came up. "Do you know if anyone else was in the building; was anyone else registered besides you two?"

"Don't know, Mel; I talked with the battalion chief, that lieutenant over there, he is in charge of one of the groups fighting the fire. He said it would be a while before they would know if anyone else was in there or not. I sure as hell hope not!" Dutch said.

Mel told them, "Things are picking up, there is more going on than I can keep up with all of a sudden. Dan Black called me about an hour ago and told me that the Vice President wants to have a meeting tomorrow morning, right there in the hospital. They have already set up a conference room and made sure it wasn't bugged. However, while doing so they did discover that the nurse's station was bugged. It was done within an hour or so after the Vice President and his wife were admitted. That tells me that whoever is running this show, doesn't know what the Vice President's condition is, how seriously he was wounded. They probably aren't sure if he is conscious or not."

Mel's phone beeped, he stepped away from the group for a couple of minutes. When he returned he looked at Penny, then at me and Dutch and said, "I'm glad that you went with Dutch and Bull, and not back to your quarters."

"Why?" Penny asked, already knowing the answer.

I spoke up in a loud voice, "If those sons-of-bitches harm her in any way, I'll personally go after them myself and drag them through hell!"

Tough, career army soldier, combat veteran, Sergeant Penny Fulbright looked at Colonel James "Bull" Miller through teary, misty eyes and smiled. She couldn't speak because of the lump that formed in her throat.

There were a couple of minutes of "quiet" silence before anyone spoke.

"You'll have a lot of company with you," Mel responded, when he broke the silence. "That call was from one of the guys I sent over to Penny's quarters; her door was wired, they found a C-4 explosive charge set to go off when the door was opened."

Then, looking at Penny, Mel told her, "If you had unlocked the door and turned the door knob it would have blown the entire room apart and probably taken a couple of other rooms with it!"

"We've got to find ourselves new quarters, at least for the night," Dutch said. "Oh, and I guess we better find us some new clothes too; uniforms, shaving gear, and stuff. Everything we brought with us was in our rooms."

Mel said, "Don't worry about a place to stay. I've got a place you can use for a couple of weeks or so; if you don't mind sharing an apartment. It has three bedrooms and three baths. We use it as a safe house at times when we bring in someone important that we don't want anybody to know about. It's kind of a hideout, just what the three of you need right now."

Gathering her thoughts, Penny said, "We can go back to the PX. They have a military clothing department. We can buy new uniforms, other clothing and items there, until we get a chance to go shopping."

"Yeah, Penny, your room has been blocked off while they check for possible evidence; your stuff will not be available either. If you need help or transportation, or anything at all, give me a call," Mel said.

Having calmed down a little I said, "I heard that Sam is out of the hospital and back at work, so I guess that means we will be back in the office tomorrow also. Maybe we will have more information then and can get a better handle on what's going on, and who is doing what. I just want to get my hands on whoever is responsible."

"Maybe I'll know more after the meeting with the Vice President tomorrow morning," Mel said.

CHAPTER THIRTY-NINE

At seven o'clock on Monday morning, Vince Dawkins walked into the lobby of the George Washington University Hospital dressed in nothing like his normal, work-day attire. He appeared much like any other business man, perhaps like one of the doctors on staff at the hospital. There was no indication that he was an Admiral, the Chief of Naval Operations, for the U.S. Navy, and a member of the Joint Chiefs of Staff for the entire U.S. military complex.

Vince looked around thinking, the entire fourth floor has only two patients—the Vice President of the United States and his wife. The fourth floor had been blocked off, cleaned physically and electronically! This is going to be a tough meeting he thought; "TOP SECRET!" "UNOFFICIAL!" No one was to know about it, only the small group the Vice President had requested.

He wondered, "How in hell does anything stay secret in DC!"

He approached the elevator and was stopped by a person in a business suit, holding a small pad in his hand, who asked for identification. The man showed Vince his own ID, Secret Service Agent, Vince nodded and produced his military ID. They shook hands and Vince entered the elevator, he pushed the 'four' button for the fourth floor. As he exited the elevator he was met by two other 'businessmen' who asked to see his ID, he complied. They both had Secret Service IDs.

One of the men said, "Sorry, Admiral, we're just like you, following orders."

Smiling, Vince replied, "I certainly understand that."

"Come on and I'll take you to the coffee shop they set up. You may even find a doughnut or two and other goodies too. I'm sure you're aware there are only two patients on this entire floor, and who they are; not sure how long we—they will be here; I understand they had only minor injuries and are ready to leave. That said, I'm sure you also know all of this is classified," he told Vince.

"From what little I know at this point, this whole set up is highly classified. You guys who are assigned here were hand-picked, as were those attending the meeting," Vince told him, much to make a point.

The agent opened the door of a room across the hall from the conference room and told Vince to make himself at home. "I'll bring the others here as they arrive," he said as he left the room.

Vince poured a cup of coffee and sat down to think and wonder what the Vice President had in mind. Vince looked up when the door opened and General Mike Holder entered, Mike was also on the Joint Chiefs, representing the National Guard. Others, Mel Pierson, Harold Reed and Dennis Wilson, slowly filtered into the coffee room, greeted each other as they arrived, then just sat and chatted among themselves about much-of-nothing; since neither knew for sure what topics the meeting would consist of.

After a few minutes, Senator Lindsey Scott entered and greeted everyone. "Good morning, Gentlemen; it does my heart good to see so many of you out so early looking bright eyed and bushy tailed for a Monday," he said smiling. The Vice President will be joining us shortly, but before he gets here, I wanted to talk with you about what's been happening. I'm sure most of you know about all the crap that's been going on; we have had several people killed, shot at, blown up or an attempt at it anyway. Also as you know, there is a very large group of our country's leaders who think, and are now saying out loud that we can't let it continue. From both sides of the political aisle, they are calling for action, albeit not too public and loudly vocal. Frankly, many are scared for their lives and their families. For quite some time now, there has been some planning, and some other meetings going on, in the background of course, to try and determine the best course of action. What we will be discussing here today may not be the very best course of action, but we feel we are out of time; things are happening too fast and too frequently to wait any longer.

"Vince I believe you have found a place for us to hold a large meeting?" Senator Scott asked.

"I have," Vince said. "Most of you are familiar with Bubba Roberts, the bar-b-que man, and his place that was attacked and fire-bombed two weeks ago. Well, Bubba has a very large farm about an hour, plus or minus, due west of here, out in the country—no neighbors, no one even close. That's where he holds his family reunions—he has a rather large family—more than a hundred fifty usually attend his reunions. He has offered his farm as a place for us to meet. It will be mostly out-of-doors. The eating place is really a couple of large, tin covered, rustic, places; it's open on all four sides but will sit well over a hundred on long, hand-made tables and benches. Also, based on the attack on his bar-b-que hut, he strongly suggests extra protection on hand before, during, and after the meeting. Not only that, he said he was sending his wife and four kids out of town and he would cook enough bar-b-que, with all the trimmings, to feed an Army!"

"Great," Lindsey said. "Mike, you recall what you and I talked about a few days ago?"

"Yes, sir, Senator, I had a meeting with several of my more reliable unit commanders, whom I know personally, and they are chomping at the bit to get something done. You just say where and when and a couple of our Guard Units will pull a 'practice training exercise.' We're always looking for ways to stay proficient and on the alert," Mike said.

Mel spoke up and added, "I'll have a number of special agents there also; we'll coordinate with Mike to be sure everything is covered. I'm sure Dan will have some of his special folks there too."

Lindsey told the group, "Okay, let's go across the hall to the conference room. The Vice President will be joining us there in a few minutes—you can take your coffee with you if you like."

They all got up and went into the conference room. In about five minutes, the door opened and Vice President Joe Bradley walked in, followed by Robert "Bob" Walters, the Deputy Secretary of Defense.

The Vice President said, "Good morning Gentleman, sorry to call you out so early but we have some very important business to discuss. I'm sure most of you know Bob Walters, Deputy Secretary of Defense over at the Pentagon. I'm not sure I know just where to begin this discussion; I do know it is serious, it is a topic that has been floating throughout the entire government for some time now, and there has been quite a bit of discussion among different people, different agencies, and departments about what to do about it. Before we get started, Mel, are you sure that this room does not have listening devices or 'bugs?' That it has been cleared and cleaned and we can proceed without any danger of being overheard?" he asked.

Mel replied, "Yes, sir, it was cleared yesterday and the entire floor blocked off and no one allowed entrance to this floor. There are guards at the elevator on the first floor, when you get off on this floor, and right now there is a guard at this door. Just as a double precaution, a clean sweep was accomplished at six thirty this morning. I think that's as certain as we can possibly be."

"Thanks, Mel," said the Vice President. "Now, folks, I'm going to get right to the gist of what we're here for. I'm will not beat around the bush or feed you a bunch of crap. You have all been sworn to secrecy, that none of us in this room will discuss any of the topics or subjects brought up; or disclose the name of anyone here. First, I'm not even going to discuss whether or not the President was born in this country! We've all heard the rumors, seen reports, and know a lot of the facts. But right now, that isn't the most important thing that we have to face! We can deal with that later. The primary focus at the moment is the overall government, and many of the agents supposedly representing us at different levels, positions, and events—foreign and domestic. We already know that there are 'bastards in high places' in this administration, pardon the language gentlemen, but it really pisses me off at what has been going on and has been for a long time now. Let me pause right here and now and apologize to you and the American people for having been a part of it. My only excuse is stupidity on my part! I became so engrossed in my own affairs and little world that I didn't see what was going on around me. I couldn't see that the country was being destroyed from within. I guess I believed that it could never happen, not to the United States anyway. Lately, I have been confronted, almost attacked, by some members of the House and Senate about the tear-down of the nation, and, gentlemen, not only by Republicans, but also Democrats. As you know, I am a Democrat, and among you are both Democrats and Republicans. We may belong to different political parties, but when it comes to this nation, we are all Americans and we will die if necessary to protect her and our heritage!"

Then the vice president added, "Some of you know that the president's chief of staff is Muslim, so is his chief of intelligence; so are many others in the administration. I'm talking about daily practicing Muslims; they have a room in the White House they use for their daily prayer to Allah—it's kind of like a 'mini-mosque,' I guess, right here in the White House! I have seen too many odd happenings and strange events taking place to just let it slide. Some time back, I talked with the president about all the protests that were going on throughout the country, that I thought they were too well-organized to be spontaneous, that I thought many were being paid to recruit and organize the protests. He laughed it off by saying that he used to be an 'organizer' and that he certainly was never paid. We all know that is bullshit! On another occasion when Congress was debating cutting the defense budget, which would obviously cut our military complex drastically, I told him how dangerous that could be, especially with North Korea trying to get nuclear weaponry. Another time, I mentioned that some of our White House staff needed to be looked into regarding their loyalty and such. This went on and on until I became suspicious and began doing a little checking, asking questions of different people whom I knew were and always would be independent, free thinking, put America first at all costs, folks whose loyalty could never be questioned!"

Then after a pause, he added, "You already know the rest of that story; on the way home from a formal White House function a few nights ago, my wife and I were attacked, literally blown up, as we drove into our residential area. Our driver and several of the agent escorts were killed in the blast that shook Northeast Washington that night. I think my wife and I had Divine Protection! We escaped with only minor injuries. At the suggestion, and direction, of the FBI Director, Mel over here, we will remain here in the hospital for the time being. Those responsible probably don't know our condition or status; for now, that is top secret!

Gentlemen, you are here because we know where you stand—you are the independent, free thinking, put America first at all costs folks we are talking about. From this point forward, it may well be 'at all costs!' I have spoken with each of you individually concerning your thoughts on what should be done and the best way to go about it. Senator Scott and I have discussed very deeply about the action that has been proposed. I had planned to resign as Vice President and step aside, but I have been convinced that my place is with you gentlemen. Like you, I pledged my life, my fortune, my sacred honor, to protect this country from all enemies foreign and domestic! It looks as though that time has come! I'm going to leave you at this point and go back to my wife, just down the hall. Senator Scott will talk further with you about the upcoming meeting that he and Admiral Dawkins have scheduled. Thank you for your service and loyalty to this great nation—this is truly the home of the free and brave! God bless each of you."

With that, the Vice President left the conference room and Lindsey Scott began speaking, "Well, gentlemen, we know where the Vice President stands. As some of you know, he and I, and our wives, have been good friends for many years even though we are miles apart on some political issues and views. But over the years, we have learned how to 'agree to disagree!' As for the subject at hand, he and I have discussed it many times but just didn't know what to do about it. We both now feel that the election of this mal-fit, community organizer to the presidency was bought and paid for. By whom we don't know; we each kind of have our own ideas, but nothing any of us could prove. But there are some unknown people, or groups of people, who do not have the best interest of this country in mind. I'm sure you have heard some of them speak; they want open borders and open elections. They want a one-world government order! They are after power—a small group of people who will tell the rest of the world what they can and can't do. They want to centralize power into their hands. All of you know of the meeting scheduled for Saturday evening at eight o'clock, and you know the directions and how to get there. Do not let anyone you do not know and trust with your life, know anything about it, or where it is being held. Between now and then, the Vice President and his family will be taken to an undisclosed location for the time being, even I don't know where he will be. Each of you know what your assignment is and also know the importance; our future, our very lives and that of our families, indeed of our very country, depends on each of us and what happens in the next few days. If there are no questions, we will dispense with this meeting and move on."

Then before ending, he added, "Oh, before we leave, you may have heard that an attempt was made on General Dutch Hall, Colonel Bull Miller and Sergeant Penny Fulbright's lives on Saturday. They were staying on Fort Meyers in the visitor's quarters; while they were out of their rooms, the whole building was blown up. They were very lucky. We are dealing with an unprecedented situation, and hard, extreme, take-over minded, criminal elements who are out to destroy this nation and anyone who gets in their way! I recommend that we not leave in a group; we never know who may be watching. I'll see you all on Saturday evening, in the meantime, watch your back! And, for God's sake, report anything you see or hear that's unusual or out of the ordinary!"

CHAPTER FORTY

Back in my office in the Pentagon on Monday morning, I was trying to wrap my mind around the happenings of the weekend. I had been shot at, the target of a wild, speeding vehicle, and subject of an attempted bombing. *It's nice to be back in a quiet, safe, peaceful "war zone,"* I thought.

My door opened and Penny came in carrying two cups of coffee on a tray. "Good morning again," she said as she sat the cups down. "General . . . Dutch . . . is on his way over and asked to have his coffee ready."

"Where's your cup?" I asked. "Grab yours and come back in, anything we have to talk about will involve you too."

Dutch entered the office, smiled, and said, "I'm thinking of transferring back to Afghanistan, where it's a little quieter and safer," he joked. "Good morning, Penny. I hope the snoring of two old Marine Corps troops didn't keep you awake last night. I thought I could hear Bull 'sawing logs' through the walls two rooms down the hall."

"You must have heard yourself," I replied. "I could hear a lot of snoring from my room, so it had to be you . . . or . . ." they both looked at Penny and laughed.

Penny laughed and said, "Don't look at me; I've had a sleep test and the doctor told me I was fine and didn't snore at all. But now that you two have mentioned it, I did wake up in the middle of the night. I thought somebody was throwing bombs, or a freight train was coming through the room."

Dutch said, "I am right impressed with our new quarters; this 'Safe House,' as Mel called it, is first class. And in the middle of the high rent district, Georgetown."

"Yeah," I replied, "Someone must have told them we were VIPs and deserved the best."

"My room is larger than my whole two bedroom apartment at GITMO," Penny added.

Rick came in and greeted them, "My crew and I have just debugged Sam Drakeford's office, so I thought we would come by and check your offices as well. The crew is over in your office now, Dutch, we're also checking in the hallway near your doors, too."

Penny, who had gone into the coffee room when Rick came in, came back with a fresh cup of coffee and handed it to Rick.

"Thanks, Penny," Rick said smiling, "This is really what I stopped by for."

"How is the debugging operation coming along, and how many have you guys done, and what kind of problems have you found, if any?" I asked.

"Well," Rick began, "Every one of you better watch your ass! So far every one of the 'good guys' have been targeted, bugged—offices, vehicles, and home places! In fact, and I have no way of knowing for sure, but I feel certain that anyone who has a government mobile phone has been under surveillance, with somebody listening to their conversations on a government secure line."

Dutch looked around at each of the others, and speaking softly said, "Folks, I don't know what all is going on, but something big is about to happen. I don't know what, where, or when; I do believe it is going to be big, bigger than anything like it, ever in this country. I don't know when either, but I also believe it is going to be real soon! We need to be prepared, but we don't know what to prepare for, how in hell do we prepare for something we know absolutely nothing about? Except that it is domestic terrorism at it's worse!"

Penny reached over and touched my hand and said, "It's pretty scary, isn't it? But you know what? As a nation, we have survived a lot of disabling attacks: cultures, ideologies, invasions, bombings like Pearl Harbor, and others, but we have stuck together as a nation, and we have survived. We have kicked butts and we will do it again if necessary!"

There was a clapping of hands behind them, shocked they turned to find General Sam Drakeford, the sitting Chairman of the Joint Chiefs of Staff, standing in the doorway, the gleam of the four-stars on his shoulder glistening in the light.

"Well said, Penny! I'm sure you speak for all of us in this fight. We're not quite sure just what the fight is just yet, but I guarantee we will kick some butt before this crap is over!" Sam Drakeford said.

We all jumped up from our seats, and Sam said, "Please, be seated; I just stopped by to check on you three since someone tried to take you out the other day. I trust you have gotten settled in to different, more secure quarters by now."

"First class accommodations, sir," Dutch replied. "Mel arranged one of his special 'safe places' for us; so we went shopping for new clothing and supplies and I believe we are settled, at least for now."

"Dan Black and Mel Pierson told me a little while ago that the Vice President and his wife have been taken from the hospital to a secret and secure place until we can figure this situation out and get it under control," Sam said. "I also understand the President has been asking about him and his wife and where they were taken. Susan Brice, the President's Chief of Staff, has gone far out of her way looking for them; she has even had the President's Intel Chief, John Beaman, trying to find him. I don't know what the SOBs have been told so far, but I do know that the Secret Service folks and the FBI do not want any of that bunch to know, or find out where Joe and his wife are. Tom Beckwith from the CIA called to warn me and let me know that they are turning over all stones and looking in bushes trying to find out anything to give them a clue where Joe is. He said I would probably be getting a phone call or a visit from one of John Beaman's cronies. You guys will also be receiving a visit or call, so be on the alert. You are aware of the meeting Saturday evening and the location I assume, and that you'll all be there," Sam asked?

"We'll be there," Dutch said.

"Wouldn't miss it for all the tea in China," I replied.

"I'll see you there," Sam said as he left the office.

CHAPTER FORTY-ONE

Chip Reese, his wife Sandi, and their two kids, Charlene age 10 and Kevin age 7, pulled into the drive of their country home, an hour's drive-plus just west of Washington in a little town that may be too small to call a town, named, probably appropriately, "Old Tavern." Named undoubtedly because back in the old days, that's where most of the men hung out. "Old Tavern" was located only about thirty miles or so from where Dave Mabry's ranch was located, and where he and his wife lived, before they were murdered.

Sandi spoke up and said, "This would have been a perfect evening together with just the family, but you had so many phone calls. What was so important that the President and his crew couldn't wait until morning? The meal in Old Town Alexandria was exquisite, and the movie would have been too, without all those interruptions."

"I know honey; but all the calls were urgent from the Intel Chief's office. The President was trying to locate Joe Bradley and didn't know if he and his wife were still in the hospital or had been released or where they were. They said the President and the Intel Chief were both upset and getting panicky because they had no idea where the Vice President was," Chip answered.

Suddenly, Chip got very quiet and stiffened. He began looking around from side to side. Then, he told Sandi and the kids to be very quiet. He slowly reached under his seat and withdrew a .45 pistol he always kept handy, just in case.

Sandi looked over at Chip and asked, "What's wrong, Chip, why are you getting your gun out?"

"Shhh," he said, as he reached to the dashboard and turned the switch for the interior lights off so they wouldn't come on; then, he quietly opened the door. "I thought I saw movement outback, by the barn. I'm going to check it out. Wait here in the car and be quiet."

Chip pulled further into the drive, drove to the rear, and stopped under the portico. It was covered with beautiful flowering vines; it was Sandi's pride and joy, one she had overseen and planted on her own. It truly was a beautiful setting.

But right now, Chip could only think about the cover it provided him; he knew someone was waiting, outback, and they wouldn't care who they hurt in trying to get to him. All of a sudden, Charlene jumped out of the car, came running up shouting, "Daddy, I saw two men running out of the side door of the house toward the back yard. Who are they? What do they want?" she screamed.

Chip yelled at her, "Stay back. Get back in the car with your mother and Kevin!"

Instead, Charlene ran toward the back of the portico through the flowery-covered archway; as she did, the archway and portico exploded in a ball of fire that tore the portico apart and sent burning pieces flying in all directions spreading the fire as it went.

"You sorry bastards," Chip screamed at the top of his lungs, he looked back just in time to see his car explode, with his wife and son still inside. He saw the glow of the trail from the RPG arch in the air then hit his car with such force the explosion shook the ground for yards around the house. "I'll get everyone of you sorry jihadist bastards," he screamed through tears. He saw another fiery arch as another RPG hit his house, shattering the walls and destroying everything in it.

He heard a noise and saw movement out toward the barn; he hunkered down and watched. He spotted two figures dressed in all black, faces covered with black ski masks. Chip fired a couple of shots; there was immediate return fire from what sounded like automatic weapons of some sort. This brought back memories of Vietnam. Chip's mind immediately focused on the enemy as he quietly began moving forward. He was no longer mentally in Washington, no longer in the United States—he was in the jungle of Vietnam.

He fumbled in his inside coat pocket and got his cellphone and speed dialed Dan Black's secure emergency number and got an immediate answer. "Where the hell are you, Chip? That sounds like gun fire in the background. What's going on? Where the hell are you? Are you in danger?" Dan yelled into the phone.

Chip screamed through his tears, "Dan, I'm under attack at my own house; the bastards have already killed my family! I need help fast. There are half a dozen or more; they have automatic weapons—it's an assault team dressed in all black. Get me some help out here fast."

"I have already hit the panic button, Chip," Dan replied. "Try to calm down and check out the situation. We'll have a team out by chopper as quickly as they can get there. The police and a team of our guys are on the way; they're tracking you by GPS on your phone. What kind of a weapon do you have?"

"I only have my .45 and two magazines; I had more in the house, but now there is no more house. The sorry bastards; they are going to pay for this! Dan, I won't be able to hold them off if they come at me all at once," Chip replied! Then, more excitedly, he added, "I see movement; I've got to go. Get some damn help out here now," he yelled!

Chip crawled on his belly through the debris where his daughter had just been blown up. He was no longer aware of where he was; he only knew the enemy was just a few yards in front of him. Suddenly, it dawned on him—**tripwire**—they had planted a tripwire hoping to get him; they got Charlene instead—his beautiful little girl. Tears welled up in his eyes. Looking through the bushes and vines, he could make out the form of two people; he got off two shots and two men went down.

Automatic fire began coming at him from three sides; they were well-armed and had plenty of fire power. To throw them off, he moved to his left, to the opposite side of the portico, and changed his position to get a better sight line to the enemy. Suddenly, he felt a strong bite in his left arm. He was hit; he felt the blood start running down his arm. He couldn't move the arm; the shot must have hit the bone and broken it. As he looked back up, he saw three more approaching his position. They were crouching; they must have known they had made a hit but not how serious though. Chip rose up just enough to see the men; he fired off three quick shots—three dropped in their tracks.

Then he heard something behind him. As he started to turn, a second round caught him in the upper left thigh knocking him backward; he felt something hit him in the back of his head and that was the last he remembered.

Sirens were screaming in the distance and the steady "whomp, whomp, whomp" of a helicopter, both drawing closer by the minute. Two men dressed in all black with black ski masks and AK-47s slung across their backs, ran to Chip and grabbed him, one under each arm and dragged him through the grass toward the back of the property, toward the barn. A large, black van came speeding in and stopped; the side door opened and the two men dragging Chip tossed him into the van and jumped in as the van sped off across the grassy field and onto the highway.

Chip awoke with a start, water splashing in his face. Unable to decipher what had happened for a few minutes, he was not conscious enough to think. All his mind could grasp was the extreme pain from his shoulder and leg. Another bucket of water hit him in the face, he gasped and moaned. *Damn*, he thought, *I feel so weak; I can't move my arm or leg.* He looked down and saw blood still flowing from his splintered, almost gone, left leg. It appeared to be just hanging by the skin. Blood flowing from his arm and shoulder didn't help any either. He thought, *I've had it; they might as well get it over with.*

Chip couldn't wrap his mind around all that was happening. He had not had the time to reflect on the killing of his wife and children; he couldn't grasp all that was going on now. There were other people in here. He could hear them talking; they had a foreign accent in their voice, mid-eastern or such. *But where the hell are we?* He was thinking as he looked around; it looked like an underground parking lot. He was sitting, leaning against a post, with a rope around his mid-body, chest, and the post.

He felt the blood still flowing down his arm and leg; it felt like his whole body was bleeding! He felt himself getting weaker by the moment. One of the men saw that he was awake and came over to him and knelt in front of him and began asking questions.

Still with the black mask on, the man asked, "What is going on? What is your group doing? Who is leading your group?"

"You go to hell," Chip replied.

"We hear that you are having a meeting very soon. Where is the meeting being held?"

Chip spat in the man's face, hitting the mask and yelled, "Screw you, you sorry bastard! You damn crazy Islamist assholes murder children. I'll see you in hell first!"

The man slapped Chip across the side of the head and opened up another wound.

"What is the purpose of your meeting and who will be attending? As soon as you answer my questions, we will get you to a hospital to a doctor and get you fixed up. We do not like to see anyone suffer," he said.

Chip struggled a little straighter in his tied down position, with the post biting into his back; he looked the masked man in the eye, spat in his face again, and said, "You can kiss my American-born ass, you jihadist son-of-a-bitch. If I could get up from here, I would stick that mask up your ass and set it on fire!"

The masked man slapped Chip across the face again, and said, "You'll never get up from anywhere, you infidel American pig! You're going to die, just like your wife and two children, only yours will be much slower. It was a pleasure to watch them blown apart and burn to death like all of you American infidels will someday."

Chip felt himself fading away, life slowly creeping from his body as his blood pooled around him. Before passing out completely, he heard the masked man tell the others, "He is dead, he is bleeding out. Take his body and dump it somewhere else, put it in a dumpster, double check, and be certain you don't leave any evidence that could possibly lead back to any of us."

Dan Black was still holding his phone with Chip still on his phone. He had heard the entire conversation. When he spoke with Chip while these masked shit-heads were shooting at him, Chip had put his phone in his shirt pocket without turning it off!

"Oh shit!" Dan shouted out loud even though there was no one else close. He placed his phone on the seat without disconnecting the call—it may come in handy later. He opened the glove compartment and brought out another of his phones and punched in his speed dial for the FBI Director Mel Pierson, who picked up on the first ring.

"Dan, what's going on to have you call me on this line?" Mel asked.

"Chip Reese, my assistant, is under attack at his house. I think his house was blown up, his wife and kids killed, he was wounded, and probably dead by now also!" Dan said. "I already have one of my teams on the way by chopper; the local county sheriff's office and uniformed police are enroute too!" he added.

Mel said, "Stay calm, Dan, I'm on my way, and I'll have a team or two meet us there; we've got to take control of this situation now! I'll see you in a few minutes," Mel said as he clicked off and hit speed dial for his special duty teams.

"Hi Chief, what's up? Must be big calling on the hotline," said John Halbert. John was Mel's Special Agent responsible for emergency operations, SWAT-team type missions and special assignments—a standby team was always on duty waiting for "THE" call to action.

Mel urgently replied, "John, how fast can you get a couple of teams out to Chip Reese's place, his home; he and his family are under attack from what sounds like an assault team of foreign speaking assholes out to take him into custody for some reason; they've already killed his family."

Mel heard a loud claxon horn go off in the background and knew that John had already pushed his "panic" button for his team to assemble in full gear on the double. Almost immediately, he heard a helicopter fire up its engines.

John came back on the line and asked, "Is this what we've been waiting for, to cover our little get-together?"

"No," Mel replied, "This is a different tactic; this is a direct attack—a military style attack on a Federal Agent and his home. We still have to be prepared for something on Saturday night, something big! In the attack on Chip, he returned fire, but he was hit a couple of times, and they were able to capture him. They tried to get information out of him about the meeting and the details of who, what, where, and when, but Chip wouldn't tell them anything so they slapped him around a few times, then let him bleed out from his wounds, and dumped his body in a dumpster somewhere; we have people trying to locate that now."

Then, Mel added, "About Saturday night; we might better 'beef' it up somewhat John. If they are willing to try something like this on one of our Secret Service agents, and they get information about the meeting, we could be in for a full scale attack! Other agencies will be covering also; just be sure ya'll coordinate who is going to do what and where each will be."

John said, "I have two teams off the ground enroute to Chip's place; their ETA is twelve minutes. I've got another chopper running and I'm about to climb aboard. Can we give you a lift?" John asked.

"Great," Mel said. "Pick me up on top of the parking garage of the FBI building; I'm on the way there now!"

The pilot sat the chopper down in the designated "heliport" spot on the top deck; Mel ran out, jumped in and the chopper lifted off immediately. John handed Mel a headset and he put it on.

John said, "I've been picking up some chatter from our crews; we have two units on the ground on opposite sides of the property and they are closing in on Chip's house now and are saying there's not much left. They will seal off the property and safeguard it until the investigators get there."

As they approached John saw his teams spread out across a wide area of the property; then he spotted one of the team leaders on the ground waving them in to land in the back yard.

"They have the place secured," John told Mel. "There must have been ten or twelve people and at least one vehicle, maybe more, can't tell at this point; we'll know more in a few minutes."

The chopper sat down on the once beautiful, grassy, manicured back yard of Chip and Sandi Reese. Mel looked around the now blackened and burned, grassy yard, he bowed his head, unbelieving what he was witnessing; he had visited with Chip and his family here on several occasions, weekend cookouts with others. Such a beautiful family and home – gone!

Dan, who had arrived first on the scene with a secret service team of agents from the White House, came over to where Mel was standing. Mel looked up and saw the red of Dan's eyes and knew he had shed some tears; he and Chip were not only 'boss' and assistant, but close friends as well.

Dan said, "This is it, Mel! This is the damn end of all this shit that's been going on; I'm not just sitting around thinking any longer; I am going to take that son-of-a-bitch out, permanently, even if I spend the rest of my life in prison or get shot trying; I've had it with these assholes!"

"I know, and I understand how you feel Dan, we all feel the same as you," Mel replied. "We are going to take him out; not only him, but the rest of his Islamic crew also. We are close, and we will be even closer, and know more about what's going on when we get together Saturday night. Keep a tight grip on your nerves and feelings until then. Try to stay out of his sight until then, take a couple of days off."

Mel's phone went off, he picked up immediately; it was Tom Beckwith from the CIA. "Mel, I just got word that something big went down at Chip Reese's place; what the hell is going on," he asked?

"My source tells me that Chip and his whole family; wife and two kids were killed in a bombing and fire-fight; that it was an actual military style assault. That's unbelievable, right here on our own soil, near the nation's capital.

"Mel I hope you'll agree with some immediate actions I took, on my own, as soon as I got the word about Chip. I called the Vice President, Senator Scott, Sam Drakeford and a few others; they agreed that we should isolate the President for a few days without anyone knowing, if possible, by keeping him busy in other areas until we finalize our thoughts and action plans in the next couple of days; however, we can't let him suspect what's going on. All of the key people have been alerted and advised of the attacks recently and they tell me their assignments, duties and areas of responsibility are fully covered and they have coordinated it with their counterparts in the other agencies."

"That's great Tom;" Mel said, "You won't believe what those shit-heads have done out here. It looks as if they were trying to either capture Chip or kill him or both. They had rigged up a 'tripwire' with enough explosives to take out a Humvee; only we think Chip's ten year old daughter ran to help her daddy and set it off; there's probably not enough parts of her body left for a funeral. Evidently they must have thought they had got Chip and started to move in; we found a number of bodies of men dressed in all black, with black ski masks; they were armed with AK-47s and grenades. Also, Tom, my people have found evidence of RPGs being used on the car and the house; that's probably how they killed Chip's wife and seven year old son."

Tom asked, "What about Chip? Did you find his body? It sounds like he got several of them before they got him."

Mel responded, "During the attack Chip managed to punch in Dan's secure number, told him the situation and pleaded for help. He didn't close his phone, instead he slipped it back into his shirt pocket; Dan heard the explosions and the gunfire; Chip got hit a couple of times, he probably blacked out, and the guys in black captured him and drove away. Dan could hear one of the guys ask Chip about our next meeting, he wanted to know the details; Chip told him where he could go so they slapped him around some more, then they just let him bleed out; the one doing all the talking told the others to take the body and put it in a dumpster someplace. We have a tracer on Chip's phone GPS and a team is out looking for it as we speak."

Tom said, "If they were trying to find out about our meeting, then the word has been leaked; but maybe they haven't found out anything. We've got to be extremely careful! They may know more than we think.

CHAPTER FORTY-TWO

Dutch Hall and I were sitting in my office when the phone rang; we heard Penny pick-up and say, "Colonel Miller's office. Yes sir, General Drakeford, Colonel Miller is in and General Hall is with him. Just a moment sir while I put your call to his phone."

"Good morning, Sam," I said as he answered. "What's the boss doing in so early on a morning like this? Yes, sir, he is right here drinking my coffee and eating my doughnuts," I laughed as I handed the phone to Dutch.

"Don't believe anything he says, Sam; I bought the coffee and doughnuts and Penny made the coffee," Dutch said laughingly. "What's going on here in the big house? Bull and I have been looking for something to do besides drinking coffee."

Sam replied, "Well, guys, some of that coffee drinking may be coming to an end. You just may have a job waiting. Bob Walters called a few minutes ago and wants us to meet with him in his office in an hour. I believe you know Bob already; you met him when we got together at that Italian restaurant down in Foggy Bottom, a couple of weeks ago. He is the Deputy Secretary of Defense and carries a lot of weight among not only the military complex, but the 'big wheels' of the House and Senate too!"

"I guess if our 'boss's boss says show up for a meeting, we show up for a meeting," Dutch said.

"I'll see you there in about an hour," Sam said.

Dutch and I made our way to the second floor office of the Secretary of Defense and waited for Sam when we spotted him coming down the hall.

"Good morning, Gentlemen. You ready to go in to see the boss?" Sam asked.

"About as ready as I'll ever be," said Dutch.

We were greeted by Bob Walters's secretary as we entered, "Good morning, gentlemen. I'll let the secretary know you're here. Would you like some coffee?"

"Yes, thank you," said Sam. "I'm sure Bob already has his."

"I think he is working on his third cup right now," the secretary said with a smile.

She went into Bob's office and came right back and said, "You gentlemen can go right in. Mr. Walters is waiting for you. I'll be back in a few moments with your coffee."

Bob stood as we entered and said, "Come on in, Sam. Dutch, Bull, how are you guys making out on your temporary duty here in the Pentagon? Are you finding enough to keep you busy?"

Dutch replied, "Well, sir, we've been right busy so far. We've had to go buy additional coffee about three times now, and I think we're getting a little low again."

"If we get any busier, and I drink much more coffee, I'll have to apply for disability," I added and then said, "It was almost a relief getting shot at and almost blown to hell and back."

"I heard about all of those attacks on you two and your secretary; I believe the Sergeant is your secretary, Bull?" Bob asked. "How is she taking it? I'm sure it shook her up pretty much,"

"Pretty much the same as Dutch and me; she is tough, and a combat veteran too. She lost her husband in Iraq, and then she was wounded in Afghanistan herself," I replied.

The door opened and Bob's secretary came in carrying a tray with a carafe and several cups on it along with a plate of sweet, breakfast treats; she sat them on a side table and said, "You gentlemen help yourself, there is plenty more; just give me a buzz if you need anything."

After everyone had their coffee cups filled and sat down, Bob began, "First, let me say that I appreciate you coming; also, as a matter of comfort, I had the offices checked for listening devices—bugs—so we can be sure what we say here stays here. In fact, one of our men who sort of does double duty here, as a contractor and as a special agent for a couple of Intel agencies brought his team in early this morning and did the sweep. I believe you know him—Rick Winstead—his office is in the basement. He is also a retired army veteran. You all are aware of, and have a designated responsibility in the meeting Saturday evening. As you know, we have a problem of real urgency facing us in this 'Land of the Free.' We are losing our freedom, our country! We are losing our very nation that so many, throughout history, have bled and died to defend! I don't have to explain any of that to you guys—you have lived it—and many cases, almost died for it! Gentlemen, we cannot let that happen; we will not let that happen! At least not while I live and breathe!

"Vice President Joe Bradley and I have talked about it for quite some time now, as have you and many others throughout every agency in the government. Well, with all that has been going on lately, it's coming to a head I believe in two ways; from the folks that believe as we do; to the ones who have the idea that they can take control of this nation, and change everything the founding fathers sought, for the benefit of the people of this country."

Just then, the phone on Bob's desk rang and he picked up. He hesitated a moment and said, "Send him on in."

The door opened and General Mike Holder, a member of the Joint Chiefs of Staff and the Chief of the National Guard, came in.

"Come on in, Mike," Bob said. "I believe you know these gentlemen and that your paths have probably crossed somewhere over the years."

"Good morning," Mike said and added laughing, "Not only crossed, but I think a couple of them have tried to run me over at times out in the field."

The secretary brought in another carafe of coffee and a cup for Mike and sat it down and Bob told her to hold his calls for a while.

"Gentlemen, the reason I called and asked you to come over to my office is to discuss, briefly, the meeting Saturday night." Bob began. "I just want to feel secure in knowing we have our ducks lined up in case any type of trouble rears its ugly head. Based on the past several days, I honestly don't know what to expect—it could be anything from nothing, to all-out war—seems some folks don't mind shooting and killing people or blowing them and their families up."

Then, turning to Mike, he asked, "Mike, how do you feel about Saturday? Do you have any thoughts or suggestions or thought of anything we might have forgotten or overlooked?"

"No, sir," Mike answered. "I have double checked with each of my field commanders and they have been briefed and have followed-up with the various unit commanders. They all assure me that they are prepared for any event that may take place. In fact, they even seemed a little anxious and hoping there would be a little fireworks. The ones I've spoken with are still pretty upset over the killing of Chip Reese and his whole family, especially when they mention Chip's kids. I think you'll find everything in order and ready to go, sir."

Bob looked around at the rest of us and asked, "What do you guys think? Is there anything we may have overlooked or not thought of?"

Dutch replied, "I think we have all the bases covered. Bull and I have gone over each step; it's really no different than laying out a battle plan, which, in actuality, it is."

I spoke out and said, "We've coordinated with Mike and some of his units and they are ready and will be in place early on Saturday." I looked to Mike and said, "I don't know how you're going to pull off moving some troops around without people noticing and asking a lot of questions."

Mike responded, "It is extremely critical that we not mention any of this to anyone outside this room; there are others that know, of course, they have assignments also. We can't let this get into the wrong hands. With the Guard, we are always moving troops around, repositioning, training, etc., so most people who pay any attention will just assume it is just another normal day in the Guard."

Bob, looking engrossed in deep thoughts, said, "You know something? We should have seen this coming several decades ago. I guess our 'little minds' don't always grasp some of the happenings that are going on around us all of the time. Back in the 1950s, Henry Kissinger wrote a book *A World Restored* on how to return the European Continent to a peaceful order. In hindsight, if we had read the book well, and maybe read a little between the lines, we could have seen days like this coming. Personally, I believe it is a prelude to what some power brokers are striving for—a new world order! A world run by a select few powerful men, with the governed having no voice in the government or who runs it."

I said, "Bob, you mean like the bunch of idiots we have in this country who are calling for open borders, anyone can vote in any election, no more immigration—everyone belongs, like, come on over, we'll feed you, educate you, heal you if you're sick, and on and on and on! Hell, we'll even pay you to live here! Yeah, I recall reading and hearing something about it off and on for several years, but to tell you the truth, I never paid that much attention to it, until now, that is. When I received the President's Executive Order telling me to release those Jihadist sons-of-bitches to a country club prison here on the mainland, it made my insides boil over. And I'll tell you, the President, or anyone else, I will not be the one to unlock the cage to let the bastards out; I'll die first," I declared!

"That goes for me too," Dutch added!

Mike stated, "That will make at least three of us! That's the very reason I accepted command of the United States National Guard, to protect the homeland; this nation that our forefathers fought so hard for, and bled, and died for. Nope! I'm with you, Bull; I won't help unlock the gates either!"

Sam, who had been sitting listening to the comments, spoke, "You folks have refreshed my memory a little; it seems that I heard something several years ago about a plan to overthrow our government, to tear it down and rebuild it in another form; I believe that is where I first heard the term: *New World Order*. If I recall correctly, it was supposed to be a ten to fifteen year plan; each step was laid out almost in an outline, to-do-list order. The first, and major part, was to weaken the United States around the world. I guess maybe the infamous 'Apologetic Tour' was to set the stage. This would be followed by other efforts that would further weaken the government; such as getting extreme liberals and nutcases elected to office; locally, state, and nationally—the U.S. Congress; I believe that has been well accomplished! Other areas are to weaken our military, and they sure as hell have accomplished that," Sam continued, "Fund terrorist groups here and abroad, flood the country with illegals, leak classified information, and help North Korea and Iran get nuclear weapons. The second part of the plan is to completely destroy the country! They have never, in the past, seemed to be in a hurry to accomplish everything. I don't have any idea why all of a sudden they seem to want to get moving. If we stop and think and look at some of the kind-of-subtle things that have been going on during the past few years, and if we start connecting the dots, it becomes quite clear. I don't remember all the different things, but just a few should make us sit up and take notice. For instance: open borders, everybody gets to come in, close military bases around the world, get rid of the Electoral College and go to a popular vote, and the list goes on. Can you imagine the U.N. as the entire world's governmental body?"

Then, after a pause, Sam added, "Anyway, let me get off my soapbox and let somebody else get up there. Let me just add one more thought to all this: we better make a difference in our venture this week or it's all over; we won't get a second chance to act."

Sam looked around and everyone nodded in agreement.

Bob spoke and said, "As Deputy Secretary of Defense, my role here is limited. Any decisions I make goes through my boss, Robert McIntire the Secretary of Defense, for final authorization. However, I'm not one hundred percent sure just where he stands, or which side he would come down on if the chips start falling. I kind of believe his heart is in the right place, but, and this is a big but, he was appointed by the President—the President gave him the job and he seems to like it. I spoke with him about the Guard's special training exercises tomorrow night, and strangely he smiled and said 'Good, they need that; just be sure to tell them to watch their ass, you never can tell who prowls around in the dark.' It surprised the hell out of me. It was almost as if he knew all about it and was giving his approval!"

Mike stood up and wandered around the office, thinking, and then said, "That explains the mystery I've been dealing with for the past several days, maybe a week. He just 'happened' to stop in my office to see how things were going with the Guard. We chatted for several minutes and he asked if I thought the Guard was well trained and 'up to snuff.' I haven't heard that phrase in many years. He sort of closed out our conversation by saying something to the effect that 'It's always comforting to know the Guard is on duty here at home to protect us.' Then as he was walking out he said 'Stay safe and keep your troops safe,'" Mike added.

"That kind of fits in," Bob said, "He has his oath of office framed and hanging on the wall in his office; the line with 'both Foreign and Domestic' is underlined."

Dutch said, "That may well tell us where he stands."

"Especially after hearing what Mike said," I added; "almost like he was warning us or perhaps giving us some advance notice. Hell, I don't really know what to think anymore!"

With that, Sam stood and told the group, "Well, gentlemen, if we've covered everything, I need to get back to my office. I've got a ton of things to get done before tomorrow. It seems we have all bases covered. I, for one, will be glad when tomorrow is behind us and we can have a drink and say, 'Well done!'"

"So will I," echoed through the room as each got up and headed for the door.

CHAPTER FORTY-THREE

As we left Bob Walter's office, I said, "Let's go back to my office while we digest some of this crap and get our heads together about tomorrow night."

"What's so special about your office? Why couldn't we just go to my office?" Dutch asked smiling.

"Well . . . General, my office has the coffee . . . and the coffee maker!" I replied.

"You really mean your office has Penny; then the coffee and anything else comes afterward," Dutch said and laughed. "I've known you too long, my friend, and I've seen the look on your face when she walks into the room. You're not kidding me. You like her and are quite fond of her, aren't you Bull? In fact, I feel quite sure the feeling is mutual. I've seen her face when she's around you. And I've seen her concern if she thinks something is going to happen to you."

"You're out of your mind, Dutch. I'm twenty years older than Penny," I replied. "She's not interested in being tied to some 'old fart' like me. Besides, she is too attractive and young; she would fit in better with someone her own age. I will admit I am very fond of her; she is very efficient as a secretary and pleasant to be around; I enjoy her company."

We entered my office and Penny jumped from her chair with a big smile on her face. "Well, I'm glad to see you two survived the big meeting and hopefully got some details about tomorrow night's shindig. Ya'll sit down and I'll make some coffee and you can tell me the gory details," she said as she went into the coffee room.

When Penny came back with three cups of coffee, Dutch asked, "Penny, do you have plans for this evening? I thought maybe the three of us could go to dinner for a change and enjoy a quiet evening."

"Me? Plans?" Penny exclaimed. "I wouldn't know what to plan for or where to plan it. I'm new to this place too. I think dinner with you two would be very nice and I would love it."

"That's great. I'll do some checking and make reservations. That suits you Bull? Georgetown is full of nice restaurants," Dutch added.

"Sounds good to me," I said.

"Does anyone have any particular preferences?" Dutch asked "You'll find a little of everything in this small 'city-within-a-city'—steaks, Italian, all-American, just name it."

"What about the place we met when we were here before? It had great Italian food; we watched them hand-make the pasta. That's also where some of the 'big-wigs' eat, people like Presidents and congressmen," I added with a laugh.

Penny said, "Pasta sounds really good to me, if it suits you guys."

Dutch took out his phone and pulled up Google and punched in maps of restaurants. "Here it is," he said; "The Filomena Ristorante." Then, he punched the call button, and a minute later he said, "We're in; reservation's for 8:30 this evening. Hope that's not too late."

"Let's head over there around seven o'clock," I suggested, "We can just stroll around the famous Foggy Bottom area and show Penny some of the sights."

"Okay; it's a date, and it sounds like fun," Penny said. "But you know how ladies are. If we're going for a night on the town, we have to have something new to wear. I'll need the afternoon off to go shopping; my field uniform just wouldn't feel right, especially if I'm in the company of two distinguished gentlemen."

I looked over at Dutch. Dutch looked back at me and I grinned and asked, "Does that mean you would like my bank account to go shopping with?"

"Well, from what I hear about the prices, I might need two bank accounts to get what I need. Remember, my other clothes were blown up and burned?" Penny replied and added laughing. "You could just sign a couple of checks and leave the amount blank."

"Maybe you just better take the afternoon and go on your shopping spree," Dutch grinned. "We'll stay here and guard the bank!" Then more seriously, he added, "But, Penny, pick out something really nice. Splurge on yourself; you deserve it. Don't worry about the price. I've seen Bull's bank account and money is no problem!"

The three of us laughed as Penny picked up her purse and started out the door. She turned and said, "I'll meet you back at the house by six o'clock," she closed the door behind her.

At seven o'clock, I heard the knock on the door between our rooms. I opened the door and suddenly caught my breath. I thought I would faint dead-away, for there stood before me the most beautiful woman I thought I had ever seen!

"Penny. . ." I stammered. "I, um, I don't know what to say. You are absolutely gorgeous; you take my breath away!"

A voice from the other doorway said, "You're off to a good start. Tell her how beautiful she really is," the voice belonged to Dutch, and he entered the room.

Penny was grinning like a teenager waiting for her prom date! "Do you like it?" she asked, looking at me, and glancing over at Dutch. "I'm not over doing it?" she added.

The two 'dumb-founded' men spoke in unison, "It's perfect!"

After catching my breath, I said, "If you two are in the mood for a little walk, we can just stroll down to the restaurant; it's only about five or six blocks or we can take a cab."

Penny held out her leg and said with a smile, "I would really like to walk, but with these new shoes, maybe we could take the taxi and get a little closer. I don't think my combat boots go very well with my new dress."

"I agree!" said Dutch.

We stepped outside and were ready to hail a taxi when one pulled up. "Taxi," the driver asked? "Jump in. Hammadi take you to the finest dining in all of DC. I recommend I take you to Farmers Fishers Restaurant, where presidents eat, even James Bond eat there, no?"

"No," I said. "Take us to the Filomena Ristorante, not too far from here, in Foggy Bottom, on Wisconsin Avenue."

"No, no. I will take you to Farmers Fishers. You will like it most well, I think! Food more good!" the cabbie replied.

I leaned forward and touched the driver on the back of the neck, saying, "You will take us to the Filomena Ristorante I think, or you will be out of this taxi, I'm sure!"

"Okay! Okay," he said in a kind of panic. He got on his radio and spoke excitedly, supposedly to his dispatcher—in his native language—Farsi or some other mid-eastern dialect; "Yes, yes, I know."

I reached behind Penny's back and poked Dutch on the shoulder; Dutch turned his head toward me and nodded that he understood.

About three blocks from the restaurant, I told the driver to pull over. I paid the driver and we three got out and began walking in the direction of the restaurant. The taxi sat in place for several minutes watching us, the driver stayed on his radio; I kept looking over my shoulder, keeping my eye on the taxi.

Walking between the two, Penny hooked her arms in the arms of me and Dutch and said, "You don't have to tell me. I know what's going on and I'm keeping my eyes open too. Don't worry about me I can take care of myself when I have to. You both be careful."

Dutch replied, "You're too darn smart, Penny."

We were about a block from the restaurant when we saw two men in long black coats step out of a doorway and begin slowly walking in our direction. I asked, "It's a little warm for such big coats, don't you think Dutch?" I reached behind my back to the waistband and slowly withdrew my old, M1911, WWII .45. The thought went through my mind, *this old fellow has been with me in a lot of scrapes, and brought me home each time.*

"Sure as hell is," Dutch replied as he reached behind his back and came out with a Smith & Wesson 9 millimeter, magazine already inserted. "I'm locked and loaded," he said quietly. "You take the one on the left I've got the one on the right."

When we were about twenty-five to thirty yards away, the two men in long coats stopped suddenly and pulled the coats back and brought up automatic weapons! Before they could get off the first burst, me and

Dutch dropped to our knees and fired point blank; the men in coats dropped where they stood without getting off a shot.

From only a few feet behind us, we heard a volley of five shots. We jerked around with weapons raised, to see Penny on one knee arm outstretched with an S&W .38 revolver in her hand. At the same moment, we heard a vehicle's engine racing, tires screeching, and then the vehicle careening across the sidewalk and slamming into the front of a small dress shop.

"What the hell," I yelled?

Penny said breathlessly, "I guess their partners were waiting in the vehicle to take them out of here before anyone could see them. When you shot the other two, the window of the vehicle went down and I saw the weapon stick out, aimed at you, I guess to finish the job. I already had my weapon out so I just fired!"

We stood over the two dead men in long coats and made sure they were no longer breathing. "Good shooting, Dutch," I said.

"Likewise, Bull," Dutch responded.

We took Penny by the arm and walked over to the vehicle which was half in, and half out of the dress shop. There were two dead men inside! The one on the passenger side, who probably was the shooter, had a hole in the middle of his forehead; the other had a hole in the right side of his head.

Dutch and I stopped in our tracks.

"Damn," I said! Where did you learn to shoot like that?" I asked Penny.

"I told you that I spend a lot of time on the range back at GITMO; it gives me something to do," she replied.

A crowd was gathering rather quickly; we had put our weapons away knowing that if we didn't get the hell out of there, the rest of the evening would be spent at the local police station, answering questions we couldn't talk about.

Dutch, spoke first and asked, "Well folks, what do we do now? I do think, however, that we should move along before the cops arrive."

"I bought a new dress and shoes for an evening out with two friends; I'm not going to let it go to waste. Besides, I'm hungry for some good pasta. I hear that this restaurant over there has the best in all of DC!" Penny said.

As soon as we were seated, we saw a gentleman approaching the table, he spoke with the Maitre'd and then turned to me, "Senator Lindsey Scott is sitting over there and he asked me to invite you to join him and his friends, if you would like. They're sitting just over there near the ballroom."

I looked to Penny and then to Dutch, both nodded their approval and slid their chairs back to get up. I noticed the entrance and saw a large number of police and others who were probably plain clothes police looking around the restaurant.

As we approached the Senator's table, he stood and greeted them. "Bull, Dutch so good to see you again. Penny—more beautiful than ever! I have known many soldiers in my time, but I have never met another soldier who looked as gorgeous; it is good to see you here in the States. Although I have my doubts about the company you keep," he added smiling.

Penny blushed, smiled, and said, "It is so nice to see you again, Senator."

Lindsey then introduced them to his dinner mates, Senator Harold Reed and Congressman Dennis Wilson.

There was a lot of friendly chit-chat around the table as we got to know each other. I was a little surprised that the group included Senator Harold Reed, the top Democrat in the Senate, a staunch opponent of Republican ideology, but a strong friend of Lindsey—complete opposites when it came to their ideology—and Dennis Wilson, Democrat Representative and next in line for Speaker of the House.

After a while, Lindsey leaned over to me and Dutch and asked, "Are we all set for the meeting tomorrow evening? I hope there won't be any trouble or real disagreements. Everyone that I have heard from who is planning to attend is in complete agreement and considers the action absolutely necessary. By the way, what was all the noise and screaming about just before you guys came in. In fact, I thought I heard gunfire, cars crashing, and who knows what else."

Me, Dutch, and Penny looked at each other then back at Lindsey; Dutch spoke first, "A couple of guys took a few shots at us as we were walking to the restaurant!"

"What?" the Senator asked in a slightly raised voice. He caught himself and lowered his voice as others at the table turned to look in his direction.

"Sorry," he said, and then turned back to us. In a whisper he asked again, "Somebody was shooting at you three? Here outside the restaurant? With all those people around? My God! Those people have to be crazy!"

Dutch looked up and saw Dan Black coming their way; he was followed several feet behind by Mel Pierson. Dutch pointed to me, Penny, and Lindsey Scott, "Anyone like to guess why the Secret Service and FBI are heading in our direction," Dutch asked?

We all turned to look.

"Nice to see you folks," Dan said as he approached the table.

Mel walked up also and greeted the group, "I'm glad I ran up on all of you together, in one place, saves a lot of time trying to locate and get two, three, or more people together in this town; it takes forever."

Lindsey said, "Hey, Dan, Mel; so good to see you. Have a seat and join us. We've been having a drink and talking, and I think we're about ready to order dinner. Please join us. I believe you know everybody here."

Mel said, "Thanks. That sounds good to me. How about you Dan? Have you had dinner yet?"

"I've just been waiting for somebody to ask," Dan replied. "But I think I'll have that drink you mentioned first. It's been a tough day and the evening isn't looking any easier either."

"What's going on?" Lindsey asked "Are you and Mel involved with all that racket we heard? People screaming and yelling. It sounded like they were coming into the restaurant, sounded like gunfire and cars crashing, too. It seems as if somebody is always shooting at somebody in this town!"

Mel said, "It seems as though these two 'highly refined' gentlemen were escorting a beautiful lady to this very restaurant, and apparently there were a couple of other men who stepped forward to protest. From what we can tell, at the moment anyway, they were going to do their protesting with automatic weapons. Evidently, from a couple of witnesses who saw them, they didn't anticipate the 'refined gentlemen' might not agree and may resist. Anyway, these 'refined gentlemen' pulled weapons of their own and about blew the heads off the other two!"

"Meanwhile," chipped in Dan, "a large, black vehicle came toward the sidewalk at a high rate of speed, evidently to run down the two gentlemen, when suddenly the, I'm sure frightened, beautiful young lady dropped to one knee, with a revolver in her hand. She squeezed off several shots; a couple caught the gunman on the passenger side in the head and another two got the driver. That's how the vehicle landed inside that small dress shop, two doors over from where we're sitting!"

Lindsey, Harold, and Dennis sat quietly, dumbfounded for a full two minutes. Finally, the Senate Majority Leader, Senator Lindsey Scott, made the profound statement of the evening, **"DAMN!"**

Just then, Dan's phone beeped. He answered but before he could say anything, somebody was giving him a lecture about something.

When he could get a word in edgewise, he said, voice rising slightly, "I don't give a shit who you want to send in there. Those three people are working directly for me and it is my job to protect them, and my folks have instructions to do so at all costs. Are we clear on that? You best keep your people away from my safe-house, better yet, tell them to stay the hell out of the Georgetown area!" And then after another pause, he added, "You know what, I don't give a shit if you are the President's Chief of Staff, and I really don't give a rat's ass what the President said or wants! I'm just doing my job and I aim to keep on doing it. If he wants to fire me, he can sure as hell do it tomorrow! In the meantime, call your 'doom' squad away from my house, and do it now!"

Then turning around to the gathering around and after he had quieted down somewhat, Dan said, "That bitch thinks she is the president."

He looked at Penny and the others and said, "Sorry, Penny, but she gets on my last nerve! I apologize for the language and getting so upset; you're not supposed to see that in me!"

Lindsey let out a chuckle and said, "Well said, Dan; I do believe you have probably expressed the opinion of all of us who know her."

Harold Reed said, "That goes for me. I can't stand having to talk with her! I avoid it every chance I get."

The food came and all indulged and changed the topic of conversation to more pleasant subjects.

After dinner, the group sat chatting about various subject matter even though they all knew that upper most in everyone's mind was the meeting tomorrow night, especially after the attack on Bull and his friends.

Dan pulled a chair between me and Penny and in a quiet voice told us, "You won't have to worry about your safety anymore, tonight at least. I have a car that will pick you up anytime you're ready to go back. Also, I have agents stationed around the safe-house 24/7 so you can rest comfortably." He looked at Penny and placed his hand over hers and said, "I apologize again for the language, Penny; however, from what I've heard so far, you are very capable of taking care of yourself. That was some pretty sure-fire shooting you did, especially in the dark at that!"

I grinned and said, "I'll tell you one thing, Dan. I wouldn't want her on the other side in any conflict. She can handle herself and a couple of others to boot!"

Penny smiled and said, "Thanks. I try to stay on ready just in case it's needed. But what happens after tomorrow night? I know about the meeting and all of that; but what if the decision doesn't go the way it's anticipated? After all, we're talking something major, in fact criminal if it's not pulled off. Heads will roll, and I don't mean figuratively, but literally! We think the shooting tonight and the attempted bombings were serious enough, but it can get a whole lot more serious afterwards!"

Everyone sat silently. We knew Penny was right!

CHAPTER FORTY-FOUR

It was pretty much a sleepless night throughout a large segment of DC; morning didn't bring much relief either. You could feel the tension in the air across the city. It was six a.m. and General Mike Holder had been up for more than two hours already, working the phones from his office. He was calling for reports from his commanders in the field; they were responding with positive information. All units were in place—under cover, camouflaged—and had been since midnight. They were ready, come what may!

He got another cup of coffee and sat down at his desk just as the phone rang. He looked and saw it was his boss, General Sam Drakeford, Chairman of the Joint Chiefs of Staff. Mike picked up the phone and said, "Good morning, General. You're in mighty early and on a weekend, at that."

"Well now, it seems as if you are in pretty early yourself, Mike," Sam responded. "Since I wasn't sleeping very well, I thought I may as well come in to the office and take care of a few little things."

"The same reason I'm in early too, Sam," he laughed; "Come on down. I've had coffee going for over an hour."

"Heat it up and I'll be right there," Sam replied.

When Sam walked into Mike's office he was greeted by a roomful of people. He looked around. Me, Dutch, and, of course, Penny were among them. Then there were Paul Moseley, Bob Walters, Rick Winstead, and Vince Dawkins. It looked as if the entire Pentagon command level team was here. Before he could get inside, Dan Black, the White House Secret Service head honcho, walked up.

Mike said in a loud voice, "Come on in and join the crowd. Who called this meeting anyway?"

Amid the laughter, Vince said, "Didn't you guys ever hear of sleepless in Seattle? This is just a small sample of sleepless in DC. This goes on every night in this city!"

"By a lot more people than are here," Rick said.

Mike looked around the room and said, "I know everybody knows one another, but just to be sure, you best get to know Sergeant Penny Fulbright. You may think you're one of the toughest military people in this crowd, but I assure you, until you meet her, you don't add up!"

Everyone turned and looked at Penny; they raised their coffee cups in salute and said "Hear, Hear!" while Penny turned ten shades of red, blushing.

Mike continued and said, "Just yesterday, while her two, armed escorts, were busy taking out a couple of attackers, Penny dropped to one knee, calmly pulled her weapon, and dropped two more who were going to run down her escorts! Now I ask you, who was taking care of whom?"

The room was filled with laughter as Penny attempted to hide behind me and Dutch.

After the group settled in for a few minutes, Sam looked over at Mike and asked, "Mike, since you were here so early and probably haven't been to bed tonight at all, why don't you update us on this evening's meeting and any special plans that you know about?"

"About all I know for sure is that the Vice President is coming also, and will speak to the group," Mike said. "I believe he will address some of the recent attacks and bombings that has killed a large number of people, mostly I think, all government-type folks. In light of all the killings, he and I, and I'm sure several others of you also, had some conversation with him about the possibility of something happening before, during, or after the meeting. So I talked with Sam and some of you about taking precautions, just in case; we don't want to be caught off-guard. If something was to happen we would be prepared to handle whatever the situation called for."

The room was very quiet when Dan spoke, "He said don't be too sure what these 'buttheads' will do, or won't do for that matter! Among my people over at the White House, we have picked up some scuttlebutt about a 'major event' that is going down very soon. My people are worried and very concerned; they reported to me that many of our agents have been taken off their regular assignments for the time-being. Some have been ordered to visit out of state offices to check on unimportant memos and suspicions. Several in Intel reported to me that IT has intercepted text messages and emails concerning the 'Big Event' is at hand, and inferences to 'time is short,' 'we are gaining ground,' and crap such as that. It has most of my people worried. Add to that, those agents who have been sent away, have all been replaced by others of shall I say, foreign descent! Not surprisingly, though!"

After a moment's pause, he added, "Then just this morning, John Beaman, whom you all know, and who is the President's Intel Chief tells me that the President will be meeting with the Joint Chiefs of Staff and other key leaders, here in the Pentagon. Sam, I'm sure you don't know about that yet, and you didn't hear it from me! None of my regular Agents or teams will be here; it is restricted to only those whom the President,

John, and that asshole, Chief of Staff, his personal guide, Susan Brice, feel are necessary!

"He hasn't given any of us a simple explanation or the slightest clue about what it's all about. That's my biggest worry at the moment. Although me, and my agents work directly for him we never know for sure what's going on; my personal opinion is there is some sort of conspiracy going on! And, I think that most of us here pretty much know what that conspiracy is—to take control of the government of this country! They intend to make the United States an Islamic nation; it's all part of the new world order that we've heard about over the years."

Dan continued, "Just think for a moment: Afghanistan used to be Buddhist, now it's Muslim;   Lebanon used to be Christian; now it's Muslim! Many European nations are beginning to see Muslim majorities in their country; they are powerless to stop the growth. Their mission is to destroy the country then rebuild it as a Muslim country. They are to prey on the weaknesses of the people of the nation by destroying the very basic beliefs our founding fathers fought for and believed so dearly that they wanted to pass it on to us. We cannot let this nation be destroyed from within! They have created mistrust between our people, they have established Mosques, grown their population, and weakened our education and religious systems. They have introduced ideas such as 'transgender, etc.; even this President has openly said, 'you are what you say you are'! In one state, they have introduced a bill instituting Sharia Law! But, gentlemen, I'll say one last thing: 'Bullshit, NOT ON MY WATCH!'"

Dan sat down as the room grew very still and quiet; no one knew what to say. They just knew the feeling was mutual throughout.

After a long quiet spell, Vince Dawkins said, "Folks we are all set for tonight, Bubba has been cooking for the past three days and says anyone who doesn't get enough bar-b-que to eat, it won't be his fault. So put on some stretch pants and enjoy."

I spoke up and told the group, "I know, or at least think, that all of you carry a weapon most of the time. And, I don't think we expect any problems tonight, I think the secret has been well kept; however, in light of what has been happening recently, I would recommend that you have your weapon on you tonight. As many people as know about the meeting, there is always that chance the word has leaked to some of the wrong folks. Just as a precaution, keep your weapon handy, all day!"

Mike added, "I believe everyone here is aware that we have some National Guard units in operational mode. Only you folks, and maybe a couple of others, are aware of that, and it is highly classified, so please don't mention it to anyone outside this room."

Dan looked to Sam before speaking. "Sam, you and me and who else, I don't know, have to get our heads together and work out a schedule for the President's meeting here on Monday. Even though I have been taken off the agents' attendee list and replaced, I am planning to be here anyway. I have spoken with the President's personal White House Physician and was told that the President hasn't been feeling too well the past week or so," he said with a sly smile on his face.

"I'll be here also; in fact, I received notice to be available to accompany the President to the podium," Sam replied.

Dan added, "Additionally, I have alerted several other agents, who have accompanied and guarded the President on his many other visits, both in-country and out, to be here, unobtrusive, but available in case of emergency. And of course, the news media will be here in all of their 'glory' to kiss the President's ass at his every word; maybe they will get a little surprise this time!" he added.

Turning to Dutch, Sam asked, "Dutch, will you take charge of the, I'll call it, the 'Pentagon Element'? And keep order and control of what happens in the conference room itself, and see that everyone is safe and security is maintained? The major problem that I can see right now is possibly with the media; they may run wild! I have already notified those who need to know, that you will be running the show from that end. You're from the 'old corps.' You know what needs to be done and when to do it. Semper Fi!"

"Semper Fi! Got it covered, Sam. I'll have Bull and Penny as my back-up!" Dutch said.

"From what I hear, if you have Penny, Sergeant Fulbright, on your side you won't need anyone else," Sam laughed.

Penny just grinned as everyone looked in her direction.

"If nobody has any further questions or comments, I guess that about covers it for now.

"Remember, somebody is out there watching each of us—individually—stay alert be aware of your surroundings at all times, stay armed; I'll see you tonight out at Bubba's."

CHAPTER FORTY-FIVE

Twelve-thirty—lunch time in the Pentagon Cafeteria; Major General Gary "Dutch" Hall, Sergeant Penny Fulbright, and Me --- Colonel James "Bull" Miller; all dressed out in Class A, military uniform, walked into the cafeteria. On any other day, a two-star general would not turn a head, much less a colonel or an enlisted person, female or not. For some reason, this day was different!

From different tables across the dining room heads turned to watch as the three entered; they looked around and saw many hands raised with a "thumbs-up" sign. Dutch and Bull looked at each other; Penny cleared her throat and spoke softly, "What's going on?"

"Beats the hell out of me," Dutch replied.

"You guys know something? I don't believe we are the only ones here who know there's going to be an event. How much they know is another story," I said!

"Well at least they're giving a 'thumbs-up' sign; they must agree with whatever they think is going to happen," Penny said.

The three of us went through the food line and started looking for a table when we saw Rick standing and motioning for us; he already had a table and was waiting on us to arrive. Rick already had his food; we sat down and joined him.

Rick grinned and said, "I assume you saw the greeting you received; you folks are celebrities right here in the Pentagon. Unbelievable!"

"Yeah, but what do they know and how much to they know, that's the million dollar question," said Dutch.

"On the other hand," Penny asked, "How did they find out? Surely, if this many people know about tonight, then the other 'buttheads' most likely know also!"

"We've got enough 'buttheads' in this place already; we don't need to add more to the population," Rick commented.

"Well . . ." I added to the fire, "If we are successful, we may be celebrities; but if we fail, we will be 'Butts' running around without the 'head.'"

Rick asked, "What time do you plan to go out to Bubba's? I understand it is about a two hour drive, depending upon traffic, of course. It is the weekend, and everybody will be rushing to get out of town.

Dutch replied, "I would like to get there before dark and have time to take a look around Bubba's farm for a bit before the meeting. I understand it is very large, a couple hundred acres or more."

"It is pretty much a commercial style farm also, from what I hear," said Rick. "I have never seen it or been near it, but I hear he has a lot of migrant workers to harvest the crops, and he grows several types of produce items. Plus, he raises his own hogs for his bar-b-que places; he has two or three restaurants scattered around the city.

"You may want to leave here around four o'clock; that will put you there just before dark, about dusk, and the field workers will be gone by then. The farm is situated in the middle of a real forest; it gets dark quickly. Bubba will have fires going and lights on, might be a little chilly after dark, too. It might be a good idea to wear a light jacket," he added looking at Penny.

Just then, Dutch's secure phone beeped and he answered. It was Dan Black. "Hi, Dan, what's up?" he asked.

"Dutch, I just wanted to check in with you guys and see what time you wanted to head out to Bubba's this afternoon. A couple of my agents will pick you up and drive you there. I would come for you myself but I'm going out earlier; besides, I think it may be best if we go separately anyway. We don't know who may be keeping an eye on us," Dan said.

"Hold on a second," Dutch told Dan and turned to the others. "What time do you want to head out this afternoon? Some of Dan's men will pick us up?"

Rick said, "I'm going to leave town around two, myself, I need to talk with Bubba and a couple of others before the crowd gets there. I would recommend you three head out no later than four; it'll give you a few minutes to look around after you get there."

I said, "Let's make it three or three thirty, I would like to get there a little early also."

"Dan, how about three o'clock?" Dutch asked.

"Okay. My folks will pick you up at the safe house at three; wear comfortable, outdoorsy type clothes. You won't be in the city," Dan replied.

"Will do; we will see you there," said Dutch, "Watch your back, Dan!"

I said, "It's after one now; we may as well leave here and go on back to the house now. By the time we get changed and ready to go, Dan's guys will be there"

As we got up and started out of the cafeteria Dan told Dutch, before he hung up, "I'll let my people know you're on the way home."

I drove and as we approached the house we spotted a man and a woman near the front; I pulled the rental car into the drive beside the house and parked near the back of the drive. I said, "They look a lot like government agents. I hope they're the friendly kind."

Penny said, "They must be the regular agents Dan has positioned here 24/7 to protect us—I hope; they don't look too mean."

We got out of the car and as we came back around to the front of the walk, the two agents came up and introduced themselves as members of Dan's group, assigned to keep an eye on the safe-house.

The male agent stuck his hand out and told us, "Hi, I'm Agent Leo Jenkins and this is Agent Marsha Jones. The house is clear; no one has been near all day. Dan sent a message that y'all were on the way and would only be here a short time and then leaving again. Another agent is at the back to keep an eye on that area; we don't want anybody hanging around. Dan also said that one of our vehicles would be coming by at three to pick you guys up; we'll keep an eye out for it."

We thanked Leo and went inside.

It was ten to three when Penny looked out the window; she told Dutch and I, "I see a large black, government-looking car pulling up and the male agent is going over to it, the window is down and he is talking with the driver. I guess they must be the good guys."

"Okay, people; let's roll," Dutch said; "We're supposed to find out what the plan is tonight." He grabbed his jacket and we headed out the door I had already opened.

As Dutch took the first step down, his left knee cracked and gave way slightly, he caught himself on the wrought iron rail; as he moved, something hit the brick next to the doorway about head high and shattered pieces of brick.

"Get down," I yelled! Leo ran up the steps toward them. As he did, the back of his head exploded! The female agent was immediately on her wrist radio, weapon drawn, looking around the area; they had not heard any sound, but training and experience told them there was a sniper looking at them.

Just as suddenly, two shots hit the vehicle but the two agents were already out on the ground behind the vehicle, weapons out and trying to determine where the shots had come from; they were both on the radio also, calling in help. Within a few minutes, they heard the sirens and police cars; within another few minutes, they heard a chopper overhead.

Me, Dutch, and Penny were all on the ground, weapons raised, ready to return fire; if only we could see where to fire and what to fire at!

I said, "That bum knee just saved your life Dutch, maybe all three of us; someone sure as hell wants us dead and out of the way."

"Evidently, we have made some-damn-body very unhappy," Dutch replied.

All of a sudden, the place was swarming with agents and police; they looked up and saw the chopper just above the buildings, ropes went down, and several agents were rappelling down.

"We're surrounded," yelled Penny above the noise. As she looked around, weapon still raised and ready to fire, she spotted the female agent on the ground, bleeding. Without another thought, Penny crawled across the grass over to where the agent lay; she was still breathing and moving. "Hang in," Penny told her, "We've got plenty of help here and we will get you out of here."

Penny saw an ambulance and medical personnel, she yelled out "Medic! Over here!"

The two medics came running carrying their medical bags. Penny already had the agent's pant leg torn open and was applying pressure to the bleeding coming from her upper left thigh.

"How bad is she hit?" one medic asked.

"I don't know, but before she passed out, she said something hit her in the leg," Penny replied.

Dutch and I, weapons still in our hands, came running up to Penny. I grabbed her hand and asked, "Penny, are you alright? Are you hurt? You really had us scared; you should never run out into an open area without knowing where the fire is coming from. You could have been hit!"

"Just scared," she replied! "Actually, it's no different than Afghanistan or Iraq; you see a friend hit you don't stop to think, you just react; it's instinct, I guess."

Two choppers were screaming up and down several blocks surrounding the safe house, watching rooftops for signs of a sniper or snipers; no idea if there may be more than one or not. Chatter was coming from the multiple radios of police, FBI, firemen, and whoever else was on the scene. After being somewhat assured the sniper had fled, we were up and moving around, weapons still in our hands.

Mel Pierson came over to us and above the radio chatter, the whomp, whomp of the choppers overhead and told us he was glad to see us unscathed and walking about.

He also said, "We've got a report coming in now that on the Northwest side of town, on a country road just off the GW Freeway, a car that had been following Senator Scott, all the way from the Capital Building, began taking shots at them! Fortunately, his guards, who are special agents, had noticed the vehicle as they left the Capital and kept an eye on it; so they were ready and expecting some sort of attack. As

Lindsey and his group approached a heavily wooded area, the vehicle, a large, black SUV, government-issue of course, started closing in on them.

"As soon as the agents saw the window go down, and the upper part of a body lean out, with what looked like an automatic weapon, they didn't wait for the first shots; the two agents leaned out of both sides of the Senator's vehicle and blew the other vehicle, and its occupants away! The last they saw of it, it was trying to go through a large stand of trees off the side of the road, upside-down! Neither the Senator nor any of his agents were injured. It looks as if we may have some big trouble in store tonight. They targeted you three and the senator on the same day, almost the same time; they must know about the meeting tonight. This is about to turn into a real skirmish or a small war. I certainly hope not, but we are prepared just in case. I have every available agent on duty and attending tonight; Dan will have all of his people there also," Mel said.

I said, "Mike has a guard unit out there for 'training' purposes; I'm pretty sure no one knows about that, at least not yet. But, if they try to interfere they will find out in a hurry, I believe."

"We have no idea what their tactics may be, but like I said, we're prepared!" Mel replied. "It looks like your driver is trying to get your attention; I believe he is ready to leave. You guys be careful and stay safe! I'll see you out there shortly, as soon as I finish up here."

Me, Dutch, and Penny got into their waiting vehicle, a large, black SUV, government-issue type, with the driver and two other agents. The driver turned his head toward the back seat where we three sat; he reached out to shake hands and said, "Hi. I'm Tom Williams; my shotgun rider is Sam and the ugly agent in the very back is John; we're your escort for the rest of the day and evening. After all the crap that's taking place around the city today, we are going to be extra careful, and we are going to keep you safe!"

The vehicle pulled away from the curb and headed west out of DC.

CHAPTER FORTY-SIX

It was a long and uneventful, two-and-a-half hour drive to someplace in the middle of nowhere, in the western part of Virginia's mountain ranges; three hours if you figure in a couple of potty stops along the way.

"Does anybody have any idea where in hell we are?" asked Dutch.

"Beats the hell out of me," Agent Williams said. "All I know is this is where the GPS told us to go; now, all we have to do is find a narrow dirt road leading off into the woods. It's supposed to have a metal farm type gate which was left open for us; also there is supposed to be a sign telling us where to turn."

They continued down the narrow, state-owned, state-paved road, paved with what looked like left over blacktop that had been re-melted and poured before it melted completely. It was as rough as an old-time washboard.

I told the driver, "There's a sign on the left, up ahead; that must be it!"

The sign read, "WELCOME MODERN DAY MINUTEMEN" The driver made the turn onto the narrow dirt road, which was more like a path in the woods—just wide enough so farm trucks and other farm equipment would have no trouble making it in and out again. In fact, the driver noticed what looked to be tracks of some heavy vehicles or machinery of some sort.

He told the others, "Looks as if we're not the first or only ones here; there has been some heavy equipment on this road recently, at least in the past couple of days anyway."

Dutch said, "We must be a couple hundred miles out of DC. I hope the folks find their way out here. You could get your ass lost out here and no one would ever find you. Sorry, Penny. I don't have the slightest idea, direction-wise, just where in hell we are."

Penny, who had been sitting quiet said, "Well, we're here anyway, wherever 'here' is; I guess we'll find out soon enough, if this road goes anywhere. We must be getting near because I can already smell the bar-b-que cooking."

As we drove on, one of the agents said, "I just saw a jeep and another military vehicle off to the right in the woods; it looks like one of those Humvees that carries troops inside."

"I wouldn't be surprised," I answered, "I think a couple of the National Guard units are on a training exercise in this area; this may be the place, if it is you may see troops on the ground," I looked over at Dutch who grinned; we knew Mike Holder was on guard!

Soon, we came to a clearing; both sides of the narrow dirt road were pretty much clear of trees; crops of some sort were planted and growing throughout the open area. We couldn't go much faster than about fifteen miles per hour, and after another fifteen to twenty minutes we came to Bubba's Pit—the pit where Bubba and his helpers barbequed the pork. In order to provide freshly cooked bar-b-que to his restaurants, they had to keep the fires going six days a week, every day except Sunday.

Off on the Southside of the field we saw quite a few cars parked, early arrivals; our driver pulled into the area and parked; we all got out and started walking toward two large, open sided buildings. Both had a concrete floor, a roof, and large wooden posts to hold it up. Two rows of long, roughly hewed tables, with matching bench seating, stretched from one end of each building to the other—enough seating space for over a hundred people to eat comfortably.

I saw Dan and Dennis Wilson in a group talking and pointed them out to Dutch and Penny so we, and Agent Williams, headed in that direction.

Agent Williams said, "I don't really know what all is going down out here tonight, but all of our available agents are out here somewhere; somebody is expecting something big to happen I believe. But I do know we are prepared if it does."

We heard cars arriving and turned to look back at the way we had come in, several cars were coming in at the same time, driving slow because of all the ruts in the dirt road. We went on up to the group standing with a coffee cup or bottled drinks in their hand, talking about the events of the day. It seems that word of their attack had preceded them; also of the attack on Lindsey Scott. Sam Drakeford, Vince Dawkins, Harold Reed, Mike Holder, and Bubba turned as we approached; there were about fifteen standing and sitting, just 'shooting the breeze.'

"Welcome to the country," Bubba said. "I'm glad you could make it; it's going to be a rather interesting evening, I believe."

Mike said, "I just got word from Senator Scott's escort agents. They have picked up the Senator's guest and are on the way—should be here within an hour."

Vehicles kept arriving and the crowd continued to get larger; there were at least a hundred people here already. Bubba asked Dutch if he, me, and Penny would like to take a quick run around part of the farm in his jeep; we jumped at the opportunity to see open acres.

Penny said, "There are a lot of very important people here. I've probably seen most of them on TV at some point, being interviewed or questioned in committee hearings, or some type of investigation. It kind of looks like Congress is meeting out here tonight. Wouldn't it be nice if both houses of Congress could get together and agree on something?"

Dutch said, "Now, that would be a miracle in itself. The two bodies haven't agreed on much of anything in the past several decades. It's amazing that any type of bill ever gets far enough for the President to sign. I guess it has been going on since the 1780s, even before the Constitution was drafted." Then after a moment of thought, he added, "But never quite this bad. There is a lot of animosity between this President and both houses. I feel sure they are being pushed on by a bunch of foreigners whose mission is to take control of our government from within."

As we returned to the center, I told the group, "There's Senator Scott arriving and that's the Vice President, Joe Bradley with him. I didn't know he was coming. I'm surprised!"

"I'm glad he is able to be here," said Bubba. "He and his wife were almost goners with that attack when they tried to blow him up; killed a bunch of agents though. I'd like to see the bastards who did it hang!"

"We all do, Bubba, and we're going to do all that we can to see that happens," I said.

Mike told them, "If any of those Jihadist sons-of-bitches try anything tonight, it'll be the last thing they'll ever try; I grant you that!"

We turned and saw several others approaching, including: General Paul Moseley, Vice Chief of Staff, the top man in the Air Force, Dan Black, Mel Pierson, and a number of others. The crowd had increased and there was probably more than a hundred-fifty. Most had already taken a seat and were waiting for the order to eat.

Bubba walked up to the podium and microphone and spoke to the crowd. "I want to thank all of ya'll for coming out here to Bubba's old farm in the woods. Getting here takes a while but when you get here you have to admit, the bar-b-que is worth it. We are going to go ahead and start eating but you'll have to serve yourself. Folks, this is extremely important stuff we're going to be talking about and it may be hard to talk about, but believe you me, it's gotta be done! When I hand over this microphone, I ain't gonna take it back anymore tonight; I'm through talking. But right now, I want to ask the Chief Pentagon Chaplain, Major General Howard Stanley, to come up and say a prayer and bless this food; we truly are a blessed nation! God bless ya'll and stay safe."

Mike Holder was on his radio talking with his unit commanders, "Stay on the alert and watch for any movement in the woods or fields and report back to me concerning anything that looks out of place or not natural to the area," he told them.

While everyone was still eating Bubba's bar-b-que, Senator Scott went to the microphone.

"Good evening, all. For those whom I haven't met, I am Lindsey Scott; I am a U.S. Senator from the state of South Carolina. Please continue eating and I will try to update you concerning this special event tonight. As I'm sure all of you well know, we are losing our country! Right now, this nation that so many have fought so hard for, and died, is going to hell in a handbasket. Congress has not been able to pass a single measure for the past six years, and it's getting worse by the day. This President has vowed not to let any conservative legislation get through the house or senate, that if one does that he doesn't agree with he will veto it. Also, as many of you who are familiar with the White House and the President's staff, know that the majority are of foreign descent; they have no real allegiance, nor respect for this country, our flag, our national anthem or anything pro-American! Personally, I believe we have a bunch of traitors running the country. What they are trying to accomplish is a coup—taking over the government completely. This has been in the planning stages for many years by a well-known multibillionaire who has formed organizations; more than a hundred of them, all over the world; but now the time has come. There is a strong element in the country trying to establish the 'One World Order' system of government; a group of individuals who see themselves as 'saviors' of the world. This small group of powerful men would control the governments of all countries. They have a ten to fifteen year plan to destroy the United States. I won't try to go into all of them, but just a few include such goals as: replace the folks in congress who are effective, replacing them with outrageous individuals who want power and are willing to stir up trouble to get it, weaken our military by closing military bases, dramatically cut military budgets, leak classified information to the media, stir up controversy by leaking rumors concerning the Supreme Court and the justices to the press, and the list goes on and on. But that is just the first phase of this plan! Then there is Phase Two of the plan; move forward as quickly as possible to the final destruction of our country! They are even willing to destroy the economy, the economy that made them multi-millionaires and multi-billionaires! And of course, they know in order to accomplish this, they must ban and control weapons; then to keep control, they must do away with the Electoral College and install the popular vote! They will try to revise the constitution to read the way they want it to. We have already seen much of this happening throughout the nation. Open borders for example and completely destroying our immigration system; I know what you're thinking—**UNBELIEVABLE! IMPOSSIBLE!** But, folks, I ask you is it?! Just think for a moment about what has already taken place. But, ladies and gentlemen, I am here tonight to tell you that we will never let it happen! That is the reason we are here, in this place right now. Every one of you has known and has been pretty sure of what this is to be about. I'm also sure that you have known and realized the possible danger it imposes of each of us. I believe it was our fore fathers who said a couple of hundred years ago, and believed it so profoundly that they included it in the constitution, 'Governments are instituted among Men, deriving their just powers from the consent of the governed, -- That whenever any Form of Government becomes destructive of these ends, it is the Right, it is the Duty of the People to alter or abolish it, and institute new Government'. Those same men, fully understanding their responsibility and the risks thereof, said, 'We mutually pledge to each other our Lives, our Fortunes and our sacred Honor'! I'm telling you; that is exactly what we are doing tonight! Now, before I introduce someone very special, I want to tell you in my very own personal words: As I stand here before you tonight, I pledge to each of you my very life, my fortune, and my sacred honor, and depending on the protection of the divine providence of Almighty God, we shall set the United States of America on the right path of freedom again!"

The crowd broke into a crescendo of applause, yelling, and responding, "Likewise for me too! I pledge all that I am and have! God Bless America!"

"Now, let me introduce you to someone you already know very well, the Vice President of the United States, Mr. Joe Bradley!"

CHAPTER FORTY-SEVEN

As the Vice President stepped forward to the podium whistles, hand clapping and yelling was enough to drown out any other sounds. Vice President Bradley waved to the crowd as the noise got louder; then he motioned for the group to begin quieting. Slowly, the noise level went down a few decibels, enough for him to begin speaking.

"My friends, my fellow countrymen, my fellow Americans, thank you for such a welcome and for coming out tonight. I realize it is a major inconvenience to drive so far and on a Friday evening at that, but I am glad that you did and that you are here. We have some important things to get accomplished. But before I get into all of that, I just want to let you know that as of midnight Monday, I will no longer be the Vice President of the United States!"

Shock went through the crowd. Some were yelling "Why not? Who is pushing you out? What is going on, Joe?"

The Vice President continued, "I have tendered my resignation effective Monday at midnight; my resignation was delivered to the President and each member of Congress at five o'clock this afternoon. I will not go into all the reasons for my decision other than to say I can no longer be a part of a movement to destroy our country! I did not know what was going on; or maybe I was too infatuated with the power that came with the position. That doesn't matter any longer. I stand here in personal disgrace and embarrassment of what I found that I have been a party to for these past several years, and I humbly apologize and solicit your forgiveness and prayers for the future of our great nation. Furthermore . . ."

But the Vice President was suddenly cut off by the sound of automatic gunfire that seemed to be coming from the wooded area back toward the highway; then the sound of explosives. A mortar round hit and exploded about twenty yards from where the Vice President was standing at the podium, kicking up dirt and shaking the earth around them; this was followed by sprays of automatic weapons fire, some hitting the building; the crowd dropped to the ground and began scattering and spreading out. The Vice President's Security Agents immediately had the Vice President on the ground and was covering him with their own bodies, weapons drawn and looking for the source of the attack. Fortunately, no one in the pit was hit or injured. No one knew the status of the troops in the field.

General Mike Holder, Commander of the National Guard, stood and yelled, "Everyone take cover; we are under attack. Stay down and get behind something, keep your head down, and stay out of sight! We have Guard troops in the field and they are returning fire as we speak." Mike was on his radio with his commanders in the field getting minute by minute reports. "Don't let them out of the field, hold them where they are! Our 'Articles of Engagement' is to return fire if fired upon; we have been fired upon—take their sorry asses out!" he said into his radio.

The group heard the sound of trucks and heavy machinery moving, men yelling commands to the troops, probably the sound of a tank or two. An RPG round or another mortar round hit closer to the buildings this time, shaking the earth around the ones who were taking shelter there. Me, Dutch, Penny, and several others who had been involved in planning the event jumped up and yelled to the group to spread out, not congregate close together. With weapons in hand, we went through the buildings spreading the word telling them that the Guard had everything under control.

A mortar round or RPG round hit the front pit building and destroyed it completely; there had been a half dozen people still inside when the rounds hit. Those inside had flattened themselves on the ground and had spread out when the fireworks first started; maybe, just maybe, none were killed!

I gasped for air and pushed some of the debris off me and crawled out from under the large table I had crawled under when the first mortar round had hit. I decided it was my smartest move of the day.

"Damn!" I said, "That was a little too close for comfort." I stood and brushed more dirt and pieces of wood from my clothes. I checked myself and found nothing bleeding or hurting, I yelled to the Vice President's Secret Service agents, "Get the Vice President and Senator over to the wooded edge of that back field; there's an underground bunker there. It's about fifty yards across the field, take that ATV or you can run it but be careful! You'll see the top of the bunker above ground level; it is heavy but has a spring loaded cover. There are stairs leading down into a large room; he will be safe there. I don't see any troops or action in that area so you shouldn't have a problem getting to it, but keep your eyes open just in case."

I started pulling debris and pieces of wood from the building and tossing them to the side and yelling, "Penny, where are you? Dutch, where are you? Can you hear me? Are you in the building? Answer me," I yelled over and over. "Penny, Penny, can you hear me? Yell out; I'm coming. I'll find you; hang on! Dutch, can you hear me? Yell out if you can!"

From the back of the open building, Dutch yelled back , "I'm back here and I can hear you loud and clear; you're yelling loud enough to wake the dead. I'm alright. Are you okay? Where's Penny?"

"I'm looking for her now, Dutch," I yelled back; "If those sons-of-bitches, ass-hole Jihadists have harmed a hair on her head, they will pay; I will blow every one of them to hell and back and then I'll kill every damn one of them again!"

Dan Black, head of the Secret Service told the agents, **"GO FOR IT!** Get the VP and Senator to the bunker now! Stay with them and don't let anybody else in or even close without my approval, got it?"

"We're all over it, Dan, don't worry; a piss ant won't be able to get through us," one of the agents said.

Penny came running up carrying an AK-47 automatic weapon. She threw her arms around Bull and cried, "I thought you had been killed when I saw the building go up and I couldn't see you or see anything move; it scared the hell out of me!"

I hugged her tight and said, "I'm okay, Penny. I was so worried about you; I couldn't find you. I thought you were in the building too. Where were you? Where did you get that AK-47?"

"Just before the last round hit, I thought I saw movement behind the building and I went to check on it. It was a couple of those Jihadist bastards trying to sneak up behind us and pick us off with this AK automatic; when they raised up, I just blew their heads off and confiscated their AK-47s. They won't be trying that again. But that's just when the mortar round hit the building; I thought it was all over. Where is Dutch? Is he alright? Have you seen him?"

I loosened my hugging arm a little and she lifted her head and loosened her grip on me; she blushed and smiled and said, "I'm sorry

Bull, I . . . I . . . I was afraid I would never see you again; I shouldn't have run up and grabbed you, I'm sorry . . . ."

I retightened my hug and interrupted, "You sure as hell should have, and need to again! Penny, I was scared too. I thought you were still in the building and I was afraid that I had lost you!"

Penny hugged him even tighter as they stood there.

A voice came from across the pile of debris and said, "Well, it is about time that you two admitted to what I have known all along—that you belong together and are good for each other. Now, no more beating around the bush! I'm happy for you!"

It was Dutch, as he stepped around to them. Penny and I backed up a little, looking somewhat embarrassed and smiling.

Penny looked up across the shoulders of me and Dutch just as dirt kicked up from the ground and wood chips few from the building where we were standing; she saw something in the air. All of a sudden, it occurred to her what it was; then, she spotted several more and she called out, "Bull, Dutch, look up and get ready! We are getting attacked from the air!"

She yelled to Dutch and tossed him one of the two AK-47s she had been carrying; she raised hers and pulled the trigger letting loose a volley into the air at the attackers.

Dutch yelled out as he raised the newly acquired AK-47, "Damn; that looks like hang gliders coming in! They're all dressed in black and hard to see; keep your eyes open! That's why we never heard them, hang gliders have no engines to make noise; they just drop the troops right into the middle of the target."

Dirt started kicking up all around the buildings, tearing holes in the roofs and playing hell with the big posts supporting the roofs of the buildings. With my .45 in my hand, I ran out of the building, looked up and saw flashes of automatic gunfire coming from the hang gliders; I couldn't see the person firing, I raised my gun and fired at the source of the flash. It flashed no more.

I ran over to where Penny was leaning against one of the support posts. With her AK-47 raised, she squeezed off several rounds in a quick volley that sent two gliders out of control and spun to the earth; above, the noise they heard screams.

"Damn good shooting, Penny. Are you alright?" I asked.

Heavy vehicles were coming out of one side of the open fields, from the woods; there must have been eight or ten heavy trucks, troop carriers. In the dim glow of gunfire and explosions, we could see dozens of men, all dressed in black jumping off the back of the large, six-by trucks; military vehicles designed to haul troops and supplies onto the battle field. But these definitely were not on our side! Suddenly, scattered from all across the open fields helmeted heads popped up and opened fire on the approaching trucks.

Grinning, Dutch said, "Man, I'm sure as hell glad that Mike Holder and his troops are on our side!"

"Our guys are really cutting their asses," Penny yelled excitedly. She had run out into an open area just as one of the gliding enemy troops landed beside her. As he hit the ground, she raised her weapon right in front of his face and pulled the trigger! Another hit the ground his AK47 ready, Penny dropped to one knee and blew his head off. She pulled the glide chute from him and grabbed his AK47.

Meanwhile, me and Dutch had picked up AK47s from other dead gliding troops.

Dutch looked around and motioned for them to look around. He said, "The civilians are taking cover; thank goodness, they are staying out of the way. I was afraid they would panic and begin running in every direction and get shot."

"They must have more than a hundred troops attacking;" I yelled above the noise, "I don't have any idea how many Mike has on the scene. There are several more of those six-bys still coming and troops in black pouring over the side."

Dutch, myself, and Penny had placed ourselves in a position to protect the people in the bar-b-que buildings, though there was only one building left. We kept our AK47s locked and loaded and finger on the trigger. We had spread out and as an enemy approached we would cut him down with a quick burst. We heard helicopters and looked up, out to the field of battle, which it had turned into, and saw four Boeing AH-64 Apache helicopters, attack gunships, slowly rising above the treetops, coming in low over the field; they flew from one side to the other to get perspective. As they made the turn to get into firing position, we saw the blazing trail of a rocket launched from one of the trucks; the first Apache, with his underbelly exposed, exploded in a ball of fire as the rocket hit the underside sending pieces of shrapnel flying in all directions. There was a crew of four on board.

I said, "Shit! That does it; you guys stay down. I'm going out to the field and take those bastards apart. That was a surface-to-air missile and I guarantee they have more. I'm going to find the truck with them and send them straight to hell!"

Penny and Dutch both yelled, "No, Bull; the troops are in the field and they know where the missile came from! Don't go running out there!"

Then, Penny pleaded, "Please, Bull, don't go out there. We've got enough troops to take care of it; please don't! You can't do it by yourself; if you go I'm going with you!"

Saying so, Penny stepped forward.

Mike who was standing nearby with his radio in his hand said, "That did it! Take the bastards out," he yelled in his radio!

In nanoseconds, two Apaches came screaming in at low level, fifty calibers firing a non-stop barrage of fifties out of both side doors at enemy troops in the field. In less than ten seconds, a rocket was launched from the lead Apache and blew the first truck into smithereens. They could hear screams and yelling as the troops on board blew apart. Those watching from the bar-b-que pit area could see body parts fly through the air as fifty caliber shells and missiles found their mark! The second Apache came screaming in right behind the first and launched one of his missiles also; that one must have hit an ammo truck. The night lit up like the midway on a busy night at the state fair in South Carolina! The troops dressed in black stood out like a sore thumb in the bright light of the explosions. Mike's Guard units were moving in and "cleaning house!"

Some of the invading troops jumped up running trying to get back to their trucks; as they began one of the Apaches sent a missile into the middle of the group of assholes as they ran—they ran no more!

Survivors started standing with their hands high over their heads with no weapon; they had thrown their weapons down and wanted to surrender. As they did, one of the trucks fired off another surface-to-air missile at the third Apache; the pilot had received warning on his radar of the launch and incoming missile. He immediately evaded and veered off to his left as fast as that Apache would move. The missile screamed by, narrowly missing, and landed in the huge wooded area—probably killed a few trees, maybe a deer or rabbit.

Meanwhile, as soon as the missile was fired, another of Mike's Apaches had locked in on the source and fired his own truck buster, it hit and the truck and its crew were, as I said, "Sent straight to hell!"

Dutch looked at me and said , "It looks as though Mike's guys have got them surrounded and are closing in to mop up this little skirmish. I think most, if not all, have put their weapons down and standing where they are with their hands on top of their heads."

"A little mop up and take these shitheads in, put them in our trucks and haul their sorry asses to a compound somewhere," I said. Then, I added, "I wish they would let me handle them, they sure as hell wouldn't attack anybody else—ever! They would never see the inside of a court-room either, which is probably where they will wind up, and they know it. I would cut their ass and send them to their virgins in Mecca," I added.

Penny, still carrying the AK47 she had taken off one of the attackers when she shot him, came back over to where me and Dutch were stand-ing. "This is damn hard to believe," she said! "A major military attack right here in the US, with missiles, bombs, attack troops dressed commando style. Are we sure we're still in the US?" she asked.

We were, standing there with AK47s resting on our hips, looked at each other and laughed.

I said, "It beats the hell out of me! The last time I got tangled up in a mess like this was probably twenty-five years or so ago, Grenada or someplace."

"I wonder how many of our guys got it," Dutch asked. "I'm sure none of the guys in the chopper got out; it pretty much exploded and killed all on board. Mike will be letting us know, I'm sure."

Mike came up about that time, still barking orders to his com-manders in the field and receiving reports. He told us, "We're just clean-ing up and completing the mission. We've had one helluva night; they had more troops than we thought they would bring in, but they were no match for our guys; hell, they started running scared and trying to get the hell out of there when we opened fire; we caught them off guard, they didn't expect to find all the resistance that hit them. We really didn't expect them to have surface-to-air missiles, and actually use them here; I'm certain that when we examine some of the shrapnel we going to find foreign markings on them, probably made in Iran or Russia or some similar place."

Mike's radio crackled and he hit the button and listened for a moment and then said, "Good, keep the prisoners separated and have the medics look at their wounded, the medics have body bags for the dead they'll handle that and take them to Guard Headquarters. We won't take them to a morgue just yet, and we certainly do not want the media to get hold of any of this yet, either."

Then, he added, "What's our casualty count, dead? Wounded? Give me a report as soon as you get it. Yeah, I know the four guys in the chopper are gone; I hope there are no more."

The air was filled with the smell of gunpowder and the stench of explosions that kill, especially your own men and friends, although even above the stink, there came the beautiful odor of cooking bar-b-que!

With the battle ended, almost all of the original guests had decided they had enough for one evening and got into their vehicles and were on the road out of the woods. Bubba came over and told the ones who were still there and just standing around talking, to keep eating; he was still cooking.

Bubba called out to Mike, "General Mike, I don't have any idea how many troops you have out here, but I think I just may have enough bar-b-que to feed the whole damn lot of them; they surely have earned it tonight. Why don't you let them know that when they get through doing whatever it is they're doing, to come on and help themselves? I'm sure we have enough to feed a couple hundred or more, and it's still hot."

Mike's troops had cordoned and roped off a large area in the middle of the field closest to the pit area and placed guards strategically around the area. The operations command team leaders came in from field positions and gathered in the bar-b-que hut.

Sam Drakeford, as Chairman of the Joint Chiefs, headed up the team with Vince Dawkins, Dutch, me, Penny, Mike Holder, Paul Moseley, Mel Pierson, Rick Winstead and Dan Black making up the rest of the team. None were in military uniforms; tonight, all of us were patriots, defending their country!

As we sat around a table with coffee cups, some eating more bar-b-que, Sam looked around and said, "We have a damn good team here. We may all be getting a little older and while some think the fight has gone out of us, I guess we have shown them. There was some great planning behind this operation and we pulled it off without a hitch. Different service branches, different ranks involved and it came together—that's American military at its best!"

Always the one, I proclaimed loudly, "Damn, we're good!"

It lightened up the mood and everyone laughed a good hearty laugh; a laugh of relieved pressure.

Sam said, "I do have to recognize one of you guys as pretty damn special. That person is the only one of us who doesn't wear eagles or stars on our uniform, but provided excellent foresight and help in the overall planning and execution of this operation. When I first met this Non-Com, enlisted Sergeant, she was as nervous as a mouse in a room full of cats; she said she was seeing too many stars and wasn't used to being around them; it made her uncomfortable. But from what I've been seeing, and what I saw of her tonight, those of us with stars or eagles ought to get nervous and uncomfortable. Penny, I saw you in action tonight; you saved dozens of lives; you got the people to take cover and stay out of the way and you posted yourself to take the brunt of any attempt of attack on them. I also saw several of those hang-gliding, jihadist almost land on top of you just before you blew them to hell; you must have shot at least half a dozen. I, and I'm very sure all of us here, are so damn proud of you and glad you are with us, not only as a fellow soldier, but also as a friend!"

Everyone jumped from their seats and clapped and cheered and toasted her with their coffee cups! They came up to her to shake her hand and congratulate her.

Dutch and I were standing off to the side watching and grinning like Cheshire cats. Dutch looked over at me, reached into his pocket and pulled out his handkerchief and handed it to me; he'd seen a couple of tears in the tough old eyes of his best friend.

CHAPTER FORTY-EIGHT

Monday morning broke bright and early for the different ones on the Special Ops Team; the weekend had finally calmed down and was quiet; no mention on any news outlet or media of any of the happenings on Friday night. Now, they had a noon meeting to look forward to with the President of the United States speaking to all leaders of the Pentagon, military, civilian, contractors, and anyone else even close to being in a leadership position.

Sam Drakeford was in his office by seven o'clock. Robert Walters and his boss, the Secretary of Defense, were in at seven also. The Secret Service driver and agents watching over me, Dutch, and Penny dropped us off at the front of the Pentagon at seven. As we entered, we saw Vince Dawkins and Paul Moseley walking in together.

I commented, "It looks as if the entire Pentagon staff is arriving early today."

"Anticipation about the big meeting at noon," Penny said.

Dutch said, "I'm not real sure it will come off; the President's personal physician has been saying for more than a week that the President hasn't been feeling very well and that he is setting him up for a complete physical next week, probably at Walter Reed. He is keeping a close eye on him and not letting many people see him. I understand the President's personal guards, his so called Secret Service agents that Susan Brice assigned, have been rather annoyed and upset about not getting in close to the President. Susan is about to lose her cool; I hear she is fit to be tied. She has been limited on her access also.

"Dan said some time back that he was going to have his agents on duty whether the President's White House staff liked it or not."

"Yes, I heard Dan say he didn't trust those SOBs," Penny said. "Remember he told us that most of them were of foreign descent and he wasn't even sure they were citizens; he remarked that some mid-eastern country was taking the country from within. I think you recall Dan had quite a bit to say about it. He was, shall we say, very strongly against those people being agents—that they certainly were not his agents."

I smiled and said, "He did use some colorful language."

As we walked down the hall toward the elevators, we passed the Secretary of Defense himself, who smiled and said, "It's good to see you, I hope you folks had a good weekend."

"Thanks, Mr. Secretary, it's nice to see you again. I trust your weekend was safe and good also," Dutch replied.

"Not a typical weekend, to say the least. But still very good when everything turns out well and right," the Secretary responded as he walked on.

The three of us stood there for a moment watching the Secretary go down the hall; we looked at each other for a second, and then kept on toward our offices.

"I believe he just told us something very important," I said.

"A very strong message, too," Dutch added.

We went into my office since it was the first we came to; Penny went to her desk, me and Dutch went into my office and put our brief-cases down. I picked up my phone and buzzed Penny's desk, "Yes, sir," she answered.

I said, "Sergeant, we've been here thirty seconds or more, is the coffee ready yet?"

"Sorry, sir, I've spent the entire morning cleaning up the mess the boss left on Friday," Penny said with a chuckle.

At about ten thirty, we received an alert of a disturbance that was taking place near the entrance of the Pentagon. Dutch and I headed out of the office and told Penny where we were going and would be back shortly. On the way down, we met Sam Drakeford and Paul Moseley.

Paul said, "I wonder what kind of disturbance they're talking about; the President is due to arrive at twelve o'clock sharp! His chief White House aide said the President wanted everything set up so there would be no down-time, he had a lot on his schedule. The aide also said that the President was bringing his personal 'aides' and security with him and that the Pentagon security team would not be needed. I'm sure all of this bullshit came from his Chief of Staff, Susan Brice. But I've got news for her and his personal 'aides'. Maybe I should say his personal attack team! If they think for a second that they are getting into this building under the guise of 'Presidential Aides,' they better think again!"

Then, after a momentary pause, he continues. "I just had a talk with Bob McIntire and he thinks somebody is trying to stir up a shitpot full of trouble by bringing in a bunch of people that aren't needed since our security teams have always provided whatever security was necessary and for whomever necessary. I understand that Dan Black, head of the White House Secret Service, is already here; he and his agents are the ones primarily responsible for the President's safety. I also hear that he is pretty pissed at this point."

When we arrived on the VIP level, we could hear discussions and conflicting comments coming from a couple of men, one of whom sounded like Dan Black, the Secret Service Director himself. It sounded as if coming from the VIP Entrance, where the President would be making his entrance. Evidently, Dan was not a happy camper with whatever was going on. As we turned the corner into the hall leading to the entrance, we could see a stand-off between two groups.

Dan was standing with five of his agents, face-to-face with eight men, dressed, incidentally in black business suits. The presumed leader was arguing with Dan, trying to convince him that his men were to take charge of checking the auditorium and points where the President would be appearing and visiting.

The vocal person told Dan, "Susan Brice and John Beaman, the President's Chief of Intel, sent us over to prepare for the visit and to post our agents in their appropriate positions, as usual."

"Bullshit!" said Dan; "You don't have a 'usual' position in setting up anything as far as the President is concerned. You can just go back to where you came from and tell whoever sent you, they can go to hell! This is my job and my department's responsibility; we already have agents in position and everything is on schedule. We're just waiting for the President to show up. Now, take your men and get the hell out of here; you're not authorized to be here."

The man glared at Dan with steely eyes and said, "I'm sure we will be back with the President and we will see whose responsibility it is."

He and his followers then turned and went back out of the door. Dan and several of his agents, as well as Dutch, me, Sam, and several other Pentagon officials, watched them drive off . . . in large, black, government-issue SUVs.

As the Pentagon onlookers dispersed, Dan came up to Dutch and the others. "Gentlemen, don't quote me on this, but I think shit is about to hit the fan in the Pentagon! It may get worse than the plane hit on 9/11," he said!

Admiral Vince Dawkins, Chief of Naval Operations, came up and called Dutch to one side. Dutch followed and asked, "What's up, Vince?"

"I would like for you to oversee the Pentagon Marine Security Detachment, starting right now and until after the President is gone. Colonel Robert Needs is Detachment Commander and he is very good, but I think he may have his hands full. He understands the job and has his troops ready and on standby."

Dutch replied, "Sure, Vince, I'll be happy to; maybe we can get this situation settled once and for all. I sure as hell hope so! Where will I find Colonel Needs?"

"He and his men are two doors down in a meeting room waiting for the word to come out, if needed," Vince said. "Get with him and you two stay in contact by radio; he will remain in the office with his troops while you are out here near the entrance. You'll need to keep a sharp eye on everybody and everything that moves—especially anything that makes a wrong move! The Pentagon Force Protection Agency will be providing back-up also. Not knowing for sure just what we might be faced with, we thought it best not to solely depend on them. They're usually a bit older than our troops and not as well trained."

Dutch said, "After Saturday night, I wouldn't be surprised at anything these jihadist bastards, and that's just what they are, home-grown terrorists, try, even here at the Pentagon! They are apt to try a full-scale invasion; I wouldn't put it past them."

Thereafter, Dutch went to contact Colonel Needs and coordinate their efforts. He found the meeting room and Colonel Needs—and thirty uniformed, well-armed, battle ready marines. He looked around and saw Colonel Needs coming toward him.

"Good morning, General," Colonel Needs said, "Admiral Dawkins told me you would be coming. I'm not sure just what we are specifically supposed to do yet, but I guess we'll find out soon enough, unless you already have the plan. I'm to give you one of the radios so we can stay in touch, and I believe with the Admiral and his team also."

He then handed Dutch the radio.

Dutch said, "Thanks. Damn Colonel! This reminds me of some old days, from years ago; I believe your men are ready to kick some ass!"

Colonel Needs and several of his men laughed, "Anytime it's necessary and they call on us, General; we stay ready! General Hall, I've heard about some of your involvements in past wars and battles, and, sir, my men and I are honored to meet you in person!"

Looking a little embarrassed, Dutch said, "Colonel Needs and men, the honor is all mine; this is a fine-looking outfit! I am happy the Admiral sent me to join you; I'll try to stay out of your way!"

"The President's entourage is pulling up to the entrance now," the radio crackled. "Everybody get in position."

The police motorcycle escort arrived first and pulled through the entrance way to the other side of the area, while four long, black, presidential limousines pulled in and stopped at the door; four large, black SUVs pulled to the other side of the limousine, and four agents, dressed in black suits, jumped out and took up positions beside the President's vehicle. Four others jumped from another vehicle and took positions at the entrance door to the Pentagon; as they did, four of Dan's Secret Service agents stepped forward and took their positions at the door, next to the ones who arrived with the president; the agents looked startled and looked back and forth at each other. Nothing was said, but everything was understood!

The President sat in his limousine while several of his entourage exited the other limos and vehicles and entered the Pentagon. The President's personal physician went to the door of the President's limo and the agent opened the door; the physician leaned inside for a moment and then came back out and the President followed. The President smiled and waved even though he looked and moved as if he could hardly make it to the entrance.

He was greeted as he entered by Vice President Joe Bradley who had arrived earlier, General Sam Drakeford, Secretary of Defense Robert McIntire, Susan Brice, his Chief of Staff, and John Beaman, his Chief of White House Intelligence. They smiled and greeted the President and began escorting him to the auditorium. The four agents who rode in his limousine, and were to escort the President, behind his personal aides, only got a few feet inside the Pentagon. Four of Dan's special agents stepped forward and assumed their positions; four more of Dan's agents moved forward and removed them to a side room near the entrance.

Dan came into the room; his agents had removed small automatic weapons from under the coats of the agents dressed in black and had them handcuffed and seated in chairs. In his earbuds, he got the message from his outside agents that six large, black SUVs, government-issue, were pulling in and they each had several people getting out. They're all dressed in black, the agent pointed out!

Dan spoke into his wrist mike, "Dutch, Colonel Needs, now, move out to the entrance!"

Five men got out of each of the SUVs and started forward toward the entrance; before they could get to the door, thirty uniformed, armed marines stepped out in their face with weapons at "port arms," ready to hit "fire" position, if necessary! The men from the SUVs were totally startled and caught off guard; before they could make a move to reach under their black coats, they were completely surrounded by marines. Colonel Needs told his men to relieve them of their weapons and thoroughly search them.

Then he said, "Lock these shithead terrorists away; if any of them make a move to leave, you know where to send them—hell is not that far from where they are standing!"

The prisoners looked around at each other, scared they might be shot where they stood. One yelled out, "You cannot do this. We are now citizens. We have rights. We will go to the courts. We will be out tomorrow; you'll see!"

The last bit, he said with a nervous laugh.

One of Colonel Needs men, a tough looking sergeant with stripes running up and down both sleeves and a chest full of medals stepped up and got in the guy's face; in a loud voice that he intended all to hear, he calmly said, "Asshole, this is the only court you will ever see; you will never see the inside of an American courtroom!"

The sergeant looked over at his squad leader; the squad leader looked over his left shoulder and instantly six Marines chambered rounds loud enough that it echoed off the walls of the Pentagon. The prisoner dropped to his knees and said, "Please, we were just following orders."

The sergeant said, "So am I, asshole!" He turned and walked away.

They heard the rumble of heavy trucks coming. General Mike Holder came out of the Pentagon. He told the group the six-bys were there to haul the trash away to a predetermined location.

The groups dispersed and went inside headed to the auditorium to hear the president speak.

CHAPTER FORTY-NINE

The auditorium was filled to capacity and everyone stood and applauded as the President entered the room. As he entered he seemed to wobble and caught himself with a hand against the wall, the other hand raised high, waving to the crowd of Pentagon employees—military and civilian. As his hand came down his physician reach forward to help steady him. As the physician's hand reached the President, the President winched as if in pain; no one saw the small needle in the physician's hand! Those accompanying him, Vice President Joe Bradley, Susan Brice, John Beaman, General Sam Drakeford and Robert McIntire, all stopped at chairs before the President reached the podium.

The President was sweating profusely and kept wiping his face with a handkerchief. Still smiling and waving to the Pentagon crowd, the President reached down and opened the folder with his speech. As he did, he wobbled again and fell against the podium and then to the floor. Immediately, his physician was by his side, as was his personal staff. The doctor checked the pulse and listened for breathing; then, he began CPR, pressing on the president's chest, and then began giving him mouth-to-mouth breathing. No response! Susan Brice and John Beaman kneeling by his side calling, "Mr. President, Mr. President, speak to me."

The whole auditorium was in turmoil. No one understood what was taking place. All they knew was that the President had fallen and had not been able to get back up.

The Pentagon EMS people arrived with their medical kits and went to work trying to resuscitate the president, to no avail. After working for what seemed like an hour, they said it's no use—the president is dead!

The auditorium was still in turmoil with the noise level so high one could not hear anybody speak. Robert McIntire spoke and told everyone to quieten down; he repeated several times before it began to get through and the people began taking their seats again. Finally, the noise subsided enough that the president's personal physician stepped to the microphone and made the announcement.

"Ladies and gentlemen, the president is dead!"

The noise level went up again with everyone talking and yelling, some into their cellphones. The noise quieted after a few minutes, after the initial shock had worn off.

The physician continued, "I am the president's personal physician and have been for the past five years. This is the worst and most devastating announcement I have ever had to make. Many of you I think knew that the President's health had been declining for several months. We can't tell yet, but we suspect the President suffered a heart attack."

Vice President Joe Bradley stepped to the microphone. "What a tragic day this is! My friend, the President of the United States of America, is dead!" He wiped a tear from his eyes. "This is so sudden, so tragic, so shocking; I . . . I . . . I don't have the words to express how I feel at the moment; like you, I am still in shock."

Robert McIntire and General Drakeford stepped forward and whispered into the Vice President's ear; he nodded agreement and turned back to the microphone.

"Ladies and gentlemen, I have just been informed, and under the provisions of Article II of the Constitution of the United States of America, upon the death of our President, I am now assuming the duties and responsibilities of this great office, the Presidency of the United States of America, effective immediately upon taking the oath of office. I see General David Graham in the audience, who is the Chief Staff Judge Advocate of the military. General Graham, would you please come forward and administer the oath of office so this Government may continue? May God have mercy! God Bless America!"

The next day, Tuesday, President Joe Bradley called his Cabinet together for a special meeting. When the Cabinet members were all seated, the President entered and everyone stood, applauded and welcomed the new President, the new Commander-in-Chief.

"This may very well be one of the shortest Cabinet meetings we will ever have," the President announced. "We will be keeping our routines for meetings each week; there will be some staff changes that I will be announcing in the next few days. I will ask that any of the staff who feels they cannot support, one hundred percent, what my administration stands for, to resign immediately. Likewise, if any of you feel that we cannot work together in harmony and accomplish great things for our country, I would ask that you consider resigning also. However, I think I know most of you well enough that you want only the best for the country. I would welcome all of you to stay and let's work together as a team."

The new president went on, "I will be making my selection for the office of Vice President later today. The name of the person I choose will be sent to both the House and Senate where they must be approved by a majority vote of both Houses. I have called a meeting with both party leaders immediately following this one to discuss the Vice Presidency. That's all I have for the moment; if no one else has anything to add, I will see you next week. Thank you for coming."

As the Cabinet members left they were met in the hall by leaders of both the Democratic and Republican Parties arriving for their meeting with the new President, who by virtue of his position, is head of the Democratic Party. The Democrats hold the majority in the House while the Republicans hold a slim majority in the Senate.

The Democratic representation included Louise Walker (D), Acting Speaker of the House since the death of Speaker Nancy Patrick, whose death was still a mystery. Representative Dennis Wilson (D); Senator Harold Reed (D), Senate Minority Leader; Senator Lindsey Scott (R), Senate Majority Leader; and Representative Bill Winters (R).

After they were seated in the Oval Office, the President walked in from one of the side doors; they all stood and greeted the President and shook hands and congratulated him, although under dire circumstances; they returned to their seats and the President sat behind his desk.

The President began, "As you are aware, I have to select a nominee for the Vice Presidency. I must admit I spent a sleepless night last night thinking about this. Also, for many years, since my days as a Senator, I have toyed with different thoughts and ideas about how our Government should operate and be governed. I will have my recommendations for Vice President later today and will make my selection then and will advise you immediately so you can act upon it. I asked you all here today in an effort for us to establish an air of unity; as a team working toward the same goals; a unified effort without regard to party politics; as servants of the people. That's why we were elected in the first place, to serve the people of the United States. Thank you for coming on such short notice, but I wanted to touch base with you. I'm sure we will be seeing a lot more of each other in the days and months to come. Again, thank you for coming."

As the party leaders were leaving, the President said, "Excuse me, gentlemen, but Senator Scott, could you stay a moment? I have a couple of questions I need the answers to."

"Yes, of course Mr. President," Senator Scott responded.

After the others had left, the President pointed to a chair and said, "Have a seat Lindsey, we can talk off the record for a little while, before someone burst through that door over there with another major problem."

Then President Joe went on, "Lindsey, we have known each other for a lot of years; we've gone fishing and hunting together, been on trips around the world together, and about any other thing two friends could do together. We have agreed and we have disagreed on many subjects; we look at politics a little differently, but we both look at what's best for this nation in the same light. I have always known you to be honest and tell things like they are. I don't believe, just because I now have the title of President, that you are going to be any different. If you agree on a topic, you'll say so; if you don't agree with me, you'll just tell me to go to hell. It's that simple!"

"Joe, you're doing all the talking, but I think you are leading down a path that you won't like," Lindsey said.

"Hear me out, Lindsey. I understand that we are of two different political parties; we differ on many issues, but we agree more than we disagree! I want to unify this nation once and for all—I intend to send your name to both Houses first thing tomorrow morning, naming you as the next Vice President of the United States! Will you accept?"

"Damn; I don't know, Joe, you are opening up a can of worms—a Democrat President and a Republican Vice President? What will the leaders of your party say? They will call you every name in the book and try to remove you from office. Are you sure you have thought this through, level headed?" Lindsey asked him.

The President smiled and looked Lindsey straight in the eye, "You may be in for a big surprise Lindsey; I half-jokingly broached the idea in a 'round about' way with a couple of my party's top names. They didn't find it funny; in fact, their comments were to the effect that the timing in this country could be just right. A couple have even said they are fed up and tired of the petty bickering and name calling that has been going on. Personally, I think so, too! What do you say?"

Lindsey sat there for several minutes; finally, he looked up and said, "Well Mr. President, since you put it that way, I can hardly say no! If that's what you want, and both Houses agree, then I will serve. Hell, Joe! That will make you my boss!"

CHAPTER FIFTY

Back in my office at GITMO, me and Sergeant Penny Fulbright were having our morning cup of coffee and discussing the events of the past few weeks.

"I still do not believe all of this happened and that I was in the middle of it," Penny declared.

I grinned and replied, "It is pretty remarkable and unbelievable!"

Just then, the door opened and Lt. Colonel Ron Phillips came in carrying a large white envelope that had big red letters stamped on the front and back "CLASSIFIED" and "TOP SECRET!"

I stood up and asked in a loud voice, "What the hell is that, Ron?"

I took the envelope, opened it, and found another envelope. This one also said "TOP SECRET!"

I opened the second envelope and pulled out the contents, the top page read, "EXECUTIVE ORDER."

"Oh shit," I yelled! "Don't tell me it has started all over again! I will tell them once more I sure as hell will never be the bastard to open the gates of this shithole and release these terrorist sons-of-bitches out on the public! No way in hell!"

Penny looked at Ron and then said; "Sir, open it and find out what we are supposed to do. Don't get so upset; you could have a heart attack. We don't need another one."

I finally calmed down a little and opened the material and began to read.

"By the authority vested in me as President by the Constitution and the laws of the United States of America, in order to effect the appropriate recognition of individuals who have distinguished themselves in in the performance of their duty with the Department of Defense during a period of crisis and throughout their military service, consistent with the national security and foreign policy interests of the United States and the interests of justice, I hereby order as follows:

Sec.3 Promotion of the following personnel to the ranks and positions as indicated. Major General Gary Hall, United States Marine Corps is promoted to the rank of General and is assigned duties of the Commandant of the Marine Corps. Further that Colonel James Miller is promoted to the rank of Major General with assignment as Commander of the Southeast Command of the United States military. And further: Sergeant Penny Fulbright is hereby given a battlefield promotion to the rank of Captain with assignment to the Southeast Command."

Just then the phone rang; Penny picked up and said, "Colonel Miller's office."

"Captain Fulbright, when will you learn to answer the phone correctly," the familiar voice said.

"I'm sorry, sir, this is Sergeant Fulbright," Penny replied.

The voice then said, "Captain Penny Fulbright, this is General Dutch Hall, all 'four-stars' of him; let me speak to that 'two-star' Major General Bull Miller, and tell him to put his phone on speaker. I want you to hear this also!"

She called out, "Colonel Miller, General Dutch Hall is on the phone; he said to put your phone on speaker."

Major General Bull Miller yelled out, "Captain Fulbright, come in here at once!

THE END

ACKNOWLEDGEMENTS

For her special patience while I devoted so much time writing this novel, and then to take on the task of reading every word, even though the genre is not something she would normally read, my very special thanks, love and appreciation to my devoted wife, Lucille. Also for her thoughtful comments throughout.

The author also wishes to thank the wisdom and technical advice of my fictitious "Double Special Ops" guy, my army-retired son, Rick Winstead, who helped work through some rough spots.

Also, thank you to my legal advisor and "keep me out of trouble" attorney, Kimberly MacCumbee (granddaughter) who holds a special compartment in my heart.